PRAISE

Sweet FILTHY BOY

"A crazy, hilarious, and surprisingly realistic and touching adventure. . . . The chemistry between [Ansel and Mia] is incredible. The team behind Lauren completely blew this reviewer away."

   —*RT Book Reviews* (Top Pick! and Seal of Excellence selection)

"Had my heart pounding from cover to cover. . . . A must read!"

—*Fangirlish*

"A deliciously filthy romp that you're going to love!"
   —*Martini Times Romance*

"Christina Lauren have taken me back to being young, in lust, and brave enough for a new adventure. I challenge you not to fall in love with Ansel's charm, looks, and that breathtaking accent."

—HenryCavill.org

"If you love Christina Lauren's super sexy and witty love stories, you won't be disappointed with this one. Ansel is just . . . yum."
   —*The Rock Stars of Romance*

"Christina Lauren fans rejoice and prepare to get hooked. If you're looking for a smokin'-hot read, look no further."
   —*Harlequin Junkie*

"No one is doing hot contemporary romance like Christina Lauren. *Sweet Filthy Boy* is beyond swoon worthy."
   —*Bookalicious*

"It's official: I'd read Christina Lauren's grocery list if they'd let me. The girls wrote the French-boy fantasy I didn't know I had."
—*That's Normal*

"The perfect combination of a flirty and dirty love story! . . . Christina Lauren are my go-to gals for when I'm in the mood for a laugh-out-loud, sizzling sexy romance."
—*Flirty and Dirty Book Blog*

"Ansel is damn near perfection. He is what those swoony YA boys grow up to be. And he speaks French. . . . Do you even need more?"
—*Too Fond of Books*

"Fun. Sexy. Captivating. *Sweet Filthy Boy* was everything I've come to expect from this dynamic duo."
—*The Autumn Review*

"*Sweet Filthy Boy* will rock your reading world. Christina Lauren has the ability to make you get lost in a story, to feel every emotion, joy or heartbreak. . . . Sexy, smart, sweet, extremely addictive, and full of humor."
—*Literati Literature Lovers*

"Funny and adorably charming. . . . [Mia and Ansel's] journey is tender, hot and even heartbreaking at times, but so worth it."
—*Heroes and Heartbreakers*

"It wouldn't be a Christina Lauren book if it wasn't laugh-out-loud funny, with lots of mind-blowing sexy scenes. All the role-playing was smoking hot while still having a touch of humor. I seriously want to plan a trip to France now and find my own (my husband won't mind, right?!) gorgeous filthy French Ansel."
—*Three Girls & a Book Obsession*

"*Sweet Filthy Boy* delivered. And, delivered huge. . . . This book truly is simplicity at its very best. Nothing was bogged down with overly complicated storylines or over-the-top drama. It was a tender-hearted romance packed full with some hot and heavy times between the sheets. A winning combination in my book."

—*Sinfully Sexy Book Reviews*

"*Sweet Filthy Boy* has everything necessary for a great romance read. Love, passion, heat, turmoil, and humor are all perfectly combined. Add in the stellar writing and there is nothing more I could ask for."

—*Bookish Temptations*

"The adorable factor is 110%. The clever moments, laugh out loud quips, and overall good feelings were there and then some. But the sex . . . good grief . . . the sex. Christina Lauren can write some sex scenes like no other. I was fanning myself and looking at my husband in a whole new light. If only he spoke French."

—*Nicely Phrased*

"This book is *chock full* of . . . everything. Hilariously mortifying situations. Playful banter. Heart. Adventure. Sexy French language, locales, art, food. French everything. Sexy everything. A gorgeous man in a suit. A gorgeous man in boxers. A gorgeous man in nothing. *Christ!* Christina and Lauren have proven time and time again that they have immense talent, an undeniable creative chemistry, romantic hearts, and deliciously dirty minds."

—*Nestled in a Book*

Books by CHRISTINA LAUREN

THE WILD SEASONS SERIES

Sweet Filthy Boy

THE BEAUTIFUL BASTARD SERIES

Beautiful Bastard

Beautiful Stranger

Beautiful Bitch

Beautiful Bombshell

Beautiful Player

Beautiful Beginning

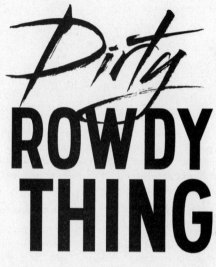

DIRTY ROWDY THING

BOOK TWO OF WILD SEASONS

CHRISTINA LAUREN

G

GALLERY BOOKS

NEW YORK   LONDON   TORONTO   SYDNEY   NEW DELHI

G

Gallery Books
A Division of Simon & Schuster, Inc.
1230 Avenue of the Americas
New York, NY 10020

First Gallery Books trade paperback edition November 2014

GALLERY BOOKS and colophon are registered trademarks
of Simon & Schuster, Inc.

For information about special discounts for bulk purchases,
please contact Simon & Schuster Special Sales at 1-866-506-1949
or business@simonandschuster.com.

The Simon & Schuster Speakers Bureau can bring authors
to your live event. For more information or to book an event
contact the Simon & Schuster Speakers Bureau at 1-866-248-3049
or visit our website at www.simonspeakers.com.

Cover art by iStockPhoto

Manufactured in the United States of America

10 9 8 7 6 5 4 3 2 1

Library of Congress Cataloging-in-Publication Data is on file.

ISBN 978-1-4767-7796-2
ISBN 978-1-4767-7797-9 (ebook)

To our dads, Pat and James,
for supporting even our wildest adventures

usually drives his mom's hand-me-down Lexus and keeps it in pristine condition. This type takes his shoes off as soon as he walks indoors and always maintains eye contact while speaking. In bed, the mama's boy offers few benefits, but at least they tend to be tidy.

Toby Amsler turned out to be the rare combination of mama's boy *and* manwhore, which somehow made him exponentially worse in bed. The only thing more awkward than his vacuum-suction oral skills was being woken by his mother bringing him tea and Cheerios—without knocking—at six in the morning. Not my finest wake-up call.

I'm not sure why I'm surprised. Despite what film and music would have women believe, these guys are *all* hopeless when it comes to the female orgasm. They learn sex from watching porn, where giving the camera a good view is the goal and no one really cares if it works for the girl, because she'll pretend it's awesome regardless. Sex happens up close, and *inside,* not at camera's length. Guys seem to forget that.

My heart rate has yet to return to normal, and the couple in front of me is ordering at a snail's pace. He wants to know, "What's good for someone who doesn't like coffee?"

Probably not a coffee shop, I want to snap. But I don't, and remind myself that it's not this particular man's fault that *all* men are clueless, that I'm frustrated and cranky.

I swear I'm not usually prone to dramatics. I'm just having a bad morning, and I need to breathe.

Closing my eyes, I take a deep breath. There. Better.

I step away and scowl at the pastry case while contemplat-

Chapter ONE

Harlow

I BURST THROUGH THE doors of this random Starbucks in this random neighborhood in the hopes of forgetting the second-worst lay of my life. Toby Amsler: Fantastically flirty, hot, and with the added bonus of being on the UCSD water polo team—he had all the makings for a night of world-class, toe-curling fun.

False advertising at its finest.

You see, when it comes to potential love interests, guys typically fall into three basic categories: the manwhore, the misunderstood, and the mama's boy. The *manwhore,* in my experience, comes in any number of shapes and sizes: dirty rock star, muscled quarterback, even the occasional irresistible hot nerd. Their strength in bed? Generally, dirty talk and endurance, both of which I'm a fan. Sadly, this doesn't always translate into skill.

The *misunderstood* often takes the shape of an artist, a quiet surfer, or a soulful musician. These boys rarely know what the hell to do, but at least they're willing to try for hours.

The *mama's boy* is the easiest to spot. Here in La Jolla, he ing my choices. And then I stop, blinking twice before narrowing my eyes and peering more closely at the case. Or, rather, at the reflection in the glass.

Is that . . . no . . . Finn Roberts *. . . standing behind me?*

Leaning forward, I can see that visible beside my own reflection, and in line just behind me is, indeed . . . Finn. My brain does the immediate mental pat-down. Why isn't he in Canada? Where am *I*? Am I awake? Am I having a Finn Roberts nightmare in Toby Amsler's twin-sized water bed?

I convince myself it's a trick of the light. Maybe my brain has finally shorted out on the one morning I'd give my left arm for an orgasm—*of course that would make me think of Finn, right?*

Finn Roberts, the *only* guy who ever managed to dodge my convenient guy-category strategy—Finn Roberts, the notorious ex-husband-of-twelve-drunken-hours-in-Vegas, who was good with hands, lips, *and* body, and who made me come so many times he told me he thought I passed out.

Finn Roberts, who turned out to be an asshole, too.

Trick of the light. It can't be him.

But when I chance a tiny glimpse over my shoulder, I realize it really *is* him. On his head is a faded blue Mariners cap pulled low over hazel eyes lined with the longest, thickest lashes I've ever seen. He's wearing the same hunter green T-shirt with his family company's white fishing logo as when I surprised him in his hometown only a little over a month ago. His arms are tanned, muscled, and crossed over his wide chest.

Finn is here. Fuck. Finn is *here*.

I close my eyes and groan. My body gives in to a horrifying reflex: Immediately, I feel soft and warm, my spine arches as if he's pressing up behind me. I remember the first moment I knew we would hook up, in Vegas. Drunk, I'd pointed to him and dropped out loud to everyone, *Probably gonna fuck him tonight.*

To which he'd leaned over and said directly into my ear, *That's sweet. But I like to be the one doing the fucking.*

And I know if I heard his voice right now—deep, calm as still water, and a little gravelly by nature—as keyed up as I am, I'd probably have an orgasm in the middle of this coffee shop.

I *knew* I should have just waited and driven over to Pannikin for my usual morning fix. I stay silent, counting to ten. One of my best friends, Mia, jokes that I'm only quiet if I'm surprised or pissed. Right now, I'm both.

The skinny barista kid catches my eye by leaning forward. "Would you like to try our pumpkin spice mocha?"

I nod blankly.

Wait, what? No, that sounds disgusting! A tiny, still-functioning corner of my brain yells at my mouth to order my usual: large coffee, black, no room. But I'm frozen in my stunned silence while the Starbucks barista squeaks out my order with a black Sharpie. In a daze, I hand over the money and shove my wallet back into my purse.

I steady myself and when I turn to go wait for my coffee, Finn catches my eye and smiles. "Hey, Ginger Snap."

Without turning to face him, I make a show of studying him over my shoulder. He hasn't shaved this morning, and his dark stubble cuts a dangerous shadow on his jaw. His neck is deeply tanned from working on the wide-open ocean all summer. I let my eyes travel lower, because—let's be real—I'd be a fool to not drink in the sight of this man before telling him to go fuck himself.

Finn is built like one of Lola's comic book superheroes— all broad chest and narrow waist, thick forearms, muscled legs. He gives off the appearance of impenetrability, as if that golden skin of his covers titanium. I mean, sweet Jesus, the man works with his hands, sweats when he works, fucks like it's his vocation, and was raised by a father who expects, above anything else, that his sons are capable fishermen. I can't imagine any of the guys I know standing next to him and looking anything other than snack-sized.

His smile slowly straightens and he tilts his head a little. "Harlow?"

Although the shadow of his hat partially hides his eyes, I can tell they widen slightly when I lift my attention from his neck. And now I remember how his gaze feels like a hook. I close my eyes and shake my head once, trying to clear it. I don't mind swooning if the situation calls for it, but I hate the feeling when it tries to shove aside my very well-deserved, righteous indignation.

"Hold. I'm contemplating my response."

His brows pull together in confusion . . . at least I *think* it's confusion. I suspect on Finn that emotion looks the same as impatience, frustration, and concentration. He's not exactly an open book. "Okay . . . ?"

Okay, here's the problem: After our matrimonial adventures in Vegas, I flew up to see him. I showed up on Vancouver Island of all places, wearing nothing but a coat. *Surprise!* We had sex for nearly ten hours straight—rowdy sex, loud, on-every-flat-surface sex—and when I told him I had to head to the airport, he just smiled, leaned over to slide his phone off the nightstand, and called me a cab. He'd just come all over my tits, and he called a *cab* to drive me to the airport. In fact, it pulled up at the curb behind Finn's brand-new, cherry-red Ford F-150.

I'd concluded, calmly, actually, that we weren't a good fit, even for the occasional border-crossing booty call, and called it a day.

So why am I so angry he's here?

The barista offers the same drink special to Finn, but he makes a mildly disgusted face before declining and ordering two large, black coffees.

This makes me even more irritated. His reasonable reaction should have been *mine*. "What the hell are you doing at my coffee shop?"

His eyes go wide, mouth forming a few different words before any actually come out. "You *own* this place?"

"Are you high, Finn? It's a *Starbucks*. I just mean it's my town."

His eyes fall closed and he laughs, and the way the light

catches the angle of his jaw, and the way I know exactly how that stubble would feel on my skin . . . *argh*.

I tilt my head, staring at him. "What's funny?"

"It was a real possibility in my mind that you *could* own this Starbucks."

With a little eye-roll, I reach for my drink and march out of the store.

Walking to my car, I stretch my neck, roll my shoulders. *Why am I so annoyed?*

It isn't like I expected a carriage to be at my disposal when I showed up unannounced at his little seaside house. I'd already slept with him in Vegas, so I knew the no-strings-attached arrangement. Clearly I was there because I wanted good sex. Actually, I wanted—no, I *needed*—confirmation that the sex was as good as I'd remembered.

It was *so* much better.

So obviously it's the bad-Toby-Amsler-sex hangover that's killing my calm. This chance meeting with Finn would have gone very differently if I hadn't *just* left the bed of the first guy I slept with after him—the first guy I'd been with in two months—and if that experience hadn't been so unsatisfying.

Footsteps slap the asphalt behind me and I start to turn just before a powerful hand curls around my bicep. Finn grabs me harder than I think he's intended, and the result is that my pumpkin coffee monstrosity tilts and spills onto the ground, barely missing my shoes.

I give him an exasperated look and toss my empty cup into a trash can near the curb.

"Oh, come on," he says with a little smile. He hands me the one cup he had balancing on top of the other. "It's not as if you were going to drink that. You wouldn't touch the instant vanilla spice stuff I had at my place."

Taking the coffee he's offering, I mumble my thanks and look to the side. I'm acting exactly like the kind of woman I never want to be: jilted, martyred, put out.

"Why are you pissed?" he asks quietly.

"I'm just preoccupied."

Ignoring this, he says, "Is it because you came all the way up to Vancouver Island, showed up at my house wearing only a trench coat in the middle of July, and I banged you hoarse?" The smirk in his voice tells me he thinks I couldn't possibly be pissed about *that*.

He'd be right.

I pause, looking up to study him for a beat. "You mean the day you couldn't even be bothered to put on some clothes to take me to the *airport?*"

He blinks, his head jerking back slightly. "I skipped an entire shift when you showed up. I *never* do that. I left for work about a minute after the cab showed."

This . . . is new information. I shift on my feet, unable to maintain eye contact anymore, instead looking past him to the busy street in the distance. "You didn't tell me you had to work."

"I did."

I feel my jaw tighten with irritation when I blink back up to his face. "Did not."

He sighs, pulling his cap off, scratching his crazy bed-head and then putting it back on. "All right, Harlow."

"What are you doing here, anyway?" I ask him.

And then it clicks into place: Ansel is in town visiting Mia, and we're all headed to the grand opening of Oliver's comic book store, Downtown Graffick, tomorrow. Canadian Finn, Parisian Ansel, and the dry-witted Aussie Oliver: the bridegrooms of Vegas. Although four of us got quick annulments after our wedding shenanigans, Mia and Ansel decided to make a real go at this marriage thing. Lola and Oliver have become friends, bonding over their shared comic and graphic novel love. So, whether we like it or not, Finn and I are expected to be a part of this band of misfit buddies. We have to learn to be civil, *with* our clothes on.

"Right," I mumble. "The opening is this weekend. You're here for that."

"I know they won't be stocking *Seventeen* and *Cosmo*, but you should come by and check it out, anyway," he says. "The store looks good."

I lift the coffee cup to my nose and sniff. Black, unadulterated coffee. Perfect. "Of course I'll be there. I *like* Oliver and Ansel."

He swipes a palm over his mouth, smiling a little. "So. You're pissed about the cab."

"I'm not *pissed*. This isn't a lovers' spat, and we aren't having a *quarrel*. I'm just having a bad morning."

Narrowing his eyes, he looks me over, from head to toe. He's so damn observant it makes me blush, and I know as soon as his smile reappears that he's deduced I didn't come from home. "Your hair is all crazy, but what's interesting is you look a little hard up. Like maybe you didn't quite get what you needed somewhere."

"Bite me."

Finn steps closer, head tilted slightly to the side with that infuriating half smile. "Say please, and I will."

With a laugh, I push him away with my palm flat to his very nice, very hard chest. "Go away."

"Because now you want it?"

"Because you need a shower."

"Listen," he says, laughing. "I won't chase you down again if you go running away, but we're going to see each other from time to time. Let's try to be grown-ups."

He turns without waiting for my reply and I hear his truck alarm chirp as he unlocks the door. I make a bratty little *fuck-you* face and display my middle finger to his retreating form. But then I pause, my heart tripping over itself with an abrupt rush of adrenaline.

Finn is climbing in the same cherry-red truck that was parked at the curb in front of his house. Only now it's covered in the dust and grime accumulated from miles and miles of driving.

Which begs the question, if he's only visiting for the weekend, then why did he bring his truck all the way here from Vancouver Island?

I don't have much time to ponder this because my phone buzzes in my pocket from my mom's text and I pull it out only to see the words, Will you come to the house right away please, written across my screen.

I AM A fixer.

When I was four and broke my mother's favorite necklace while trying it on, I spent three hours in my tree house trying to glue it back together. I succeeded only in gluing several fingers together. Senior year when Mia was hit by the truck and nearly paralyzed, I sat by her side every day for the entire summer she spent in a toe-to-waist cast. I knew that if I sat there long enough she would need something and I would be there, ready. I brought her DVDs and ridiculous teen magazines. I painted her nails and went so far as to smuggle the oddest things into her room—wine coolers; her boyfriend, Luke; her cat—just to see her smile. When Lola's father was sent to Afghanistan—and then when he returned, shaken and different, and Lola's mom abandoned them both for good—I brought groceries and dinners, anything that would take the tiniest burden off them. And when Ansel was too man-brained to fix things with Mia, I forced my way in there, too.

When my friends need something, I do it. When someone I love can't solve a problem, I find a way. For better or worse, it's what I do.

So when I pull into the drive and sit down beside my little sister and across from our parents in our light, airy, *happy* family room—a room that, right now, feels like a tomb—I'm immediately on high alert. On an average day, our family is boisterous. Right now, we are silent. I feel like I should whisper my hellos. The curtains are open, but the thick fog of the marine layer outside makes the room feel gloomy and dark.

My family is—and has always been—the center of my world. My mom was an actress when my parents got married, and Dad's career didn't take off until I hit high school. So when I was little, Dad and I would travel with Mom from one set to the next. Until my sister Bellamy was born when I was six, it was just the three of us most of the time.

Dad is the emotionally intuitive, nurturing one, all creative energy and passion. Mom is the beautiful, calm centering force in our family, leading the house with a wink behind my father's broad shoulders. But right now she sits next to him, gripping his hand in both of hers, and I can see from across the low coffee table that she's sweating.

I have it in my head that they're going to tell us they're selling the house. (I would picket in the driveway until they backed down.) That they're moving to Los Angeles. (I will lose my shit.) That they're having some trouble and are going to spend some time apart. (This I can't even fathom.)

"What's going on?" I ask slowly.

Mom closes her eyes, takes a deep breath, and then looks right at us, saying, "I have breast cancer."

After these four words, the hundreds that follow sound fuzzy and shapeless. But I understand enough to know that Mom has a tumor that is roughly three centimeters in her breast, and that cancerous cells were found in several lymph nodes. Dad found the mass while they were in the shower one morning—I'm too relieved he found it to be weirded out by this information—and she didn't want to tell us anything until she knew more. She's opted for a mastectomy, followed by chemotherapy, and they've scheduled surgery for Monday . . . three days from now.

It's all somehow moving too fast, and, for a fixer like me, not fast enough. I can rattle off questions as if I'm reading from a book: Have you gotten a second opinion on the pathology? What is the recovery time for the surgery? How soon after can you start chemo? What medications will they give you? But I'm too stunned to know if my rapid-fire questions are an appropriate reaction at all.

When Dad mentioned he found the lump, Bellamy burst out laughing and then immediately broke down into hysterical sobs. Mom sounded like an automaton for the first time in her entire life as she detailed what the doctor had told her. Dad remained uncharacteristically mute.

So this is what I'm saying: What *is* an appropriate reaction when the center of your world finds out she's mortal?

Once she's finished telling us everything she knows—and once she's promised us that she feels strong, and *fine just fine*—she tells us she wants to go lie down and be alone for a little while. But I can hardly breathe, and from the look on my father's face, he's faring much, *much* worse.

Bellamy and I sit and watch *Clue* with the volume practically on mute. She's curled in my lap, and Dad has disappeared down the hall to their bedroom. On my phone's browser, I read every website I can find on stage-three breast cancer, and with every new piece of information I mentally update the odds of my mother's survival. The credits are rolling and then the screen goes blank before I realize the movie is over.

BUT THERE'S NOTHING I can do now. Mom doesn't want us to do anything; she doesn't want me *taking care* of her. She wants us to "live our lives" and "not let this monopolize our thoughts."

Does she not know Dad and me at all?

Only a few hours after she tells us, this cancer has become a *thing*, a living, breathing entity that takes up just as much space in our house as any of us do. It's all I can think about, all I see when I look at her. And so I have no idea what to do with myself.

"I thought there was a party at Lola's new place tonight," Mom says, and I snap back to the conversation. She looks perfectly normal, if not a little tired, flipping a grilled cheese and glancing at me over her shoulder. You know, making us dinner as if it's a normal Friday night, nothing different. I can tell all three of us are watching her cook and suppressing our need to suggest she go sit down, relax, let us bring her something to eat.

She would kill us.

"There *is* . . ." I hedge and steal a few shreds of cheese from her bowl. "But I'm staying here."

"No, you're not." Mom turns and gives me her best don't-argue-with-me face. "Oliver's store opens tomorrow."

"I know."

"You're going out, and you're staying at your place tonight," Dad insists. "I'm taking Mom to a movie and then I'm bringing her home and"—he does a slick little dance move behind her—"you won't want to be home for what comes next."

Oh God. I press my hands over my ears as Bellamy ducks and pretends to hide under the breakfast bar.

"You win," I tell him, trying to keep my tone light and shove down the panic I feel welling up inside of me. I don't want to be away from my mom. "But tomorrow we're doing something with all four of us."

Dad nods and smiles bravely at me.

I've never seen him look so shaken.

———————

IT'S ACTUALLY GOOD to get out, if I'm being honest. The worst thing we could do for Mom is sit around and watch every move she makes with our worried, woeful expressions. Dad assured me my role will come in the next few weeks and months. I can work with that. Bellamy is sweet, but she's only eighteen and also oddly incapable. Every small errand stresses her out. It makes her good for the role of *Stay Positive!* I'm the daughter who gets shit done. I'll be the daughter who drives Mom to appointments, asks too many questions, takes care of her when Dad needs to work, and will probably drive her crazy.

But right now, I feel awful.

And if there is anyone I want to see other than my family tonight, it's my girls.

Lola's new apartment is a *huge* step up from the dorms. I expected her to move in with me when we graduated, but she wanted to be downtown, and every time I visit I can't really blame her. It's situated just north of the Gaslamp Quarter in a new, giant-windowed high-rise with wide-open rooms, a view of the harbor, and a location only blocks away from the Donut Bar. Lucky woman.

"Harlowwwww!" My name is shouted across the large living room and quickly I'm surrounded by four arms. Two are Lola's, and two belong to London, Lola's new roommate and the most adorable all-American girl you can imagine: sandy blond hair, freckles, dimples and a constant smile. She cools it down perfectly with her hot nerd girl glasses and wild clothes. Tonight, for example, I see she's wearing a blue Tardis T-shirt, a polka-dot green and yellow skirt, and black-and-white–striped kneesocks. With Lola's retro black dress and sleek Bettie Page thing going on, they make the rest of us look tragically unhip.

"Hi Lola-London," I say, pressing my face into Lola's neck. *I needed this.*

Lola's voice is muffled against my hair. "That sounds like a stripper name."

London laughs, extracting herself from the tangle. "Or the name of a drink?"

"One Lola-London on the rocks," I say.

"Well," London says, pointing to the cooler on the kitchen floor. "We can try inventing it tonight. I swear I bought everything. Mixers and booze and beer and nuts and—" She closes her eyes, raises her right hand in a rocker salute, and belts out, *"Fritos!"*

She turns running off to answer the door and I give Lola my nod of approval. "I like that girl."

"Someone told me there is a fiesta in this *casa*!"

I turn to the sound of Ansel's deep, accented voice, and every sound in the apartment dips for a beat before applause and laughter break out. He's wearing a sombrero filled with tortilla chips. Because he's an adorable idiot.

Mia breaks away from him, making a beeline to me, and wraps her arms around my shoulders. "You okay?"

I called Lola and Mia earlier, gave them both the truncated update, and they know me well enough to anticipate the magnitude of my panic.

I blink away from the delightful spectacle of Ansel doing some weird little bullfighter dance. "Eh. You know."

She pulls back and studies my face before deciding, accurately, that I'm here for distraction and not to discuss my mom. We all turn to watch Ansel as he offers sombrero chips to someone. Seriously, his inner child is definitely alive and kicking.

I draw a circle in the air around my head. "What is with the—"

"No idea." Mia cuts me off. "He and Finn went out for beers earlier and back he comes with it. He hasn't taken it off in hours, but *has* refilled it three times. Stand back ladies"—she bends, digging a beer out of the cooler—"he's all mine."

And at the mention of his name, I catch sight of Finn across the room. He must have come in with them. My stomach does an annoying clench-warm-flip move when he laughs over something Ansel says and lifts his arm to adjust his baseball hat. His bicep flexes and my stomach ignites. I chug half my beer to make the feeling go away, imagining the hiss and steam as the metaphorical flames are put out.

"I didn't know Finn was coming tonight." But what was I thinking? That they would leave him at home alone? Finn is just one more complication my already frazzled brain can't quite handle right now.

Mia twists the cap off her beer and watches me, a little smile in her eyes. "Is that okay?"

Civil. Band of misfit buddies, I remind myself. "You know it's fine."

"As long as it doesn't try to speak, right?"

Laughing, I nod. "Right."

Lola rubs my back and then tilts her head, indicating she's going to join the people gathering to play cards. "You good here?"

"Yeah," I tell her. "I'll probably just hang back and watch you guys be awesome."

After making sure I don't need company, Mia follows her, and I'm left alone in the brightly lit kitchen, watching the small group around the dining table. Ansel licks his thumb and then begins dealing cards, tossing them expertly across the table to each player. I feel a little lost, like I shouldn't be here but unable to go home, either. I'm too tight in my skin, too warm in this apartment.

A shadow dips past me and when I turn, I find a bleached-blond mohawked guy bending to pull a wine cooler out of the fridge.

"Interesting beverage choice," I say. "Passion punch!"

He turns and laughs, nodding in total agreement. He's gorgeous, if not a little dirty, but his smile showcases a mouthful of perfect, white teeth—a La Jolla hippie boy. Of course. "Have you ever had these? They taste like *juice*!"

The cheap wine cooler is a newfound, amusing novelty? Definitely a La Jolla hippie boy.

"I'm Harlow," I say, extending my hand. "And if you want juice, why don't you just drink juice?"

He shakes it. "There is very little trouble to be had in juice," he says, before pointing the bottle at his chest and adding, "Not-Joe."

"'Nacho'?"

"No. *Not. Joe.* Oliver, my new boss? Calls me Joey. I think he's fucking with me, like a kangaroo thing because he's Australian? But it isn't my name."

I wait for him to give me his real name—obviously he can't have known Oliver long enough for him to be called Not-Joe more than a few months—but he doesn't. "So you go by Not-Joe?"

"Yeah!"

"All the time?"

"Yep."

"Well, okay then, it's nice to meet you." Despite the fact that I fear Not-Joe is a few synapses short of an invertebrate, I look him over and instantly like him, anyway. He's wearing board shorts and a T-shirt and clearly has absolutely nothing but earnest giddiness to be right here, doing exactly this. "So you're going to work at the store?"

When he nods, gulping down half his wine cooler in a single swallow, I add, "Tomorrow should be pretty exciting for you guys."

"It's gonna be good. Oliver is the best boss. Or, I can tell he's going to be. He's just so laid-back."

I look across the room at where Oliver is concentrating so hard on the cards in his hand I fear they might incinerate. Unlike Finn, who doesn't seem to worry much about his appearance, but tilts the odds in his favor by keeping his hair cut short, his face usually clean-shaven, Oliver is hot in an accidental sort of way. I haven't really decided if he's as oblivious about it as he seems, but I do know he's a pretty intense guy, and given that he's only thirty and opening a high-profile comic store in the hippest area of San Diego, I don't think he's quite as *laid-back* as Not-Joe is hoping.

I look back to the hippie boy. "What are you going to be doing there?"

"Selling comics and stuff."

I laugh. This guy unsupervised must be a sight to behold. "Oh, you mean working the front?"

"Yep. Working the front. And sometimes the back." He laughs to himself. "The re-gis-ter," he sings.

"Exactly how high are you, Not-Joe?"

He stops moving and seems to do a lengthy mental inspection. "Pretty high."

"Want to do some shots?"

Because really, there's no way I'm ever having sex with Not-Joe, but my second favorite thing to do with guys is watch them get drunk.

We line up a couple and toss them back, just as I see Finn stand from the table. He tosses down his cards, clearly folding as he pulls off his cap, scratches his head with the same hand, and then slips it back on again. I hate that I find the maneuver so completely sexy. When he looks up and sees me in the kitchen with Not-Joe, he narrows his eyes for a beat and then starts to walk toward us.

"Oh, shit," I mumble under my breath.

"Does the Hulk belong to you?" Not-Joe asks, tilting his head.

"Not even a little."

"Still. Look at the intensity in his *eyes*," he whispers drunkenly. "The lion prowls." With a little shiver, he seems to clear his trance and chirps, "I'm headed to the little boys' room."

"Thanks," I grumble to his retreating back, as Finn slides between me and the counter, leaning a hip against it.

Tonight I'm missing my usual armor—my social enthusiasm, my confidence, and the ease that comes with knowing life is okay for everyone I love. A tiny alarm in my brain signals that talking to Finn right now might be a terrible idea. We will either end up fighting or fucking, and Finn does neither with any sort of tenderness. But I refuse to step back and can feel the heat coming off his chest. His hat is pulled low over his eyes, so I have to rely on the curve of his mouth to interpret his mood. So far, he seems . . . bored, angry, pensive, or asleep.

"Fancy meeting you here."

"Finn." I acknowledge him with a little nod.

His smile starts at one corner and twists across his lips. Damn him and his amazingly flirty mouth. "Harlow."

I saw my teeth over my bottom lip as I consider him.

Mindless chatter won't work here, but I'm not entirely sure I can handle his rough edges tonight when I'm feeling so threadbare myself. Finn doesn't fit into any of my easily predetermined boy-categories, and maybe there's a challenge in that.

He is hard to read, easy to look at, and no matter how bad an idea it may be, it's nearly impossible to resist pulling him closer.

Fighting or fucking.

Both of those options are starting to sound pretty good.

Chapter TWO

Finn

I DON'T REMEMBER THE last time I was at a house party surrounded by a bunch of obnoxious twentysomethings on their way to varying degrees of hammered. I am not a party guy, but I agreed to come along because Ansel is in town, and the last time we saw each other was Vegas, when the end of a fun reunion crumbled into matrimonial chaos. But somehow tonight I end up nowhere near the kid, with a keg cup in my hand, and halfway to buzzed for the first time in months, standing close enough to Harlow Vega to touch her.

It doesn't surprise me that we're standing this close or that I'd really like to touch her.

What surprises me is that Harlow is the one separated from the rest of the party, hanging out in the kitchen with Oliver's stoner employee. Despite our Vegas nuptials and Vancouver Island bangfest, it's fair to say I don't really know much about her. But I *do* know her type, and if there's a table at a party, girls like her are usually pounding, lying, or dancing on it.

"Why are you in here and not wiping the floor with us at poker?"

Harlow shrugs, placing her hands on my waist so she can move me aside and open the cabinet overhead. "I'm distracted tonight." She frowns up into the crowded cupboard. "And why is this such a mess? Dear God."

"You going to rearrange their kitchen for them?" I ask, smiling at the clinking sounds as she moves glasses around. "In the middle of a party?"

"Maybe."

Dark auburn hair frames her face, which she tucks behind her ear as she stretches for the top shelf, exposing her long neck. I immediately think of sucking little marks into her skin, from her ear to her collarbone.

"Preoccupied this morning," I say, drinking in the sight of her bare shoulders. "Distracted tonight."

She retrieves two clean shot glasses and pulls back to look at me silently in response. And now I remember the heat of her oddly hypnotic eyes—more amber than brown—and the temptation of her full, flirty lips. Unscrewing the cap from a bottle of pretty stellar tequila, Harlow blinks away before pouring each glass to the brim.

"Well, I can tell Not-Joe is doing a great job undistracting you," I tell her, "but you might want to slow down on shots with the guy who pierced his own penis." Honestly, when Oliver told me that story, I nearly choked on my sandwich.

Harlow was beginning to hand *me* a shot, but her hand pauses, midair. "He . . . what now?"

"Twice. One in the tip, one in the shaft."

She blinks.

I lean in a little and the way she's staring at my mouth is making my skin hum. "According to Oliver, 'things happen' when Not-Joe gets drunk."

She tears her eyes from my mouth and looks up at me, lifting her chin to indicate the table of people still playing cards across the room. "You're suggesting instead I go play cards with the people who're giving out shots of Clamato as penalty?"

"It's even better than that," I say with a shudder. "It's Budweiser *with* Clamato. It's called chelada, and it's pretty warm now."

She makes the exact same face she made when the barista offered her a pumpkin spice mocha this morning—complete and total horror—and that drink she *ordered*. "Someone actually made that into a thing? There are people who drink and enjoy that?"

Laughing, I tell her, "You know, despite my better judgment I find it really funny when you act like a diva."

With her head tilted to the side, eyes incredulous, she asks, "Being turned off by Budweiser mixed with tomato and *clam* juice makes me a diva?"

Apparently I'm buzzed enough to belt out a few lines of the only diva song I can think of at the moment: "I Will Always Love You." And then I lift my shot and down it.

Harlow looks at me like I've lost my mind, but I can tell she's amused. A smile lingers in her eyes, even if her brows are pulled together disapprovingly. "You can't sing to save your life."

Wiping a hand across my mouth, I say, "That's nothing. You should hear me play the piano."

She narrows her eyes further. "Did you just quote the Smiths?"

"I'm surprised you got that. It wasn't from a song eventually sampled by P. Diddy."

Laughing, she says, "You have a pretty fantastic impression of me."

"I really do." The tequila slips into my bloodstream, warming me from my chest outward. I lean closer so I can get a good whiff of her. She always smells *warm,* somehow, and a little earthy and sweet. Like the beach, and sunscreen and honeysuckle. I've said more nonsex words to Harlow in the past five minutes than I did the entire time she was in Canada, but I'm surprised to find that not only is she easy to talk to, she's fun. "And, my impression of you is ever evolving, now that you aren't just a pretty face in my lap."

"You're one classy motherfucker, Finn."

"This speaking thing does wonders for expanding our horizons."

She takes her shot, swallows, and winces before saying, "Don't get ahead of yourself, Sunshine. I like our arrangement."

"We have an arrangement?"

Nodding, she turns to pour us each another shot. "We fight, or we bang. I think I prefer the banging part."

"Well, then I would have to agree."

When she hands me the second shot—on top of the three beers I've already had with Ansel—I ask, "Why did you come up my way anyway? I never got around to asking you that because you were sitting on my face most of the time. The visit was . . . unexpected."

"But awesome?" she asks, brows raised as if she knows I'd never deny it.

"Sure."

She licks the side of her hand, shakes some salt on it this time, and studies it, thinking. "Honestly? I guess I wasn't sure I could trust my memory from Vegas."

"You mean your memory that the sex was so good?"

"Yeah."

"It was," I assure her.

"I know that now." She licks the salt, takes the shot, and grabs a slice of lime from the counter, sucking it briefly before murmuring through wet, puckered lips, "Too bad the man attached to the penis is such an epic loser."

I nod sympathetically. "True."

"You're fun," she tells me, pulling back a little as if she's only really looking at me now. "You're fun in this sort of easy, unexpected way."

"You're *drunk*."

She snaps her fingers in front of my face. "That must be it. The tequila I've had is making you fun."

I laugh, wiping a hand over my mouth. "You seem to be in a better mood tonight," I say.

"Just have some stuff going on and trying not to think about it. And besides," she says, raising her empty shot glass, "this helps immensely."

"How many have you had?"

"Enough that I don't care much, not so many that I don't care at all."

This seems like a pretty bleak response for someone I've assumed all along was chirpy and sexy and carefree. Really, though, I don't actually know much about Harlow's life. I know she's a pretty little rich girl, and probably has a line of pretty little rich boys lined up at her door. I know she's a loyal friend to Lola and Mia, and because she's apparently one of those people that need to help every human alive, she was a driving force in getting Ansel and Mia back together again. But outside of that, there's not much. I don't even know what she does for work . . . or whether she works at all.

"Anything you want to talk about?" I offer halfheartedly.

"Nope," she says, and tosses back another shot.

My phone vibrates in my pocket and my warm, drunken comfort is quickly replaced by a sense of dread. Without having to look, I know this is the message I've been waiting for. Back home my youngest brother, Levi, is running a safety check on the largest boat in our fleet, the *Linda,* named after our mother, and with the way things have been going, I'm willing to bet the news isn't going to be good.

Short in the wheelhouse, none of the controls are working.

Fuck.

Although there are about a hundred curse words I want

to type right now, I don't answer right away. Instead, I slip my phone back into my pocket, pour myself a shot, and throw it back. It helps.

"You okay there?" Harlow asks, watching me.

I clench my jaw against the burn, feeling it warm my body as it settles in my stomach. "Just a little distracted myself."

"Well then—let's have another!" She pours two more shots and hands me one. I know this isn't really going to help. I'm going to sober up in the morning—or maybe a bit later in the day than that—and the controls in the boat will still be down, and our whole fucking livelihood will still be just as in jeopardy as it is now. But, damn, I'd really like to forget all that for a while.

I pick it up, look at the clear liquid before I lean into her, my lips almost brushing the shell of her ear. "I think you and I both know the last time we drank tequila together it didn't end so well."

"True," she says, pulling back just far enough to meet my eyes. "But there's no twenty-four-hour chapel nearby manned by some reckless idiot willing to marry us, so I think we're safe."

Point made.

Harlow knocks back her shot and winces. "Ooooh . . . I don't think I can do any more." She holds up her hands, pretends to count out about thirty shots, and then smiles up at me. "One more and I'd face-plant into the bowl of these Fritos London is so excited about."

She may have lost count, but I haven't. Four shots into my time in the kitchen with Harlow and—besides Vegas—I'm drunk for the first time in years.

It feels like he's been gone for an hour, but Not-Joe finally returns in a cloud of weed-smell. As he approaches, he extends his hand to me, saying very slowly, "I'm Not-Joe . . . it's nice to meet you."

Laughing, I remind him, "We met earlier at the store, when Oliver was doing the final walk-through?"

Not-Joe makes a little clucking sound, saying, "*That's* why you looked familiar."

It was three hours ago. This guy must not breathe unless it's through a joint.

"You're the lumberjack from Nova Scotia?" he asks.

"Fisherman from Vancouver Island."

Harlow bursts out laughing. "Poor Finn."

He looks back and forth between me and Harlow. "So do you guys know each other through Oliver, too?" he asks.

"Not exactly," she says, and then looks at me with a silly grin. "Finn is my ex-husband."

Not-Joe's eyes go as wide as saucers. "Ex-*husband*?"

Nodding, I confirm, "That's right."

The kid looks at Harlow, and then *really* looks at her. Like eyes moving up and down her body in a way that makes me want to slap him into awareness and so he'll stop fucking *leering* at her like that.

"You don't look old enough to be divorced," he finally concludes.

I lean forward to break his attention away from her chest. "But I do?"

Now he looks at me, but with far less interest. "Yeah, actually. You're older than her, right?"

"Right," I say, laughing as Harlow giggles delightedly next to me. "Thanks."

Not-Joe digs his hand into a bag of corn chips on the counter, asking, "It must be weird hanging out at a party with your ex."

She waves him off, saying, "Nah. Finn is an easygoing guy."

"Am I now?" I ask her, and this makes me laugh because if there has ever been a phrase to describe me, it's not *easygoing*. Easygoing is Ansel. I often get "contained." I am, admittedly, sometimes a little closed off. I am not *easygoing*.

Nodding, she studies me for a breath and then says, "Yeah. You like long walks on the dock, making little dream catchers out of your extra fishing line, and evenings spent yukking it up with some Mountie MILFs at the local Mooseknuckle Bar."

I burst out laughing. "I do, huh?"

Her lips come together in a sweet, thoughtful pout. "Mm-hmm."

"Well," I reply, "you're pretty easy to be around yourself. It helps that you're a fun-loving gal who likes shopping, nail polish, and . . ." I pretend to think some more before finally repeating, "Shopping."

She puts her hand on my cheek, wearing a playfully adoring expression. "I love how well we know each other."

"Same."

In unison, we lift our empty shot glasses and clink them.

"Why did you guys get divorced?" Not-Joe asks. "You
seem to really like each other."

"Do we?" I ask, not taking my eyes off Harlow. I didn't
actually think I liked her all that much until tonight.

She finally breaks our shared look to tell Not-Joe, "The
truth is, we were only married for a night and, like, half a day
in Vegas. We've probably only spent a combined twenty-four
hours together, most of it drunk or naked."

"Or both," I add.

"Seriously?"

We both nod.

"That is *wicked*."

"It was, trust me," she agrees, and then pretends to glare
at me. "*Very* wicked."

I look at her lips just as she licks them and it sends a
shock of electricity down across my skin and straight to my
cock. In fact, I'm nearly drunk enough to suggest she reintro-
duce that tongue to that cock.

"It's something I think everyone should do once in their
life," Not-Joe muses, pulling my attention away from Harlow's now-smiling mouth. "Everyone should: run a marathon, read *Candide,* and get married in Vegas."

Harlow laughs and begins to explain to him that it was
fucking expensive and actually not all that convenient. We

could have banged and parted ways for free. As she tells Not-Joe about the misadventures in Vegas, I excuse myself to go hit the head.

Outside the kitchen area, the party is loud and drunk. London is belting out a song at the poker table; Mia is playing cards and wearing the sombrero while sitting on Ansel's lap. Lola and Oliver are the only ones who seem sober, and I laugh watching them for a few seconds. Oliver is notoriously competitive about cards, and here I can see the same determination on Lola's face. The rest of the table has dissolved into drunken debauchery, but the two of them seem to be trying their hardest to keep the game organized. It's like trying to tie a string around raindrops.

When I come out of the bathroom, Harlow is there waiting for a turn. She slips past me with a cheeky little smile and when I turn to do something—fuck, I don't even know, crack a joke, stare at her, *kiss* her—she closes the door in my face.

I forgot how drinking makes me feel blurry at the edges, a little unwound. It's freeing, but in the corner of my mind I can sense the red flashing light: *Danger. Danger.*

Looking down the hall, I consider going back to the poker table or to the kitchen, but my feet are planted, and even while I think about how fun it would be to play some cards with Ansel and Oliver, I don't go anywhere.

Harlow opens the bathroom door to find me leaning against the wall opposite and she doesn't look even a little surprised. Not one little bit. She stands in the doorway studying me and then takes a couple of steps closer.

She just stares up at me, and this is all so fucking new. She feels like a different woman than the wild Vegas party girl, than the hungry vixen who nearly broke down my front door. *This* Harlow feels patient, and seductive, and fucking *fascinating*. Beneath the surface of her gaze I see something there I hadn't seen before, some depth she usually keeps hidden, as if tonight, some shield was stripped away. It can't just be the alcohol, because I've seen her drunk. It can't just be that she wants to get off, because we've done that before, too.

The longer Harlow stares at me, the more it feels like my heart has become an inflatable raft she's slowly filling with air. My chest just gets tighter and tighter and tighter.

I can tell she put on some more lip gloss in the bathroom, and her mouth shines red when she smiles a little. "Are we gonna rumble?"

This breaks me from my trance and I reach for her arm, pulling her with me and turning us into the bedroom just to my left.

The room is empty but for a pile of bedding, a low dresser, and some cardboard boxes in the corner.

"Who the hell has an empty bedroom in a place like this?" I ask, walking to the floor-to-ceiling loft windows that line one wall. This place has three bedrooms and is twice the size of my *house* on Vancouver Island. There's a sweeping view of the harbor and, in the distance, what I think must be Coronado.

"This was Ruby's room," Harlow says, leaning against the wall to my right. "London inherited this apartment a few years back. Ruby just moved out a couple of weeks ago, right after Lola moved in. She got some amazing internship in London."

I look over at her, feeling confused. Drunk, mostly. "Ruby . . . and London?"

"Ruby moved to London, England," she says more slowly. "And yeah, I know. Her roommate was London; she moved to London. The jokes were endless. It was like Abbott and Costello up in here." Pushing off the wall, she takes a couple of steps closer to me and looks out the window at the water. "They're looking for a new roommate so if you know anyone who wants to flee the oppressive regime in Canada . . ."

"You won't move in?" I ask.

"I like my space. I like living alone."

I nod. I like living alone, too. My hometown is small enough as it is; sometimes it's nice to imagine I can close my door and get some distance.

Not that even at a thousand miles away I can really distance my thoughts from all the bullshit going on at home. My phone feels like a lead weight in my pocket, and I slip it out, putting it on the flat top of a cardboard box. Harlow watches me do it, and then does the same, pulling her phone from the pocket of her frayed-hem denim skirt and laying it facedown beside mine.

I step forward and she turns her face up to me, closing her eyes when I slide my hand along her neck and into her hair. "You smell like a fucking dream."

"Yeah?"

I nod, but she misses it, eyes still closed. "Give me your underwear."

No pretense, no warm-up, and she doesn't even startle. My worries are safely placed on top of a cardboard box four feet away, and what I have in front of me is a soft, warm girl to make everything else evaporate. With a little glance up at my face, she reaches under her skirt and shimmies out of her panties, giving me the tiny blue handful of lace. I slide them into my pocket, and then bend, kissing her.

This, too, is new. It's sweeter, more honest than the wild, biting, savage kisses we knew before. I kiss her once, just a touch, and then again, groaning as her hands slide up my chest and around my neck. Her lips fall into an easy rhythm against mine—there's no physical negotiation or uncertainty, only Harlow offering me her full bottom lip, little strokes of her tongue, and her eager little gasps. I can taste a hint of cherry lip gloss, the shots we did together in the kitchen. She's not sloppy drunk, but her cheeks are warm from the alcohol, her body pliable and relaxed. I'm sure I could bend her however I want. I could spread her out on the floor, put her legs over my shoulders, and fuck her so hard that people out in the living room would hear the slap of my skin against hers.

"You think about fucking me sometimes?" I ask, pressing a kiss to her neck, slipping a strap off her shoulder, and trailing my lips and teeth along her skin.

"Yeah."

"Tell me."

"It's my go-to when I get myself off," she admits without hesitation.

"So you think of me like five times a day?"

Harlow laughs and it catches in a little hiccup when I push her skirt over her hips and lift her onto the dresser, spreading her legs and stepping forward. I'm already hard and the feel of the bare warmth of her pussy against the denim over my cock is enough to have me hissing against her mouth, pushing my hips forward.

She presses into me and I slide my hand between us, reaching to touch the soft, slick skin between her thighs.

Fuck.

She's gasping these perfect little breaths and shaking against me, and I'm so hard it's all I can do to not reach for my fly, pull out my dick, and rub all over this, but instead I slide my fingers over her unbelievably soft body. She's the only woman I've felt in so long. It's hard to not let my mind instinctively tattoo her with *mine* when I kiss her neck, her lips, her shoulder. And it's easy to pretend everything beyond this room has evaporated or, at the very least, been put on pause, and that relief—even if imagined—sends a thrill down my spine, coiling tightly at the base. I'm so hard for this girl; she makes me harder than anything I can remember. I swear I can still feel the echo from almost two months ago of her lips kissing down my cock, her hands guiding me into her.

"You have any idea how this feels to me?" I step back enough to watch my fingers slide up and over her clit and back down, lower, inside. I fucking love how they look when they're wet with her. "God, when did your pussy get so sweet?" I look up to her downcast eyes, the lip trapped savagely between her teeth as she's watching me touch her. A searing fire iron of a thought stabs at me: "You let that asshole kid lick you here last night?"

She closes her eyes, pushing into my hand, and I lean in to kiss her neck. Her silence is as good as a *yes* and it further sparks a fire in my chest. And then I remember how she looked this morning: like she simultaneously wanted to fuck me and beat me.

"Tell me you like my mouth."

She whimpers, choking out, "I like your mouth."

"Tell me you remember coming on it."

"I do."

"How many times?"

Harlow coughs out a laugh and it turns into a groan when I slide my thumb around and around and around her clit. "A *lot*."

"I remember telling you to crawl across the room to get it."

Her nails dig into my shoulder. *"Dick."*

"But you did." I kiss her neck, her jaw. "And I love licking it. I love your obscene little sounds."

A knock on the door cracks through the quiet room and we both startle. Against me, Harlow tenses, reaching to hold my arm so I don't stop touching her.

"Finn?"

Fuck. It's Ansel.

"Yeah?"

"Hey, uh . . . we are leaving, in case you wanted a ride back to Oliver's."

I can practically feel Harlow waiting for my response; her body is tense all around me. "When is Oliver going?" I ask, contemplating my options.

"He left about ten minutes ago to swing past the store one more time."

I groan and, without realizing it, move my hand away and use it to wipe my mouth. But my fingers are covered in Harlow. And now I can smell her, and taste her, and I'm so fucking hard my jaw clenches tightly with tension.

She watches me, but it's hard to see her face since she's backlit from the city lights. If I don't leave with them, I'll need to cab it. And the Roberts family business needs every one of the measly five thousand we have in the bank, so I really don't think I should pay thirty bucks for a cab tonight.

"I gotta head out with them," I tell her.

"I know." She doesn't sound angry or even all that disappointed . . . just tired.

"Don't try to drive home," I tell her. "You've had too much to drink."

She blinks, and when she looks back up at me, I can see whatever shutter she keeps over her emotions has been slotted back in place. Disappointment cools me when she says, "Do you think I'm an idiot?"

"No." I move to retrieve my phone, sliding it into my back pocket. Oddly, I feel a little like she's played me tonight. "Do you want a ride home with us?"

She shakes her head. "I'm good."

"I'll see you tomorrow?" I lean in to kiss her, but she turns her head away and pushes me. It's half annoyed, half playful.

"Go away, Sunshine. Goodbyes with emotion aren't part of the arrangement."

Right. This detached Harlow is much more familiar. I adjust my cap and give her a little nod before walking to the door.

Chapter THREE

Harlow

I'M STARTING TO see that despite Oliver's gentle and mildly aloof demeanor, he really is a pretty shrewd businessman. After scouting for months for the best location for his store, he settled on an updated, bright space on G Street in the Gaslamp, nestled between a trendy tattoo parlor and a bar.

The place is amazing, and I can tell this even without the gathering crowd or the row of apparently famous comic artists sitting at a table in the back signing books.

Catching Lola's eye from where she stands several feet away, I can tell she's impressed, too.

I can count on zero hands the number of times I've been inside a comic book store, but I immediately get the sense that the layout is genius. I expected cluttered and narrow rows filled with floor-to-ceiling racks of brightly colored books and magazines, but Oliver has built-in cube-shelves—asymmetric, with panels of different sizes to look like pages of a comic book—along the walls. They're filled with books and merchandise, but there's also lots of open space for tables shaped like a stack of upward-curving pages displaying featured titles. Up front and nestled in a bank of giant windows are a couch and a matching set of bright red leather lounge chairs. A space just for reading.

"Won't people just sit and read and not buy anything?" I ask Oliver, who's just finished giving me the tour.

But he's already stepped away to greet a customer—the place is getting busy—and instead I hear Finn's voice. "I asked him the same thing."

The sound is gravelly, and faint, like it was overused last night. I can feel the echo of his fingers on me, the thrill of the dirty things he said, a feeling that only intensifies when I hear him take a step closer.

Turning, I meet his eyes. I expect it to be a little awkward after last night's cockblock, but he holds my gaze and smiles. His eyes are greener than brown today, and his lashes seem thicker, even darker. His lips look a little swollen, but the effect is to make me want to suck on them, soothe them.

I make out with him in a drunken haze and he gets hotter? Unfair, Universe.

I can tell we're both trying to play it cool, but I wonder if I'm failing as badly as he is. His attention dips to my lips for a beat before he says, "But Oliver says comic geeks like to have hard copies of their favorite books. He wants people to hang out, maybe find new titles. He wants newbies to feel comfortable taking the time to find a book they'll want to follow."

With this explanation, I think Finn has just used more words in one breath than he has with me up to now, cumulatively. "Did you memorize that?"

"Yep."

"Makes sense. I like the feel of it."

I pause, waiting. He closes his eyes, pinching the bridge of his nose.

"You okay there, Roberts?" I ask. "You're passing up a pretty epic *that's-what-she-said* opportunity."

He opens one eye. "Never drinking again."

This makes me laugh. Finn the Invincible has a wittle hangover? "You're too old to say that now."

"Practically middle-aged," he agrees. "Might as well skip out and go get a beer for breakfast."

"Breakfast?" I make a point of lifting his wrist and looking at his giant, manly waterproof watch. "It's almost *eleven*."

"I was a little slow to start this morning. Late night," he growls, smiling darkly. When he looks at me like that, I immediately recall the way he slid his fingers over and inside me—*God, when did your pussy get so sweet?*—the way his breath warmed my neck. I remember the feel of his hungry mouth sucking at my neck, my shoulders, the hard press of him through his jeans between my legs.

And then he left. And I nearly screamed in sexual frustration.

It shouldn't feel so easy with him today. Why does it feel so easy?

After a quiet pause, he asks, "Did you get home okay?"

I look past him, my head swimming a little with the jarring transition in mental images his question brings. Bellamy was still up when I tripped in at nearly two in the morning. I found her sitting in the kitchen, staring blankly at the space in

front of her. *I went out. I tried to just . . . have a good night,*
she'd said. *But I felt sort of like a bobblehead. Disjointed, you*
know? And now I can't sleep.

I felt immediately guilty for going out and forgetting everything in the middle of Lola's kitchen, and with Finn of all
people. But Mom kicked me out again after breakfast this
morning, telling me she hadn't seen me indoors on a Saturday since I was an infant and I wasn't allowed to miss Oliver's
grand opening.

"I slept in Lola's bed for a little bit, then took a cab," I
tell Finn, giving him a pointed look. "It's what I do after we
hook up, apparently."

"Right." He doesn't seem to think I'm as funny as I do.

When he looks over my shoulder at the store beyond, I
take the opportunity to check him out. I can't find a single
flaw with the man's body, and I'm woman enough to admit
that I'm completely obsessed with his forearms. They're
roped, thick, every single muscle defined. I want to see him
haul a big net onto the deck of his ship. God, he would make
majestic fisherman porn.

"What are you thinking?" he asks and I blink up to his
face.

"Trying to decide if I want to buy this pair of boots I saw
on the way here." A lie, but one he'd believe. Obviously Finn
is comfortable with me in the role of airhead shopaholic, and
for sure doesn't need to know that I was just casting him in
the role of Salty Fisherman #1 in the small-screen production
of *Swabbing the Decks Aboard Her Royal Thighness.*

"When in doubt, buy the boots," he says dryly. "Isn't that what I'm supposed to say here?"

"I don't think you need an opinion on the boots."

"Thank God," he mumbles and then heads across the room when he sees Ansel and Mia walk in. Such an unceremonious departure. I'm sort of relieved with how easy that was. See? No need to rehash or trip through some stilted, day-after *I-was-so-drunk* conversation. Finn and I have already done that in much greater magnitude, what with the getting married and sexual consummation. Talk about next-day awkward.

Mia passes Finn, giving him a knowing little wink before handing me a plastic cup with the Whole Foods logo and filled with a green juice concoction.

"Ansel wanted to see what the juice craze was all about," she says. "So of course he goes purist and gets sixteen ounces of straight kale juice. I thought he was going to vomit in my car."

I look at my cup with suspicion.

"Yours also has banana, mango, and pineapple." She nudges me with her elbow. "I hear it cleanses the body of the toxic effects of shady decisions."

"Actually, last night was a *fun* decision. Lord, I can't help but enjoy that physique," I admit. Instinctively I look over to where Finn has met up with Oliver and Ansel, and he looks over at me at exactly the same time. He quickly blinks away when our eyes meet, and the two other guys lean in to listen to what he's saying. Clearly he's doing some sexplaining of his own.

"Did it speak last night?" Mia whispers. "I know how it vexes you when it tries to converse."

"It spoke some—never much—but it was acceptable. Mostly dirty sex words." I lean in closer to tell her, "We didn't have sex, though."

"Yeah, I figured," she says, nodding. "Finn sort of drunk-grumbled something about blue balls in the car. Where's Lola?"

I look toward the side of the store where I'd last seen her, lifting my chin so Mia's eyes follow mine. Lola is completely absorbed in reading a book and doesn't seem to realize that an *actual celebration* is happening, with people talking, pictures being taken, Not-Joe showing customers around, and everyone congratulating Oliver on what he's pulled off here.

I can tell Finn has successfully assured the other guys that we aren't approaching Awkward Group Dynamic territory when Ansel comes to join Mia, looping a long arm around her shoulders. He squeezes her to his side before bending for a kiss. She's so petite, and he's so tall, that the effect is pretty comical; Mia practically disappears from my view for the length of it.

"Did you guys need some privacy?" I ask.

Ansel speaks against her mouth. "That would be wonderful, thank you. Order everyone away."

Laughing, I shove his shoulder playfully and he pulls her back up, steadying her. She presses two fingers to her lips as she stares up at him, flushed and a little breathless, and for just a beat—only a teeny, *tiny* heartbeat—I want what they have so intensely it makes my chest pinch.

And then it's gone.

"We're thinking of grabbing some lunch," Finn says from behind me, and—*dammit!*—that tiny spike of heat jabs right back through my chest. Mia's gaze zeros in on my face to gauge my reaction. He's standing directly behind me and I widen my eyes, telling her with my expression, *It's fine. I'm perfectly fine.*

"We only got here fifteen minutes ago," I tell him, slowly turning. Slow, and cool. "Shouldn't we stay a little longer?"

He looks around meaningfully. "This place is packed. Friends show up to these things to fill space. We're just in the way now."

I should go with them, and I'm sure it would be fun, but I really want to be home, pretending not to hover over my mom.

"Are you leaving tonight or tomorrow?" I ask him.

"Um." He glances at Ansel, who has tilted his head and is wearing the world's most hilarious expression of amused expectation. Mia is staring at me wide-eyed, as if I'm a grenade and Finn is about to remove my pin.

He reaches up to scratch his jaw. "I'm actually staying with Oliver for the next couple weeks."

MY THOUGHTS ARE stacked like a deck of cards and I have to continually shuffle the top one to the back of the pile.

I can't obsess about Mom's surgery on Monday. I can't think about the possibility of more sexcapades with Finn. I don't want to shop. I don't want to surf. I don't want to eat. And my part-time job is a joke. So, I go to my parents' house on Saturday afternoon, change into my bathing suit, and head out to the pool to swim until my limbs are like noodles. At least there I can be close by, but not hovering.

Apparently Dad had the same idea. He finishes his lap, surfacing when he sees me and folding his arms at the edge of the pool. Water drips from his salt-and-pepper hair onto his tanned skin and he pushes his goggles onto his forehead before closing his eyes, tilting his face up to the sky. I would do anything to not have to see my father this worried.

I sit down, sliding my feet into the water next to him. We sit in easy silence while he catches his breath.

"Hey, Tulip."

"Hey, dude."

I slip the rest of the way into the pool, relishing the mild chill of the unheated water in September. When I break through the surface, I ask, "You hanging in there?"

He laughs without much humor, stripping his goggles off completely and tossing them onto his towel a few feet away. "Not really." He's still breathless. Dad is in unbelievable shape; he must have been swimming like a maniac. "You?"

I shrug. For some reason, I don't feel like I have a right to be as shaken by all of this as Dad is. After all, he in particular has always been my most involved parent. Mom's career exploded when I was only two and tapered just as I was entering college. Dad's took off my sophomore year of high school, the first year he won an Oscar. He loves us with a ferocity that amazes me, but I know without question that Mom is his sun, moon, and stars.

"Did you go into the office this morning?" I ask.

He smiles, clearly noting my diversionary tactic. "Only for about an hour. Thinking about getting involved with Sal's next project. It'd keep me home until April, at least."

Salvatore Marìn is a producer/director who is Dad's closest friend and most frequent work colleague. I know the question of work has to have been weighing on Dad: how to balance his career while still *being there* for Mom in every sense of the word. Dad's never in one place for long, and so I'm sure the idea of having to leave right now, of missing anything with Mom, must be terrifying.

"That sounds ideal," I say simply, going for light.

"I think you'd like this one." His smile changes into one I haven't seen for a while, genuine and mischievous. "It's about a bunch of guys on a *boat*."

"Very funny." I splash him. I've missed his laughter and his easy smiles, so if letting him hassle me about Finn, or any other boy, makes them happen more often, he can do it as much as he wants.

"So what'd you end up doing last night?"

I dunk underwater quickly, slicking my hair back. "Went to Lola's."

I can feel him watching me, waiting. He's used to getting every detail. "And? Was it fun?"

"It was okay," I hedge and look at him, squinting into the sun. "Funny thing, actually . . . Finn was there."

His eyebrows slowly inch up. "Finn, huh?"

I've always relied on Dad's brain to help me sort through my day, my frustrations, my adventures. So of course he knows the PG-rated details of my Vegas trip: We met at a bar, got drunk and married. After a sharp cut-to-black in the version of the story he got, I told him about how we went together to get the marriage annulled the next afternoon.

But he also knows I flew up to visit Finn for less than a day. So when I mention that he was at the party last night, I'm pretty sure my dad puts two and two together.

"It was a good distraction . . ." I mumble, even more quietly admitting, "not that much happened."

His eyes dance with restrained teasing. "He's in town for the grand opening?"

I nod, leaving out the part where it seems Finn is staying for a couple weeks. I can't decide if I'm excited about this news, or irritated. As if I don't already have enough to think about, now I'm going to be forced into seeing him every time I want to socialize?

Dad watches me as I doodle in the dry concrete with a wet fingertip. I've never had to hide my interest in boys, my distress over girl-dramas, or my fears and anxiety about life from him. Growing up, our deal was that as long as I always came to him first with the big things, he would do his best not to lecture, judge, or go into what mom calls his Protective Latin Rage.

"Distractions are sometimes nice," he says, watching me.

The problem with being raised by such an amazing man is that it's nearly impossible not to compare every boy I meet to him. Every single one falls short.

I shrug.

"With everything going on in your life, it's too bad he lives so far away."

I look over at him. "He's here for a couple of weeks."

Dad laughs at my grim expression and lifts himself out of the pool. Water pours off him into puddles at his feet, reflecting a hundred dots of sun on the ground.

"I adore you, my beautiful, fierce girl." He bends for a towel and dries off his chest and arms as he says, "And I know you. I bet you're thinking of all the reasons why you shouldn't spend time with him."

"Of course I shouldn't—"

He cuts me off with a hand gently raised in the air. "I know you never let anything come before family; that's how I raised you. But soon you'll want to be at every appointment, sitting nearby for every possible second. You'll be online, reading every detail you can find. You'll be hovering, offering her food, a sweater, movies, gifts. I'll be doing the same. And together we will drive your mother crazy." Crouching down in front of me, he whispers, "Please, Tulip, let yourself be distracted when you can. Have some fun. I envy you."

OLIVER'S HOUSE IS a tiny, single-story stucco cottage in Pacific Beach, with ocean-breeze-dulled blue paint and faded, chipped red windowsills. The sidewalk out front is cracked and uneven, and the lawn is a mottled calico of yellow, green, and brown. Unlike his glossy new store downtown, this place isn't much to look at. But I know the area well enough to guess what it cost him and that being able to climb up to his roof at night and see the sunset over the ocean is part of the appeal.

After swimming for a while, I'd gone inside to find Mom and Dad in the living room, cuddled together on the couch and reading their books in easy silence.

I offered to make them lunch. They weren't hungry. I offered to run some errands. They had nothing for me to do. So I stood, fidgeting at the perimeter of the room until Dad looked up at me and gave me a sad little smile.

Mom *will* need me, but she doesn't need me today. She doesn't need anyone but her guy, and what he needs is to be her entire world right now.

I drove to Oliver's in a fog, on autopilot, trying not to second-guess what I was going to do. My father was basically telling me to enjoy Finn—though not in those exact words—and why not? It isn't like Finn and I have misaligned expectations. We've spent a combined total of maybe one full day together, and have been naked for most of that. Before this weekend, our most meaningful conversation occurred when I showed up at his house and he told me to help myself to anything in the fridge while he ran out to get condoms.

I smile at the R2-D2 knocker and rap twice at the door with it.

The house inside is silent, and all around me the ocean wind whips past the tall, willowy palms. Finally, I hear footsteps just in front of the door and it swings open.

Finn pulls a dish towel off his shoulder, using it to dry his hands. He's shirtless, and his jeans hang low on his hips, revealing the black waistband of his boxers.

"Hey, Ginger Barbie."

In one heartbeat I've gone from relieved anticipation, to hating this moment. I feel vulnerable and on the verge of tears, but there's nothing particularly sympathetic about Finn. Drunk Finn was an anomaly, all soft expressions and playful. Daylight Finn is efficient and brusque, good for fishing, fucking, and—apparently—washing dishes.

"You know what?" I say, looking at my car parked at the curb. "This was a stupid idea."

"Wait. You came here to see me, not Oliver?" He takes one step closer.

"Yeah . . ."

"Did you come here to finish what we started last night?"

I turn to leave, having no idea what to say to such a blunt question. I mean, yes, I did come for that. But it's bigger than just wanting to fool around: What I want with Finn is the sex that absorbs me and shuts off my brain. I don't want to play cat-and-mouse, I don't want to discuss it. I just want to *do* it.

I can hear the playful mocking in his voice when he calls, "If that's what you want, you just need to say it, Harlow."

I stand, facing the street for several deep breaths. A car

drifts by, its frame lowered so it almost touches the asphalt, stereo bass blaring, vibrating up through my feet. The car slows, and the man in the passenger seat lifts his chin to me.

"The next young freak I met was Red," Too $hort raps from the car, his voice distorted through the crappy speakers.

I square my shoulders, staring down the guys as their attention moves past my face to my chest.

"I took her to the house and she gave me head."

At the lyric, the man in the passenger seat smiles lewdly, raising his eyebrows at the next line as if to ask me whether it's true, whether *I* like to freak, and the car stops, idling in the middle of the street as if the driver expects me to jump in and party with them. I want to walk to my car but feel trapped between these guys and the cocky asshole behind me.

Finn steps out of the house, pulling the dishrag off his shoulder as he comes to stand with one shoulder in front of me, and stares down the men in the car.

"The fuck are they looking at?" he growls under his breath.

I no longer care about the guys in the car. I've never had a man other than my father take a protective stance around me. The boys I'm used to would just pretend they didn't see the car at all, or anxiously whisper-hiss that we should get back inside. Beside me, Finn is huge. I've never seen his skin in the sun, but the sun has seen *him* a thousand times. I'm tall, but he's inches taller, and nearly twice as wide. His chest is tanned and bulky, clear of a single tattoo, but marked with the occasional tiny scar. A snag here, a cut there. He seems larger than life on this street full of salty surfer boys and skinny thugs.

The car accelerates with a rumble, driving off down the street.

"Those assholes wouldn't know the first thing to do with you," he says quietly, looking me over as if I'd been handled. And with that look, I see the same expression he gave me last night—possessiveness, interest, hunger—as if I'm not quite what he'd assumed . . . and that, maybe, he liked it.

My heart is hammering wildly and—with the pulse of adrenaline in my blood—even more than before I want to go inside with him and let him take over every single thought.

"Okay yes. I'm here to finish what we started."

He waits, thinking. For the first time, I realize he's not wearing a hat. I can see his eyes in the sun—*really* see them, without shadow or the diffused light filtered through the heavy marine layer. I find that I like the way he studies things, especially me.

His eyes seem so much smarter than his mouth.

Case in point: "A girl like you is way more trouble than she's worth," he says with a little smile.

God, he's such a dick. But the twinkle in his eyes tells me he's pretty fucking happy I'm here, and the truth is, he can think I'm a high-maintenance diva as long as he's able to make me forget for a little while. "I see."

"We can have sex, that's fine. But just so we're clear, that's all it is."

I laugh. "I'm here for sex, not some deep bonding ritual."

He makes a gentlemanly sweep of his arm, indicating I lead us both inside.

It takes my eyes a few seconds to adjust once I'm out of the bright sun. Finn closes the door behind him, leaning against it with his arms crossed over his chest. I turn away, pulse tripping in wild throbs in my neck, trying to calm my thoughts as I pretend to survey the room. The sheer unexpectedness of it all catches me off guard, and for a beat I forget to be nervous.

Light shoots in through the oceanside windows, causing slanted shadows to be cast across the acacia wood flooring throughout the living room and small dining room. The furniture looks vintage, but refurbished, and surprisingly well coordinated. The couch and chairs are various shades of blue. A large Aztec woven ottoman serves as a coffee table. A few framed photographs stand on a side table adjacent to the sofa, and there is a small urn with twisting bamboo growing in intricate curls on a stunning multi-tone wooden dining room table. The table's made from random cuts of wood, light and dark wood intermingling, and although the long side is smooth and polished, the jagged edges of the short sides give the table a striking, artistic feel.

"Oliver surprises me," I say. "This place doesn't look like a bachelor pad."

Finn laughs. "He's tidy."

I glance at the dish towel draped over his shoulder. "You're doing dishes."

With a little one-shouldered shrug, he murmurs, "I'm tidy, too."

"So Ansel is the slob?" I ask with a smile. My heart is beating so hard I can hear the whoosh of it in my ears. I miss the ease of conversation after tequila. His brows pull together, and I clarify: "One of you must be messy . . . based on my completely sexist statistics."

"Actually, he's the biggest neat freak I know. Perry is the slob. There goes your theory."

"Of course she's a slob. She's the Beast."

Finn stays quiet, his expression unreadable. I don't exactly expect him to start bashing one of his best friends, no matter how horrible she might be.

"Why are you still in town?" I ask finally. "I thought you never missed a shift at work."

He smooths a hand down his mouth, over his chin, holding my gaze for a beat. "You seem to always be present for the exception to that rule."

"That's not really an answer."

"Business."

"Business?"

"Yeah." He takes a couple of slow steps closer to me. "Why are *you* here?"

"I thought we clarified that outside."

"I know *what* you're here for, but not *why*."

"My . . ." I stop, changing my mind against telling him what I'm really doing here. Too heavy. Too much. "I just wanted to get out of the house."

His brows draw together, and more questions seem perched on his tongue, but instead of asking them, he holds his hands out, taking one last step closer. Palms up, he moves his hands in a seesaw gesture. "Finn . . . shoe shopping . . . Finn . . . shoe shopping."

"I guess you won."

He gives in to the smile he's been fighting. "Tell me why *me*. You've got a city full of rich kids waiting for you to climb between their sheets."

Heat seeps into my bloodstream and he reaches out, toying with the strap of my dress. "None of them are any good," I admit.

"Oh, really?" He doesn't sound at all surprised.

"I've never been with a guy who made me come. Without my help."

I ignore the smug tilt of his lips when I say this. At least, I try to hide the way I'm shaking inside, so desperate for the sensation overload that happens when he touches me. But maybe he *should* see. Maybe it'll make him want to outdo himself today.

"So, just to be clear," I whisper. "I'm using you for sex."

Finn reaches behind me and I feel my eyes falling closed, my senses rising in anticipation of his first touch. He gently gathers my hair in his hands, barely brushes his fingers against the nape of my neck as he bunches the strands into a twist and closes a single fist around it. "Then start by kissing me."

He's holding my head by my hair; I try, but I can't move any closer.

I try again but he's holding me still, smiling darkly at my lips. I close my eyes and reach out, running my hands up his bare stomach and over his chest. His skin is impossibly warm. He's hard and smooth, nipples tightening under my palms, and he lets out a sharp hiss when I scratch my nails over them, loosening his hold on my hair. This feels familiar, and also not: This time the sex isn't rushed or cramped, drunken or spontaneous.

It's intentional, and we have all afternoon.

At least, I think we do. Uncertainty about his business here tickles my thoughts, but that evaporates when my hands move up his neck, and I brush my mouth over his. With a groan he slides his lips across mine, easing his tongue inside, and all at once it's fevered. He pushes me back, turning me, and we stumble down a hall, knocking against a wall, where he stills, pressing the length of his body to mine.

"Last night I wanted to eat your pussy," he says directly into my ear. "I still want it. I want you wild, squirming all over my face. What do you think of that?"

I think it sounds like an excellent plan.

As Finn pulls away and tugs me down the hall, I count three bedrooms—three *tiny* bedrooms—with his at the end, on the street side of the house. It's pretty empty, other than a full-size IKEA bed against one wall and matching dresser against the other. Finn's suitcase rests just next to the closet door.

Removed from the sun streaming through the windows, this side of the house is cool, and we trip in and stop, only inches apart. His warmth grows and ebbs with each of his heavy breaths. I'm practically gasping, my heart is thudding so hard.

I almost never feel intimidated—and I'll be damned if I ever let a guy get the upper hand—but if there is an alpha dog in this room, it isn't me. Tossing the dish towel back over his shoulder, Finn lets his eyes move from my mouth, to my neck, and lower. My nipples harden beneath my thin dress, and he licks his lips, humming.

"I'm going to tie you up this time," he tells me, slipping one strap of my dress off my shoulder. With his lips trailing across my neck, he asks, "You into that?"

I blink up to him, a little caught off guard. I . . . *might be?* I've never been tied up. But to be completely honest, I'm not all that surprised Finn wants this. In Vegas, and again in Canada, he was rough and tender in equal, drastic measure. He spanked me, pinned my hands over my head, and withheld orgasms, only to push back inside and kiss me so tenderly I came with a scream. And then he pulled out and made me come again with his mouth.

The first night we were together, we only had sex one time before we passed out cold, but he made it last three hours. Finn likes to call the shots, and right now, I'm going to let him.

"I can be."

"Last time you showed up unannounced, I was just down to fuck," he says. "Today, I think I want to savor this. Unless you've got somewhere to be?"

I shake my head, closing my eyes. It feels so good to just put it all in his hands. To shrug away every single worry and let him tie me up, eat me out, fuck me until I can't walk. I don't know him well enough to trust him with anything else, but I trust this man with my body.

"What's that?" he asks with a tiny edge to his voice, ducking to meet my eyes.

"No," I say, eyes fluttering open and my voice coming out thick before I clear my throat. "I don't have anywhere else to be."

He nods, walking over to the closet and pulling a length of red rope from a high shelf.

"You just happened to have *rope* in the closet?" I ask, my voice high and reedy.

"Didn't want to leave it in my truck in case someone took it." He grins at me. "This is really nice rope."

I'm pretty sure few people in Pacific Beach would have any idea that the rope in the back of a pickup truck is *really nice rope*, but I can hardly complain. I'm glad he didn't have to leave the room to go get it.

But when I look down at it, this rope doesn't seem like something he'd use on a boat. It's soft, has the sheen of silk.

"You carry silky rope around in the bed of your pickup? Should I Google you, Finn?"

He laughs a little, dropping it at the foot of the bed. "I was pretty sure I'd get you naked while I was here." He lifts his chin, silently telling me to do just that.

"How confident of you."

His eyebrow flickers up, as if to say, *Well?* and he pulls the towel from his shoulder, walking a slow circle around me as I pull my dress up and over my head. When I slide my underwear down my legs and step out of them, I feel a whisper of fabric against the back of my thigh.

And then a sharp pop against the exact same spot.

With a gasp, I turn and gape at him. He's snapped the *towel* at me, like a fucking teenager in the kitchen. The sting turns warm, making me more aware of the cool air in his room.

"Come here," he says, ignoring my surprised expression.

"You're not going to whip me with a *dish towel*."

"You're right, I'm not." When I start to take a step closer, he snaps it again, barely grazing my hip. "I'm going to tease you with it."

"What happened to just getting naked and—"

He pops me again, this time on my upper thigh. "You came to me, not some skinny-dicked kid in Del Mar. And I'm doing this how I want." His eyes soften. "It's not like I'm going to leave you needy, sweet thing. I wouldn't do that."

I exhale a jagged breath and nod. Whatever he wants to do . . . it's why I'm here. I close my eyes, giving in to the semi-drunk sensation I get when I'm this close to him, and he's the only thing I can sense in the room.

He wraps his fingers around a small lock of my hair and glides them down to the end, tugging gently. "Look at me."

I blink up to him, eyes wide and focused on nothing but the bow of his bottom lip, the appearance of his ironic little smile as I wait to hear what instruction comes next.

"Kiss my neck," he whispers, so I do. I stretch on my toes and press my lips against his pulse point. It's an excuse, maybe, to see how I affect him and whether his blood trips the same way mine does when we are this close. But his pulse is a steady and slow *dum . . . dum . . . dum* beneath my touch.

"Lick me." His fingers slide up my neck and over my necklace, pressing into my scalp and gripping handfuls of my hair.

My tongue sweeps out, just barely touching his skin, and he groans, a low, hungry sound. He tastes like salt and air, as if the ocean wrapped around him when he was small and never let go.

"Go lie down." His fingers release me but his gaze doesn't. Right now, I remember that Finn is ten years older than me; I must look wide-eyed and naïve. I wonder if he has any idea the extent of my inexperience with lovers like him. "I'm gonna tie you up and kiss that sweet pussy for a while. I want to hear you say my name when you come on my lips."

I back up to the bed and then turn, moving toward the middle. Having grown up on the beach, I'm used to being in bikinis around people, but Finn and I have only ever hooked up in the dark. It's a little weird to be completely naked—with him mostly clothed—and crawling on my hands and knees on a bed in broad daylight.

When I kneel and wait for him to join me, he shakes his head. "Lie back. Close your eyes." At my suspicious expression, he says in a quiet, deep voice, "You want it or not?"

Before I do what he says, I blink down to the worn button fly of his jeans, faded and soft over time and now distorted with the shape of him, hard beneath. He's always made sure my body was ready, and I know that's what we're doing, but the threat of panic and fear lingering at the edges, and my need to get lost in something other than my own thoughts, makes me impatient.

He sees where my attention has gone and rubs the heel of his hand down the thick line of his cock, gripping it. "You'll get it in a little bit. Lie back."

The pillow is full and hard, but the cotton comforter is soft and warm against my bare skin. Between my legs, the mattress dips as Finn climbs up from the foot of the bed, his palms smoothing up my shins.

Finn drags the length of red rope up over my torso, coiling it around his hand. Reaching behind me, he slides the center of its length under my body and then crisscrosses it back and forth down across my torso. Looping it around one hand he coils it up one arm and then back over my chest to the other side. Wrapping it down around my other arm, he's softly bound my arms so each of my wrists stays at the sides of my hips. In the center, just below my belly button, he ties an intricate—and beautiful—knot. I watch him the entire time; he's focused and careful not to bind me too tight. I can tell, too, that he loves what he sees. When he's done, he sighs, running his hands up over my hips and across my stomach, my breasts, my neck.

"I had no idea you were into this," I whisper.

He shrugs a little, but doesn't say anything. My breasts are displayed on either side of an X across my breastbone, and the rope is soft but sturdy; I can feel it pressing into the tender skin all along my torso.

"Is it too tight?" he asks, drawing a finger in a small circle around my nipple.

I swallow back a gasp. "No."

"Do you like it?"

I hear genuine concern in his voice. I can tell from his trembling hand, intense gaze, and the pressing shape of his cock beneath his jeans that Finn likes this. A *lot*. But it matters to him that I do, too.

And fuck, I do. I don't mind having my arms pinned at my sides as much as I thought I would. And I feel *everything*: the silken slide of the rope as I wiggle a little under his inspection, the cool air over my breasts, the thudding echo of my pulse in my neck, chest, between my legs.

I forgot how rough his hands are, calloused from constant work—rough and so huge he covers much of my body as his splayed fingers slide up my legs to my inner thighs, spreading me.

I resist, and he makes a quiet *tsk* sound, easily overpowering me as he shakes his head. He's not looking at my face, he's looking at me, *there*, between my legs.

I like to consider myself a pretty progressive woman—lots of talk about being comfortable with anything and trying everything once—but mostly, so far, it's only been theory. At twenty-two, I've never had a lover who was experienced enough to be slow and force me to still under his acute attention. I've never been with anyone who was confident enough to be still and calm while he just *looks* at me. I've certainly never been tied up. And I've never had someone savor me the way Finn is right now, not even the Finn I thought I knew from before.

He settles, propped on his elbows between my legs, and kisses my thigh, looking up the length of my body at the red rope against my skin. "You look amazing."

I whisper out a raspy "Thanks," watching rapt as he bends, lips parted. And, God, I believe him.

He groans a split second before he makes contact, and when he does it's like a bomb goes off inside me. Something seems to break loose with the wet slide of his tongue. I fall back, arms stiffening in their hold, back bowing off the mattress so I can arch closer. I know now that I haven't just been waiting for this since last night; I've been waiting for it every second since I last felt his tongue between my legs. His mouth is warm and strong. Kissing there like he would my mouth, small kisses and gentle licks release my first cry, and he grunts, pushing his tongue up into me and just . . . *losing* it.

Finn was always borderline rough and clearly wanted control the two other times we were together, but this . . . this is different. It isn't just the rope around my arms or the way he has me pinned beneath him. It's the way it feels like we've crossed into a different space—before it was just a one-time thing, a two-time thing, just sex. But this time, it's like he's peeling away the layers to show me a secret side of him.

For a flash, I'm aware of how loud he is, sucking and smacking, and how loud *I* am, crying out and saying his name and other garbled words—but I can't hold on to the inclination to be self-conscious. I can't because with the vibration of his groan spreading through me, and the way he uses the knot at my belly to rhythmically pull me against his mouth, I'm coming so soon, so hard it claws up my thighs and explodes like heat and wet and pure fucking bliss, sliding silvery all along every inch of my legs. My skin feels flushed and electric, and I can hear my own hoarse cries echo sharply in the mostly empty room. Finn keeps going, diligently working his mouth over me, but I'm gasping as I come down, my legs trembling and weak. I want to push them together, but his hands spread across my thighs, holding me open, pressing them flat to the bed.

He grunts out a *No* and reaches beneath me with one hand to deliver a sharp smack on the outside of my thigh.

I'm too far gone to be shocked. When he spreads his hand over where he's just struck me, and rubs his rough palm in slow, soothing circles as he hums, I immediately want the sharp crack *again* because of the way it melted into delicious heat under his sweeter touch.

Finn is watching me, his lips pressed gently against my clit, concentrating his gaze on my face. He pulls away just enough to whisper, "Tell me how that felt."

Does he mean the spanking or the mind-numbing orgasm? Or the way I can barely move after he made every muscle in my body clench? Regardless, the answer is the same.

Blinking, I open my mouth, slowly stringing the words, *So . . . fucking . . . good*, together in my head. Before I can get them out, he smiles against me, returning to the maddening kisses, the licks and tugging on the knotted rope. I let the words and every thought in my head fall away and push into him, circling my hips closer to his mouth.

My face feels hot, my cheeks flushed. The rope tickles along my skin, pulling up and down in a rhythm that matches the teasing flicks of his tongue. My nipples are hard, aching, and I want his fingers to find them, his mouth to find them. I want him everywhere at once. I feel heavy and desperate, my entire world oriented by where he's touching me and where he's not.

I must be saying something because the sound of his voice breaks through the fog. "That's right," he says, murmuring softly. "Fuck, *look* at you."

But I'm looking at *him*. His soft hair is between my legs and his eyes, those fucking eyes are staring right back at me, waiting. He curls a finger inside and bends his head to continue sucking, and that's all it takes. My back arches off the mattress and I cry out, falling to pieces again inside his web of silken rope.

I feel like melted chocolate poured across this bed and moan quietly when Finn's hands smooth up over my belly, gently unfastening the knot.

"It may tingle a little when I take it off." He kisses where the knot was, where there's now an indentation of what almost looks like a flower on my skin. "It'll be sensitive."

"Okay," I say on a long exhale. And it does; as he unwinds the soft rope from my arms, reversing the intricate crisscross pattern across my body, I can feel the air hit the delicate lines on my skin, but only for a split second before Finn's mouth slides along the same path, licking, kissing, soothing everywhere it feels so sensitive.

It's overwhelming how good this feels, and how gentle he is. When my hands are free, I slide them both over his shoulders and up his neck, holding his face to my chest as he licks and sucks at the rope lines beneath my breasts.

Finally, he pulls my nipple into his mouth, tongue circling. "So fucking good," he murmurs, switching to my other breast, fingers ghosting along the fading lines.

His hands find my wrists and he guides my arms over my head, looping the rope around them again.

"Okay?" he whispers.

"Yeah."

Bound like this, I can leave my arms over my head or loop them around his neck. But for now I leave them where they are and relish the feel of the comforter beneath my back as Finn grips my hips and drags me to the foot of the bed.

Reaching between my legs, he strokes me with two fingers, making a V as he slides over my clit and then inside, repeating the pattern again, and again.

"You're so damn warm." He bends, kissing my hip.

Finn pulls away and steps back so I can watch him push his jeans and boxers down his hips, kicking them onto the floor. He grabs a condom from a box in the top drawer of the dresser but doesn't put it on yet.

Instead, he climbs up on the bed, straddling my chest. Above me, he feels like fire, the heat emanating from his skin unlike anything I've ever felt. I feel like I've grown extra nerve endings over the parts of my body that were covered by rope.

He braces a hand beside my head, gripping his cock with the other. "Kiss me."

When the broad head of his cock touches my lips, I let my eyes fall closed at the sound of his groan. I love the tight flare of the crown, the taste of him. I lick around the tip, opening wider when he slides more into my mouth, rocking just in and out while I play, getting him wet enough to slide easily past my lips.

"You like it?" he asks, voice rasping. "The feel of my cock on your tongue?"

Nodding, I open my eyes to see an expression on his face I've never seen before: frenzied adoration, as if he's never seen anything more amazing in his life.

"I never came in your mouth," he says quietly. "I kept thinking about it, but then I always ended up wanting something else instead."

Backing away, and proving the point he just made, he straddles my hips as he tears open the condom and rolls it down his length. If this was a movie, I would rewind and watch those three seconds again and again. I like the way he looks down as he puts the latex on, gripping himself, reaching down absently to run his palm across his balls. With a little growl, he moves the rest of the way down my body and stands at the foot of the bed, between my legs.

"Wrap them around my waist. Hold on to me with your legs."

I do everything he says because I don't know anything else but that I need Finn inside me right now. He holds his cock straight and rests one palm on the mattress beside my hip, sliding the head just in.

Just out.

Just in.

Watching me with his lips parted, eyes heavy, he pulls just out again.

I groan, pushing my head back into the mattress and gritting my teeth.

"I like seeing you so impatient," he whispers, bending to kiss my collarbone. "You have any idea how you look right now? Dripping wet all over me?"

He knows I don't have words and doesn't really seem to expect an answer as he pushes in, inch by inch, reaching down to circle his thumb around my clit, murmuring, "Ah, ah, ah, don't come yet."

But when he pulls back, he barely takes a breath before thrusting back in and then I know it's *on*. He gives me all of it, his hard thrusts and those low, animals sounds he makes with every one. His hands, so big, curled around my body, holding me steady as he fucks so hard.

I relish this man telling me to wait.

Wait.

Not yet, Harlow. Don't you fucking go without me.

I said wait. I'm close. I'm so fucking close.

He pulls out just when I've almost burst into a thousand tiny pieces, and then he eases back inside, whispering, "Wanna come?" against my neck. And I do. *I do, please please,* I'm begging, and I realize it only on the second, maybe the third *please,* and he loves it, I can tell, because he's wild again, and for a tiny, frantic pulse I'm startled by the memory that *there is something bigger than this.* I squeeze my eyes closed and fall back into feeling like there isn't anything else in the world but Finn and the way he makes me feel.

Rational thought vanishes as quickly as it peeked in, and I'm screaming as he moves back into me, grinding, grinding, grinding until I come. His palm is cupping my ass to pull me into him, his lips are on my shoulder, and his cock is so deep inside I don't think I ever knew I could feel so full.

Finn jerks over me, his body tense as he groans against my skin. I feel the twitching of him inside me, the pounding of his heart between us—or is it mine?—I can't even tell anymore. I have no idea where he ends and I begin.

I'm not sure which of us is more exhausted. Finn did all the work, moving over and into me, pushing and pulling me where he wanted, and yet I feel totally drained. My legs are heavy, my bones composed entirely of rubber. I could sleep for days.

It's exactly why I'm here.

At some point Finn has unbound my wrists, rubbed his thumb along the faint red marks.

"These will fade," he says, examining them, a hint of regret in his voice. "Probably within an hour."

Nodding, I close my eyes, count to ten, and then move to stand. I begin to dress, feeling his eyes on me from the bed.

"Jesus, Harlow. You don't have to rush off," he says, his voice thick and sleepy. The sky outside is deep lavender post-sunset. "Oliver won't be home until late."

I open my mouth, saying, "I should . . ." and pointing vaguely north, toward home.

He nods, watching me put everything back on before he pats a heavy hand on the bed. "Harlow, you shouldn't run off." Pushing to sit at the edge of the mattress, he says, "Stay. Let me . . . fuck, I don't know. Set up a bath for you, or . . . just stay here. It was intense. Wasn't it intense?"

It was. It was so intense that I'm suddenly second-guessing everything that brought me here.

As I gather my things to leave, I'm not sure if being with Finn is an escape, or a new dangerous obsession.

Chapter FOUR

Finn

*T*HE LIGHT CHANGES and I step off the curb, crossing the street in the middle of a small crowd. With my phone pressed to my ear, I listen as my brother Colton rattles off a list of things that will have to be repaired, most of which need to be done before the boats can leave the dock again.

"And you're sure the wiring's shot?" I ask. My stomach churns and I feel the need to clarify. "Do you know if it's the wiring itself, or have you checked the fuse panel?"

I hear him sigh and can imagine him taking off his hat, using the brim to scratch the top of his head. It's Tuesday and he's worked straight through the weekend on this. I'm sure he's beat. "Checked the panel myself while Levi was in the wheelhouse with a meter. We replaced any bad fuses and every goddamn one of them blew as soon as we flipped the breakers."

"Fuck."

"Pretty much."

"So what's the plan?" I ask, stepping into the shade of a bright red canvas awning. The sun is high this time of day, the sidewalks clean and nearly empty of shadows.

"I need to replace a bunch of wires, figure out how to pigtail them in on the damaged lines. It's gonna take some time."

"Jesus. I need to be home, not in fucking California of all places."

I lean against the wall of a brick building, trying to figure out exactly how all this happened. It feels like it's been one thing after another this year; add that to a long line of years with not enough fish and not enough money and well, I'm in fucking California.

But Colt isn't having it. "Stop," he says. "We've got it handled here. We need you there, figuring out the next step. We've made it through worse. We'll make it through this, too."

I take a moment before I ask the question I'm dreading. "So how long?"

He blows out a breath and I can practically hear him calculating. "I need to unbolt and pull panels from the wheelhouse floor," he says. "At least a couple of days."

It could be better. It could definitely be worse. I do the mental calculation of how much money we'll lose being off the water. "You serviced the engine?" I ask.

"We serviced number one," he says.

"And? Same? Worse?"

He hesitates. "A little worse."

"Fuck. How long will it hold?"

"Report says at least six months. But it said that six months before that, Finn. And six months before that. There's only two percent more shavings in this oil sample than there was the last time. I'd say we have *at least* a year, easy. By then we'll have finished the season and we'll be good. We can do this."

"Right," I say, and push off the building. I pass several shops, restaurants, and small bars, the sidewalks growing more crowded the farther I go. The San Diego sun beats down, and I feel the heat of it seep into my black T-shirt, through the thick denim of my jeans. Colton is right; we've been through worse. We don't need to push the nuclear button quite yet.

Why the fuck am I here, then?

"So you're all ready for the meeting?" he asks, a hint of anxiety finally coloring his tone.

"Doesn't sound like I need to be."

His nervous laugh rings through the line. "Finn, let's keep the option open, okay?"

"I know, Colt. I'm just fucking with you." Though I'm not. Not really. I want my business to stay the way it always has, and the L.A. Option, as I've been calling it, is *not* an option.

"When do you go?" he asks, like he doesn't have the date burned into his brain. Like we all don't.

"Next week." I lean against a building, scrubbing my face. "Why did I come down so fucking early? I could be there fixing shit and—"

He groans. "God, would you stop worrying? Spend some time with Ansel and Oliver, have *fun*. Remember fun, Finn? And for all our sakes, please, get laid before you head up to

L.A." I almost trip when he says this because Jesus Christ, my abs are still sore from the marathon sex with Harlow the other afternoon. "All this will still be waiting for you when you get back. Got it? Fun?"

There's a run-down large brick building to my right, and I glance inside the windows as I pass. My reflection looks back at me against the busy street, but I stop in my tracks. Because there, sitting at a table and frowning down at her laptop, is Harlow.

Fun, I think.

"Yeah, I got you."

THE HOSTESS AT the little podium smiles as I walk inside. She's hot, in that cool, pinup kind of way, and like she'd be perfectly at home stretched across the hood of a vintage muscle car. Her purple hair is cut short and clipped with little barrettes at the sides; her lip is pierced and so is her nose; splashes of bright-colored ink cover both of her arms. I almost consider calling Colton back; this girl is exactly his type.

"I'm over there," I tell her with a smile, and point to where Harlow is sitting, still alone, still staring at her screen and scrolling mindlessly through whatever she's looking at. Every once in a while she picks up her phone, scrolls some more on that, and sets it down again.

The hostess smiles back and motions for me to go ahead, handing me a menu and winking before I turn away. It's dark and blessedly cool inside. October on Vancouver Island is chilly.

In San Diego, it's as if the summer is only just getting started. Perpetual summer. No wonder everyone here is so laid-back.

Sleek black cushions and couches line the walls and create little seating areas in the front half of the restaurant, while long, well-worn tables and stools fill the back. It looks more like a club than a place you'd have pizza.

Harlow is at a long wooden table in the corner. She's in some sort of yellow skirt thing today, her tan legs stretched out, wrapped in a pair of tall brown sandals, and resting on a stool across from her. Her hair is pulled back from her face in a knot that seems simultaneously messy and complicated, and as I near the table, I'm more than a little pleased to spot what looks to be a small hickey on her shoulder.

"Hello, Miss Vega," I say.

She jumps at the sound of my voice and looks up, her smile vanishing and replaced by an expression of surprise . . . and maybe defeat.

"Finn." I don't miss the way she angles her laptop away as I slide onto a seat across from her. "Please," she says dryly. "Have a seat."

"You know, I think I actually heard your eyes roll when you said that," I reply. "That's talent."

A waitress steps up to the table and I glance down, seeing that Harlow has only a glass of iced tea in front of her.

"I'll have the same." I blink back to find Harlow watching me.

"Planning on staying?"

"Why not? This place seems kind of cool."

She hums in response—neck flushed but otherwise definitely pretending I didn't tie her up and fuck her three days ago—and glances down to her phone again.

"What time do you need to head back?" I ask.

She shakes her head. "I don't have anywhere to be."

I make a show of looking at my watch. "I don't mean to be nosy—"

"I find that hard to believe," she interrupts in a mumble.

"—but don't you have a job?"

"I do," she says, more to the screen than to me. Her eyes are still down and the little pendant she wears swings ever so slightly with each of her exhales. It's too easy to remember how she looked on her back, nothing but that necklace resting above her breastbone and my rope around her—

Focus, Finn.

"Then shouldn't you be in an office, or out with ladies who lunch?"

She makes a show of closing her laptop slowly. "Not today."

"Why?"

She's definitely growing irritated with my questions, which—let's be honest—only makes me more curious. "Because I don't work today. My mom isn't feeling well. I was just looking some stuff up."

"So when you work, what exactly do you *do*?" I ask.

"I'm an intern at NBC."

I make another show of looking at my watch—more dramatically this time—at the fact that it's one twenty in the afternoon on a Tuesday, and she's sitting in a pizza place staring at a laptop and playing on her phone.

"Part-time," she clarifies, adding, "I work about twelve hours a week." *Twelve?* At my less than impressed expression she throws in, "What?"

"Unpaid?"

"In-tern?" she says, as if saying the word more slowly will help me understand. "I want to work in the film industry but you have to start somewhere, and NBC is local."

"I see. So you, like, get coffee and stuff."

"Occasionally."

"Doesn't that bug you? You're the kid of a famous actress and a big Hollywood guy, and yet they make you the lowly coffee girl?"

I'm only partly serious. I mean I *am* curious, but in truth, she's just really fun to wind up.

"That's not all I do," she says, and then reconsiders, smiling at me with surprising self-deprecation. "Actually, yeah, they love to make me do the grunt work because of who my dad is. I've worked on his sets for as long as I can remember, and probably know more about how movies are made than most of the people I work under now. But Dad always told me my first lesson in work should be how to earn respect through humility, so I guess that's what I'm doing here. It won't always be this way."

Huh. Wasn't expecting that. And it's a little disquieting how much it sounds like something my own dad would say. "So you went to college and majored in . . . ?"

"Communications."

"Communications, ah. What is that, like majoring in Twitter and Facebook?"

She purses her lips playfully studying me. "You've *heard* of Twitter?"

I consider flipping her off for this.

"What are you doing downtown, anyway?" she asks, slipping her fancy silver laptop into her even fancier bag. "Is your mysterious *business* here?"

"Grabbing lunch and then making a few calls," I say, scanning the menu. "Why? Got some other ideas on how to pass the time? I'm sure I could think of a few."

"Well, since we *are* at Basic and you're already here, I feel it's my duty as a San Diegan to make you stay and eat. The food is good *and* they have beer."

"Beer would definitely make it easier to have lunch with you."

I hear her playful gasp but fail to dodge her fist connecting with my shoulder.

IT TURNS OUT, Harlow was right.

"Did I really just eat mashed potatoes on pizza?" I ask, reaching for my beer.

"Yep, and wasn't it the best pizza ever?"

It was pretty close, I think, but I'm not telling her that. I finished off half a mozzarella, mashed potato, and bacon pizza by myself. Harlow wasn't that far behind. "It was good."

"'Good,'" she repeats, shaking her head. "Don't hurt yourself with the enthusiasm there, Finn."

"I can give plenty of compliments when the situation warrants."

"Example?"

"I seem to remember telling you how good your pussy feels."

Her eyes go wide from across the table and *there,* that's what I've been waiting for. There's something about eliciting a reaction from Harlow—whether it be shock or abandon or rage—that tugs at a baser instinct in my chest. I know that makes me some sort of a caveman-asshole, but it feels good and gets both of us off. I'm really not interested in psychoanalyzing it.

"Speaking of which, why *did* you leave so abruptly on Saturday? I give great back rubs."

I can tell she's not prepared for more of this blunt-force honesty because she blinks at me a few times, speechless, but she recovers. "Because it was intense. And I just wanted to get laid."

I hum into a small remaining bite of pizza crust. "What are you going to do about that libido when I leave town?"

Shrugging, she says, "Masturbate more," and then takes a huge bite of her own slice.

I laugh. I do really like being around her. "So you majored in communications and your dad is a big-shot cinematographer. What else should I know about you?"

"Finn, don't you remember our arrangement? You should know I like *orgasms.* Don't strain yourself."

"Come on, Ginger Snap."

"Fine." She wipes her hands on a napkin and then tosses it down on the table. "I have a sister, Bellamy."

"Is she cute?"

Harlow looks at me with disgust. "She's eighteen, you predator."

"I mean for my *brother* Levi. Jesus, trigger finger."

Laughing she shrugs. "She's gorgeous but totally crazy."

I raise an eyebrow, saying, "Genetics are a bitch, huh?"

"Har."

"Is she in school around here?"

Shrugging, she says, "She's doing an art school thing I'm pretty sure is just a front for a giant pot operation."

"Seriously?" I feel my eyes go wide. I'd heard stories about California, but . . .

"No. I'm kidding, settle down Canadian DEA. But it seems like a pretty flaky program. I'm sure her degree will make her only marginally more employable at Burger King."

"And you live at home still?"

She narrows her eyes at me. "I'm twenty-two, Finn."

"But your parents are here and you're an unpaid intern working twelve hours a week fetching coffee. Pardon my harebrained assumption that you may rely on them for shelter."

"I have a trust fund." She shakes her head, pointing her pizza at me. "Don't make that face like you're surprised."

"I'm only surprised you *admitted* it."

"Because I should feel bad my parents were responsible

with money and that I, in turn, was responsible by investing in California real estate and own my condo?"

"Should I congratulate you for knowing how to properly spend your parents' money?" I ask through a laugh.

She leans forward. "It's cute you think I'm a rich airhead, but I'm no more an airhead than you are a dumb lumberjack."

"Fisherman."

"What?"

"I'm a fisherman, Harlow."

She licks her lips before growling, "Same. Fucking. Thing. My job might not be very glamorous but I am damn good at it. Best fucking coffee fetcher out there."

I burst out laughing. "You're a trip."

"You're a hot piece of ass."

I lean my chair back, balancing on two legs, watching her watching me. She's hands down the sexiest girl I've ever seen. Surprisingly, she may also be the smartest. "Yeah. I know."

"So what about you? Do you have siblings? Brothers, right?"

I nod, reaching for my glass to take a sip of beer. "Colton and Levi."

"You guys work together?"

"Yeah, plus my dad. He had a heart attack and a stroke a few years back, so he's not as hands-on as he used to be, but he's still always around."

"What about your mom?"

I shake my head. "Died when I was twelve. Breast cancer."

Her face seems to literally fall and she lifts her iced tea to her lips, taking a sip with a shaking hand before she manages to say, "Finn. God, I am . . ." She shakes her head, takes a deep breath, and then closes her eyes. "That is *heartbreaking*."

What else can I say but, "Yeah. Long time ago."

She blinks away and for the first time it occurs to me that she looks exhausted. "So what has you looking so beat?" I ask. "A grueling Facebooking session during your day off work?"

I can tell she's on the verge of saying something smart in response, but her expression softens and she says, "Just looking some stuff up."

"Next season's top shoe picks?"

"Something along those lines." And *wow*. Harlow is a terrible liar.

But if she's not sharing, then I suspect I shouldn't push, anyway. Lord knows I don't really want to lay my woes on this table, either.

"Come on."

Looking up at me, she draws her brows together.

I stand, holding out my hand. "Let's go."

———

SO WE'RE DISCOVERING a pattern. We fall into the hallway at Oliver's again, hands in hair and mouths everywhere. Her body is warm, her skin soft and smelling so fucking good.

Harlow leads this time and steers us down the hall, stumbling blindly in the direction of my bedroom.

"Oliver?" she asks, breaking away just long enough to glance around, and listening to the empty house. Her lips look bitten and her cheeks pink. Her hair has come loose from the bun and some smooth strands fall around her face and shoulders.

"Not home yet," I say, and pull her back to my mouth. Our feet shuffle along the wood floors and I wonder if I'd have time to fuck her right here, bent over the couch or with her hands pressed to the wall, the sound of her screams ringing through the silent rooms. "Not sure when, though; think you can be quick?" I circle my thumb around her nipple and she groans.

"Mmm, I didn't come all the way over here to be quick."

I don't want to, either. In fact, I'm beginning to wish we'd gone to her place. Someplace we can take our time like we did the other day.

We get to my room and I close the door, flipping the lock behind me.

"On the bed," I say.

Harlow pulls away with a final kiss and—surprisingly— does what I tell her, making a show of kicking off her shoes and climbing up onto the mattress. I cross the room and stand over her, meeting her gaze as I unfasten my belt.

"Take your clothes off."

Harlow nods and we each begin to undress: shirts first, her bra, my jeans. She takes hers off slowly, not like she's putting on a show, but like she's relishing the way my eyes move over every inch of newly exposed skin and is trying to make the feeling last. Her tits are fucking fabulous, high and full—a generous handful, and I have big hands—with tight pink nipples that make my mouth water. She has to lie back to shimmy out of her skirt and I step over, reaching forward and pulling it down her legs.

"Wonder what you'd look like with these ankles tied up in the air," I say, bringing her leg to my shoulder and pressing a kiss to her calf. I don't mean it—not right now, anyway— Oliver could be home any minute, and for something like that I want to tease her, take my time until both of us are absolutely wild. But remembering last time, the suggestion is enough to do the trick, and Harlow's eyes widen, her breath picking up.

With an arm braced near her head, I reach between our bodies, slipping my finger into her panties.

She gasps and I push in more, adding a second alongside it and moving my thumb in circles over her clit.

"Look how wet you are," I say. "Just from taking off our clothes. I've barely touched you and you're ready to come all over my hand."

Harlow huffs out a breath, like she can't decide if she wants to deny it or not, but still she rocks her hips, taking more of my fingers. I kiss along her ribs and up, taking a nipple between my lips, sucking until she's wet and slippery. She gasps in a breath as I use my teeth, easy at first and then just a bit sharper.

"More," she groans, and I move to the other, sucking, biting. I don't want to hurt her—that's never what this has been about—but I do want her to feel it later. Those small, lingering aches that catch her off guard. "Finn, *more*."

"Roll over," I say, and grip her hips, helping her to her stomach. Her lace panties are barely a scrap and I reach for them, slipping them down and off her body, leaving her completely, gloriously naked in front of me.

"Fuck. This ass," I say, squeezing it, not even knowing where to look. I grip her tighter, a little rougher, rubbing my palm over her again and again to prepare her for what's to come. "Seem to remember I had plans for it."

Her entire body is tense, practically vibrating, every muscle poised and waiting. I move my hand over her hip and up to her lower back, dragging my short nails along the skin there. She lets out a little sound, and I can hear each of her breaths, how they're almost even and controlled but still just the slightest bit shaky.

"Has anyone ever spanked you, Ginger Snap?"

She shakes her head against my pillow, loose strands of dark hair following the arch of her back. "Only you."

I try not to think too much about the spark of pride I feel when she says this, and attempt to tamp down the curl of possessive heat in my stomach. "You want this?" I ask.

She nods, but it's not what I need, and I slice my hand upward through the air, landing with a quick smack on her backside, just enough to get her attention.

"Say it, Harlow."

"Y-yes," she says. "Yes."

I do it again, my palm connecting with her skin, a little harder this time.

Harlow gasps, her fist closed tight around the sheets, and she arches her hips, pushing back toward me. Wanting more.

"Didn't I tell you I'd give you what you need?" I say, and bring my hand down again, on the other side. The sound she makes is louder this time, more desperate. I spank her a few more times, just until her skin is warm and pink, and she moans as I soothe the flushed skin with my palm. I wonder if she's ever thought about this kind of thing before, had any idea how much she'd like it.

There's no doubt Harlow Vega gets off on a little man-handling, or that I very much enjoy being the one to do it. There's just something so hot about the way she *lets* me. She knows she could take control at any moment, but I'm sensing that she doesn't want to. I'm sensing that maybe she needs someone else to lead right now.

By the tenth spanking, Harlow is wet down her thighs, and I'm not sure I've ever been harder. Her hand has disappeared between her legs, fingers slipping over the slick skin.

"You do like it," I say. "Feel that." I lean forward, touch where she's working herself over. My fingers push in alongside hers and *fuck*. I need a condom right now.

Straightening, I reach for the box I'd hastily tossed into the dresser drawer. Harlow moves to her back and watches, eyes fixed to where I slide the condom down and over my dick.

I climb over her, lifting her arms above her head, helping her reach for the bed frame. "Keep them here, okay?"

She nods, and I see the way she tightens her grip, knuckles turning white with the effort.

I press the head of my cock against her, moving it back and forth before beginning to push in. "Think you can be quiet?" I ask, gauging her expression as I continue to move. "Oliver could come home anytime. You need to be quiet. Okay?"

She looks down the length of her body, where my palm slides over her skin, and nods.

I reach for the pillow next to her head and lift her hips to position it just beneath her ass. "That's right," I say, pressing deeper and deeper, watching as I disappear entirely inside her.

Her teeth bite into her bottom lip and she moans around it. I shush her gently. "Look so good like this," I tell her, watching her breasts bounce with each snap of my hips. I place my hand on her sternum to hold her down, and admire the color of my skin against hers, tan and rough against golden softness. A rough engine sounds outside and I recognize Oliver's car, hear it move up the street and pull into the driveway.

Harlow's little gasps are still too loud, and so I reach near her hip for her panties, ball them up in my fist, and, after I kiss her on the lips, I stuff them into her mouth.

Her eyes close like she's *grateful,* and she moans around it—and it's enough that I nearly come.

"I said quiet, Ginger Snap." I spread her legs even more. I tilt her hips in a way that my pelvis doesn't rub against her clit while I fuck her.

And again, she moans, a deep, desperate sound that makes me fuck into her harder, wanting to make her do it again.

"You definitely like this," I whisper into her ear. "I bet you think I won't be able to stop thinking about this later, how wet you're getting my cock." I suck along her neck, careful to leave the skin red, but not marked. "Can you tell I like it, too? You nearly made me come before I was good and ready."

She groans around the fabric and presses her knees to my waist, using the leverage to bring me closer, harder.

"I wonder if you'll get wetter?" I say. "Should we see if I can make you wetter when you come?"

She nods urgently.

I can hear Oliver outside, laughing and shouting something over to a neighbor. I hitch Harlow's leg up higher and reach down, smacking her ass again. She cries out, clenching around me. Her skin is flushed, her nipples hard and goose bumps spread along her skin.

"He'll be inside any second. Do you think you can be quiet? I can make it so good for you if you can."

She nods and I fuck her harder, my arms shaking, neck corded and tense as I hold myself back. I see the moment it happens: Harlow's eyes widen before they close again, a tear slipping down her cheek as she struggles not to make a noise.

It's enough to send me spiraling after her. I lean down, nearly bending her in half with my thrusts—just one more time before I'm coming and have to muffle my sounds against her skin.

When I can move, when my heart doesn't feel like it might burst out of my chest, I push up, slipping out of her carefully before tying off the condom. I take her in my arms, kissing her fingers, her wrists, the corners of her mouth.

"You did so good." I press my lips to her shoulder, drag my nose up her neck, and growl in her ear. "You did so fucking good, sweet girl."

Chapter FIVE

I DON'T REALLY KNOW how I would feel three days after having both of my breasts removed, but given what an important part of my body they are, I can imagine I'd be doing the exact same thing my mother has done since Monday: sleep, and cry.

And there is nothing, literally *nothing* any of us can do to make her feel better. Mom has never been particularly vain, but her career was obviously dependent on her body. So even though at forty-five she would be unlikely to get a bikini-dependent film role, anyway, and the newsmagazines are highlighting her bravery and strength, she really just hates no longer having what was admittedly an awesome pair of boobs. Plus—and Mom is tougher than nails—I can tell how painful her recovery from surgery is.

She's released from the hospital on Wednesday morning, and Dad, Bellamy, and I spend most of the day sitting in bed with her, watching reruns of *Law & Order* while she sleeps. By Thursday afternoon, we're all restless, unshowered, and picking at each other.

I now know what would go down if the four of us were ever trapped together in a bomb shelter: murder. The incessant chirping of Bellamy's cell phone is making Dad homicidal. Bellamy keeps talking about how hot the room is. And Mom tells me, "If you offer me food one more time I'm going to throw this remote at your head. Sorry, sweetie."

For the family that never really fights, we sure are a testy bunch.

Finally, Dad pulls us both aside in the hall. "Girls, I love you," he says, laying a hand on each of our shoulders. "But please get out of my house. Just go get back to your lives for a couple of days. I'll call you with any updates."

The problem is it's not really that easy. I detest the morbid, niggling sense I have after talking to Finn at lunch on Tuesday that my mother is going to *die*. I can't talk about it with anyone, and even if I could, giving voice to it would only make me feel like I was validating the possibility or—worse— turning it into reality, somehow. I have too much free time to think; my part-time job isn't nearly absorbing enough, I can only run or spend so many hours at the beach, and my friends have packed schedules from morning to night. All of them, that is, except Finn.

Once Bellamy has driven away, I stand on my parents' driveway and forcibly pull myself together. It feels literal: Pick up the pieces and put them where they belong. Pull the spine straight. Tie my still-wet hair back in a messy bun. Smooth my hands down the rumpled front of my T-shirt and jeans. Slap on a smile.

I'm making everyone join me at Fred's, and I won't take no for an answer.

————————

"NO," LOLA SAYS, and then I hear a loud clang in the background. "I can't tonight. I need to finish these panels. And Mia said she and Ansel are staying in, since he's leaving tomorrow and won't be back for a few weeks."

"I'm barely keeping my shit together, Lorelei Louise Castle."

"You're going to bust out my full name?"

"I didn't brush my hair after I showered, I'm wearing one of Bellamy's Hello Kitty titty shirts because I forgot all my clothes at home, and the Latin Love Machine"—Lola and Mia have a bit of a thing for my dad—"kicked me out of the house until further notice. Get your ass to the Regal Beagle."

She sighs. "Fine."

Fred Furley opened Fred's Bar in 1969, when he was only twenty-seven. Now he's seventy-two, has been married (and divorced) six times, and loves my mother maybe only a fraction less than my father does. I celebrated my twenty-first birthday here, and Mr. Furley only let me have two shots. Perhaps relatedly, I went home sober and alone. He's loosened up somewhat, but he still likes to play the role of father figure, which is probably why I'm so comfortable being here. Besides, it's a way better regular hangout than a coffee shop because, hello, booze.

It took him about seven years to understand why my dad called the bar the Regal Beagle, but the name stuck even if Mr. Furley is nothing like the guy from *Three's Company*. He's calm, tanned, and fit and gives me almost anything I want.

Like Thursday Ladies Nights.

Ansel and Mia picked up Lola and Finn on their way over here, and they arrive around the same time Not-Joe stumbles from his beach cruiser, parking it haphazardly against the side of the building.

"Where's Olls, Ollie, Olzifer?" I ask with a silly grin.

Lola pulls back, studying me. "Are you already drunk?"

"No. Just . . . in a weird mood." And it's true. I feel a little unsteady, like if I stop moving I'll crack and the crazy will spill out onto the street like a pool of oil. "I'll probably be *better* once I'm drunk, actually."

"Oliver's meeting us here," Ansel says. He's the only one who isn't looking at me like my hair's on fire and I'm full of nitroglycerin.

Finn is watching me, his eyes hidden by the brim of his hat. "You okay, Ginger Snap?"

I nod. "No." I take his arm and use the opportunity to grope his bulgy-hot bicep. "Yes? I guess. Weird day?"

"I hear that," he says, leading me inside.

Mr. Furley renovated the interior of Fred's a few years back, but at my mother's insistence he kept the décor almost exactly the same and just brought in new tables, chairs and booths, fresh paint, and flooring. Like I said, Fred loves

Mom. Yet another reason to love this place: We have our own booth in the back corner with a RESERVED card keeping people out whenever we're not here. The truth is, Fred's is rarely busy enough for someone to try to snag our table, but the gesture still makes me feel like a bit of a badass.

We greet Mr. Furley, order our drinks, and head to the booth en masse. Finn follows, unsure.

"This seems very ritualistic," he says, opting to lean against the side of the booth rather than sit next to me.

"You stay here long enough and you'll get the routine down. It's a little complicated, though." I hold up my fingers and count off the steps for him: "You walk into the bar. You order whatever you want as you pass Fred over there. You then walk to this table."

He nods slowly. "Walk, order, walk."

"Good puppy."

Finn surprises me by touching his thumb and forefinger to my chin and gazing down at me sweetly before turning to Ansel.

Our drinks show up, and we decide to order some food, and then Lola and I spend some time catching up in the comfort of the booth. She recently signed a contract with Dark Horse for a comic book series, and my first response, pre-Google, was "I'm so happy for you!"

My second response, post-Google, was to nearly crap myself. Although this happened almost as soon as we got back from Vegas, I still sometimes can't get over what a big change this is going to be for her life. In only a few months, the press will start: She has some interviews, a couple of trips to little boutique shops, and then her baby, *Razor Fish*—for which she's been drawing characters since she could hold a crayon—will be launched into the wild.

While we talk, Finn wanders back over, leaning against the booth and listening to the tail end of our catch-up.

I peek over his shoulder. "Your drink is empty."

He shakes his glass, looking at the liquid sloshing over the ice. "No, I have a little left."

"Oh, just mine is empty, then." I hand it to him, eyes wide and innocent.

He laughs, taking the glass.

"Tell them to put it on my tab," I call to him as he heads over to the bar.

Finn throws me a dirty look over his shoulder. "I got it."

"Smooth, Mistress Vega," Lola says, her eyebrows raised.

"Harlow *Vega*?" Not-Joe asks, blond brow quirked.

I nod, popping an olive into my mouth and repeating, "Harlow Vega," around it.

"Did your parents ever want you to go to college, or did they plan for you to go straight to the pole?"

I cluck my tongue at him, licking my fingers. "Careful, Not-Joe. Your boner is showing."

"Oh!" Not-Joe says, turning to Lola. "Speaking of boners. I'm excited for your book to be out and selling like crazy, and then at Comic Con it will be unreal. You'll be in your chick author getup, strutting around. Wearing a sexy mask, and spand—"

"Are you *high*?" Lola asks.

I realize it's rhetorical so it cracks me up when Not-Joe answers, "Well . . . yeah."

"I'm not going to deep-throat a corn dog and then go make out with a bunch of chesty girls in Catwoman costumes just to show I can hang with the comic guys."

Oliver chose this moment to arrive and looks a little stunned, eyes wide behind his thick frames. He stares at her, gaze softening with what clearly appears to be admiration. His speechless reaction makes me do a slight double take. Is quiet, sweet Oliver beginning to fancy *Lola*? I meet Mia's wide eyes and can tell she's wondering the exact same thing. Swear to God, if my head weren't so fucked-up right now, I'd be *all* over getting these two together.

"But would you let a comic book *guy* make out with you if *he* wore a Catwoman costume and deep-throated a corn dog?" Ansel asks, tilting his head to Oliver. "Theoretically speaking."

"Reckon the fanboys will be gobsmacked regardless," Oliver deflects, collecting himself. "Corn dog deep-throating or not."

Mia scrunches her nose, shaking her head at Oliver. She almost never understands his thick Aussie accent, which is ironic considering she's married to someone who speaks English as a second language.

"Happy fanboys no matter what," Lola translates in shorthand.

I remember the first night we hung out with Oliver—

after Mia and Ansel disappeared down the hall and it was just me and Lola, way drunker than the two strangers in front of us. After closer inspection, we realized Oliver had a black Sharpie flower drawn on his cheek.

"I'm curious about the flower," Lola said when he'd settled onto the seat next to her. He wore his usual thick-rimmed glasses, black straight jeans, dark T-shirt. I was almost positive it wasn't a face tattoo . . . almost.

"Loss a bit," he said cryptically, and then returned to silence. It took several beats for me to recognize that he'd said, "Lost a bet."

"Details," Lola said.

And Finn supplied them happily. Apparently they'd just done an abbreviated version of the biking trip across the States that brought them together six years earlier. "The deal was, whoever went through the most tire tubes had to get a Sharpie face tattoo. Oliver here can't help but treat a road bike like a mountain bike. I'm surprised his tire rims don't look like tacos."

Oliver shrugged, and it was clear to me he couldn't care less that he had a flower drawn on his face. He was definitely not there to impress anyone.

"Do people call you Ollie?" Lola asked.

Oliver looked at her, completely dumbfounded by the possibility of this nickname. She may as well have asked him if people call him Garth, or Andrew, or Timothy.

"No," he said flatly, and the only thing charming about him was the way his accent seemed to run through every vowel with one syllable. Lola's eyebrow twitched in her single tell—mildly annoyed—and she lifted her flashing LED drink cup to her lips.

Lola wears mostly black, including her glossy dark hair, and has a tiny diamond pierced into her lip, but, even still, she's never been able to pull off the full physical manifestation of the angry Riot Grrrl. With her perfect porcelain skin and the longest eyelashes in the world, she's simply too delicate. But once she decides you're an asshole, it no longer matters to her what you think. She gives good glare.

"The flower suits you," she said, tilting her head to study him. "And you have pretty hands, kind of soft. Maybe we should call you Olive."

He grunted out a dry laugh.

"And a really beautiful mouth," I added. "Gentle. Like a woman's."

"Aw fuck off." He was laughing outright by then.

Somehow we all went from tipsy strangers to hammered best friends to spouses that night. But Lola and Oliver were the only couple that didn't consummate anything, and, even at the time, Lola was pretty convinced Oliver wasn't interested at all.

Now I'm pretty sure she was wrong.

"Where's Finn?" Oliver asks, sliding into the booth, then saying, "Hey, Joe," to Not-Joe.

"Driving Miss Harlow," I say.

He stares at me, confused.

"Getting Harlow a drink," Lola translates again.

Oliver nods once, satisfied, glancing over at the bar and then back to me. "Be nice to my boy," he says, giving me a wink, but his tone tells me he's serious.

"Because he's delicate? Please," I scoff. "I'm just using him for his enormous penis and surprising skills with rope. Don't worry about his finespun man feelings."

Oliver groans, covering his face. "More than I needed to know," he says, at the exact same moment Lola shouts, "Overshare alert!"

"That'll teach you to lecture me," I tell them with a grin. "How's the store?"

"Good. Really busy. I reckon it'll be right if it keeps up like this, yeah?"

I see Mia lean to Ansel, who laughs as he repeats more slowly what Oliver has just said.

"Do I need to speak slowly, Mee-ahh?" Oliver drawls in his exaggerated version of an American accent.

"Yes!" she yells.

"How's the front reading nook?" I ask. "Bringing in lots of newbies?"

"I think so?" he says, stealing Mia's untouched beer. "I need to get a feel for who my regulars will be."

"How long until you bang someone up there after hours?" I ask, leaning my chin on my hands.

He laughs, shaking his head. "That front window is pretty enormous. Reckon never."

"Some girls are into that."

He shrugs, grinning down at the coaster he's playing

with, not glancing at Lola even once. I will break this boy if it kills me.

"Maybe Oliver's first go-round there will be in the stock-room," Ansel joins in and *oh,* he is my *favorite.*

Mia leans into Ansel's side, and he bends to say something near her ear. Her happiness is the *best* distraction from my own worries. Maybe the alcohol helps, too. I'm so happy for her that her guy's here for more than just the usual day and a half. He seems to come visit every couple of weeks, but it's a mix of giddiness when he arrives and the constant dread of another goodbye when he leaves.

"You guys look so good together," I say, leaning halfway across the curved bench to kiss Mia's cheek.

"Imagine what we look like when we're having sex!" Ansel yells across the table. "It's unreal!"

I ball up my cocktail napkin and hurl it at him. "Too far."

"It's my superpower."

"What's mine?" I ask.

Ansel cups his hands around his mouth, calling out over the music, "Doing shots?"

He nods to the shot that Finn apparently snuck in front of me. Despite our wild night at Lola and London's, and my spectacular drunkenness in Vegas, I rarely drink more than a couple of cocktails. But I guess Ansel is right: When I do it, I really commit. I toss back the drink in front of me, tasting sweet and sour and then the burn of vodka as it warms a path to my stomach.

Letting out a roar, I stand, announcing, "I'm drunk and I'm going to dance." Pointing to Finn, I say, "You. Follow."

He shakes his head.

"Oh, come *on*," I groan, running my hands up his chest. God he feels good—so sturdy and hard, his pectorals tensing under my touch—and now I'm on fire for him.

Thursday night at Fred's is Ladies Night, and they play music for dancing because we ladies like to dance. Also? I like Drunk Me. Drunk Me doesn't have any problems, and Sober Harlow might be too proud to turn on the coy, begging female act. But put a little liquor in her? Showtime.

"Please?" I whisper, stretching to kiss his neck. "Pretty please, with Harlow naked on top?"

"Is she always like this?" Finn asks my girlfriends without taking his eyes off me. He's watching my mouth, looking at me like he might throw me over his shoulder and carry me the five miles to Oliver's house.

"With almost every damn guy she meets," Lola lies. "It's exhausting tracking her down in seedy Tijuana motel rooms."

Finn's brows draw together. I scratch my nails down his chest the way I think he likes, and I can feel him shiver once beneath my hands. He blinks away, to the dance floor. "Then I'm sure there's another guy out there who'll dance with you."

I study him for a beat, hoping my disappointment doesn't show too plainly on my face. "I'm sure there is."

I lift my chin to Mia and she pulls Ansel out of the booth with her. The three of us head to the mostly empty dance floor, where—despite Finn's prediction—there's only a half dozen other people: an older couple slow-sex-dancing to a fast song and a small group of girls whose IDs I would seriously like to check.

I love everything about this bar—the worn velvet seats, the cheesy chandeliers, the strong pours—but I especially love the music. When we get out there, the DJ, who happens to be Fred's newly minted twenty-one-year-old grandson, Kyle, cranks the bass-heavy song, nodding at me.

I don't need someone to dance with, I just need to *move*. I raise my hands in the air, bouncing to the beat and closing my eyes. I fucking love this song, love the pulsing bass and the obscenely sexual lyrics. Ansel and Mia try to dance with me as a group, but maybe they can tell that I don't care if I'm alone or surrounded, because they turn into each other and move in this perfect pair of rolling hips, weaving arms, and smiles.

God, they look so good together. Of course Mia is an amazing dancer because she was born for it, but Ansel moves like someone who has control over every single cell in his body. I'm so happy and so miserable. I'm not a miserable person. My life has been easy, wild, filled with adventure after adventure. Why do I feel like my chest is slowly filling with cold water?

Warm hands slide around my hips and to my stomach, pulling me back against a broad, solid body. "Hey," Finn growls quietly.

Like he's pulled a plug, the cold feeling drains from beneath my ribs and I'm surrounded with nothing but Finn's unreal heat. He presses into me, barely swaying to the music.

Turning in his arms, I dance against him, let him hold on to me. I feel the most basic need to fuck. To couple. To have him inside.

"You're driving me crazy, dancing out here." He bends, ghosting his lips across my ear. "Goddamn you look good."

I stretch to reach his ear with my lips, hearing my voice crack on the first word: "Come home with me."

———

LUCKILY FINN IS sober and can drive my car. I direct him back to my place, but otherwise we just stare out the windshield, not really speaking. I'm glad we're not speaking. It would distract me from the feel of his hand on my thigh, the heel of his hand pressed firmly near my hip, his fingertips touching what feels like the softest, most intimate inner part of my leg. It's as if he's thrown his anchor overboard, grounding me here.

"You okay, Ginger Snap?"

I like that he calls me that, like he's branded some part of me all his own.

I nod, managing a "Fine, just . . ."

"Just suffering your quarter-life crisis?" he says, smiling over at me. It's not a mocking smile, and I put my attitude away. Apparently I look as desperate for more distraction as I feel.

"Yeah."

"I don't mean to sound like . . ." He pulls his hand away from me just long enough to wipe his face, leaving on my skin a cold shadow in the shape of each of his fingers. But then it's back, and I can breathe again. "I don't mean to sound condescending. I just remember feeling so pissed-off when I was in my early twenties, like why wasn't everything already figured out."

I nod, worrying my voice would come out strangled with emotion if I tried to speak.

"It's around that time when Dad and Colt made me go on the bike trip."

"Are you glad you went?"

He nods, but doesn't say anything, and I guide him to turn right, down Eads Avenue. We pull into a spot in front of my building, and he reaches to turn the ignition off.

"Yeah," he says, looking at me and handing me my keys. "I'm glad. But life is always complicated. It just looks different from older angles."

He follows me to the elevator in the lobby of my building, raising his eyebrows but not saying anything. His hands are shoved deep in the pocket of his jeans, his worn cap pulled low over his eyes. "How drunk are you?"

I shrug. "Pretty drunk."

I can tell he doesn't like this answer, but again, he stays quiet and follows me into the elevator, watching me push the button for the fourth floor.

"This means nothing, coming back to my place," I say. "Could just as easily have been at Oliver's again. This was closer."

He ignores this. "You don't have a roommate, right?"

"Right."

"You like what we did the other day?"

"Which?" I ask, leaning against the wall of the elevator as it slowly climbs. I swear I can feel his body heat from three feet away. "With the rope or without?"

He smiles, licking his lips. "Both. But I guess I meant with the rope."

"You mean you couldn't tell?"

The elevator doors open and he motions for me to get out first. From behind me he explains, "I haven't done that with a girl in a long time." I start to respond to this—I mean, now my curiosity is spiked; he's got to give me more than *that*—but he keeps talking, "And the way you always leave right after . . . you're not exactly easy to read."

"Jesus, Finn." Stopping in front of my door, I turn to look at him. "Isn't this just hooking up? What's there to 'read'?" I mean this to come out a little flippant, a little jokey, but instead my drunk voice is slurred and slow. He scowls, taking my keys from me and using them to let us into my apartment.

Inside, Finn drops the keys on the little table by the door and looks around. My apartment has two bedrooms off a large main loft area with a view over a couple of city blocks and out across the ocean.

"Wow," he says quietly. "Nice investment."

Laughing, I push his shoulder from behind, making him take a step forward into my living room.

"I'm going to ask something that's going to make me

sound like kind of a dick," he warns, looking over his shoulder at me.

"For *once*."

With a little smirk at this, he says, "What was it like growing up never having to worry about money?"

I smile at Finn and let him stew in what he's just asked for a bit. Because . . . seriously? "What makes you think we always had money?"

He looks around the apartment and then back at me, raising his eyebrows meaningfully.

"When my mom first started out in television, I remember my parents really scraping by," I tell him. "She commuted for filming. Dad was here doing, like, little indie movies and stuff in his friend's backyard. Maybe when I was in junior high they got more comfortable." I shrug, holding his gaze. "When Dad won the first Oscar, it sort of took off. But that wasn't until I was a freshman in college."

He nods, and the silence stretches for a long, weird beat until he says, "I'm going to go use your restroom." He looks down the hall and then back at me, gaze moving from my face down to my feet. "You go get a big glass of water, a piece of toast, and a couple of ibuprofen or something. I'm not going to fuck you until you're steady."

He turns without waiting for my reaction to his bossy tone, walking down the hall and ducking his head into the bathroom before slipping fully inside, closing the door behind him with a quiet click.

Because it's a good idea and *not* because Finn told me

to—a fact I have to restrain myself from shouting over my shoulder—I go to the kitchen for water, food, and two ibuprofen.

I hear the faucet turn on, the bathroom door open, and then he calls from the hallway, "Where do you keep your sports and surfing shit?"

"My what?" I ask around a mouthful of toast.

"I don't mean your board." I hear him open the hall closet and mumble an "Ah. Got it."

I chug my water and watch him emerge from the hallway. My heart trips. His shoulders fill the doorway and I feel oddly intimidated. It's only odd because I *like* it. I like the idea of him being a little scary, a little out of control. I like the idea of him crashing into my life and pushing everything else out of frame.

He's got a spool of bungee cord in his hand.

"How did I know you were looking for something like that?" I ask.

"It could be the subtle way I asked you about the rope, earlier." He wraps his hand around my upper arm and leads me to the living room.

I weave a little on my feet and he studies me, pushing his hat off his head and mussing his hair with one hand. "You gonna remember this?"

It's troubling how his voice affects me. It's raspy, and reminds me of a good rich whiskey, the scratch of it in my throat, its warmth in my blood. I don't think I can pretend anymore that I'm not completely obsessed with Finn Roberts.

"Probably," I whisper, stretching to kiss his jawline.

"I can't wait for you to beg me to come." He lifts his chin the tiniest bit, running his tongue over his bottom lip. "And I can't wait for you to beg me to let you stop."

I have the sense of sobering up just so I can get high off the feeling of him inside.

Nodding at my clothes, he murmurs, "Take them off."

I pull my T-shirt off, slip out of my shoes and jeans. He watches every move, absently unwrapping the new roll of bungee cord. I bought it a couple of weeks ago to transport my surfboard after my last cord started to fray, but hell. This works, too.

"This won't be as soft," he says, motioning to the cord, but I sort of hope he's also talking about how he's going to fuck me.

Once I'm naked, he steps closer, bending to kiss me. I love his taste—tonight it's the faint taste of beer mixed with mint—and he hums quietly. "Tell me you want this."

"I *definitely* want it."

Carefully, he wraps the cord around my chest, above my breasts, then behind my back. Pulling it up over my shoulder, and down across my breastbone, he wraps it around my back. After he's framed both breasts, he guides my hands behind my back so I'm holding my opposite elbow in each palm, and he binds my upper arms before tying the entire length of the cord together near my spine, just below my shoulder blades.

My breasts are framed by the cord crisscrossing over my sternum, and my arms are pinned at my back. The way Finn looks at me . . .

I feel like a fucking queen.

He presses his hand to my chest, each finger splayed so that I register just how big his hands are. I feel carved out, and now I'm famished. I don't think I've ever wanted to feel someone as untethered as I want him to be with me.

He runs the tip of his tongue across my lower lip. As if reading my mind, he says, "You like it when I'm a little rough, don't you?"

I nod. I have so much need. I crave the edge, the point just before I fall where I know the relief comes and he gives my body everything. But I know he'll make me wait for it, and the anticipation has me shaking.

"You want me just a little rough?" he asks, hands shaking where he cups my face. "Or you want me fucking *wild*?"

"Wild."

He inhales, his flaring nostrils and scent making me feel as urgent as fire.

Finn reaches behind him, pulling his shirt over his head and then quickly unfastening his pants, pushing them and his boxers down his hips. He's watching my face, my breasts, gauging my reaction as he undresses in front of me. Taking a step back, he lowers himself until he's sitting on my couch, and curls his index finger.

"Come sit on my lap."

I walk to him, straddling his thighs, and he steadies me with his hands on my waist.

"You good?" he asks in a quiet rasp.

When I nod, his hands slide up my sides and he grips my

breasts, eyes on me as he sucks and licks, fingers moving up and over my chest, cupping me. Tongue flat, teasing.

With my arms bound, he pulls me up his body as he turns and lies on the couch, resting his head on the arm, legs stretched out behind me. Finn positions me with my legs spread over his mouth, rocking me there, and moaning, grunting against my skin. He keeps talking while he licks me, telling me he likes it, I taste good. Telling me *I* like it, that he can tell I'm going to come. I'm flushed, I'm shaking. He barely moves at all, just whispering and kissing and licking and somehow . . . somehow just his breath and the heat, the press of his tongue against my clit . . . I'm starting to sweat from the effort of holding my body upright. His eyes flame, hands reaching away from my breasts to grip the cord behind my back, somehow both holding me upright and pulling me farther onto him.

I can't grip the sofa. I can't grip him. I can't focus on *anything*, anything at all, and it feels so good to just let go. To hand it all over. I'm writhing against the intense pleasure, legs wide, body so hungry I want more pressure and more wet and more of *him*. All of my weight is on him or held up by his arms and I'm coming so hard my legs are shaking, my back curling sharply away as I cry out. Maybe I scream—I don't have any idea other than I feel like I've exploded, melted, been put back together and he's still talking, saying,

Good girl

Oh so fucking good

You like that?

You like it?

You're candy on my mouth, fucking sweet

Wet, so ready

You wanna get fucked now?

Somehow, the last question presses into my thoughts and pulls a "Yes, please . . . *now*" from me. His hands wrap around my hips, mouth sliding along my belly, my breasts, over my neck as he sits up and backs me onto his lap.

"Wait, wait, wait," he groans when his cock slides between my legs. I whimper, wanting him inside, wanting to feel him tear loose and pound up into me.

Whispering, "Shh, shh, almost ready, almost," Finn reaches to grab the condom at his hip and quickly tears it open. I'm gasping, feeling the sweat run down my neck and between my breasts. Feeling the cool air on my forehead, my stomach. I'm trembling against him, trying to focus on one thing, but it's impossible. Finn is gorgeous, his chest broad, every muscle tense, skin slick with sweat as he rolls the condom on.

"Oh God," I gasp, when he kisses my breast, sucking the peak and groaning.

I've never felt this desperation—I'm bound, he's huge, he could do anything he wants but . . . *look*—look how careful and focused he is, look how he makes me come and talks to me and praises me. A tiny pulsing suspicion at the back of my mind tells me this urgency isn't about escaping reality right now.

It's about *him*.

"Hurry," I whimper.

He steadies me with a hand on my thigh, holding his cock with the other hand, and whispers, "Okay, shh, *shh*, I'm ready, I'm ready. Here. Come here."

I lower my body with his help, taking him in and *oh God*. It takes forever to feel the length of him ease into me. I'm shaking and a little wild, wanting to ride him, but he's holding me down on him with one fist curled around the cord at my back, the other knotted in my hair. He's so deep, so deep inside—and I swear I can feel his pulse, can taste his need to buck up into me.

He groans, rocking his hips just the slightest bit. "Don't make any sounds," he murmurs into my neck. "Your little sounds will make me come before I'm ready."

I have to bite my lip to stay quiet, and he praises me for the effort with a kiss. With his hands spread wide on my hips and across my ass, he raises me, and lowers me, and when he raises me again, he holds me there, and then starts a fast, relentless rhythm up into me. He speaks the whole time, and it isn't even really about what he's saying, because half the time I'm lost and can't process anyway. It's the sound of his voice. The richness of it, the reassurance of it. Words like *pretty* and *good* and *strong* and *lose it, oh fuck I'm gonna lose it* filter in through the haze of pleasure.

It's so good. It's so good.

This is the only thing I can think, over and over. He's making me stare right into his eyes—at least it feels that way, though I don't think he's actually told me to. But the way he's looking at me . . . it's intense and obsessed and tender and adoring. I can't look away, I don't *want* to.

I don't remember ever coming like this, where I can't localize the sensation, can't pinpoint where it starts, or even how long it lasts. I'm trying to be quiet, trying so hard, but my cries slip out even as I taste blood on my lip. I give up, screaming and pulling against the binding as the wild bliss tears through me.

Finn growls, thrusting up hard and fast—and then he bellows, pulling at the cord behind my back and shoving so deep in me as he comes that I feel bent in two.

He slows, and then stills, wrapping his arms around me and grunting into my neck with every quiet exhale—*fuck, fuck, fuck*—long after he's already come. Around me, his big arms are shaking from exertion, wet with sweat, and I've never felt more overwhelmed by someone in my entire life.

I realize I'm going to cry only a split second before I feel the tears spill and run down my cheeks.

But his face is still pressed to my neck, his breaths slowly evening out. "Harlow. Don't move. I can't . . . just give me a second."

I don't think I could even if I wanted. I don't ever want to move off him.

His mouth slides over my shoulder, and he begins to slowly massage my thighs, my ass, my lower back. Lifting me carefully, he reaches between us and takes off the condom, quickly tying it and dropping it somewhere on the couch next to us.

And then he's loosening the knot at my back.

"*No,*" I choke.

He looks at me, sees the tears on my cheeks and maybe thinks I'm crying because I don't want him to free me. *I don't even know why I'm crying.* I'm just *spent*, and if he can't be inside me anymore I need to be tied up, and if I can't be tied up I need another way to know that, right now, I'm his and he'll take care of me. That he'll take over and fix everything because I'm not sure I know how.

Finn swipes at my face with his thumbs. "I have to, sweetheart, you can't be bound up any longer."

It just feels like it's the only thing holding me together.

"I know," he says.

Oh God. I said it out loud.

"Shh, shh, come here." He unwraps me like a gift, running a gentle fingertip along every groove the bungee cord left in my skin, and then he picks me up like I weigh nothing—I have no bones, no muscles, only skin and lust and blood—and carries me to my bedroom.

"This one?" he asks at the end of the hall.

I nod and he ducks in, pulling back the covers with one hand and sliding me under. I'm terrified he's going to leave, but he doesn't. He climbs in behind me, spooning me, running a reassuring hand down my side, over my hip, up my stomach, until he's soothing the cord lines around my breasts with his tender, rough hands and kissing my neck.

"I need to hear you're okay," he rasps. "Tell me you don't hurt."

"I'm okay." I take a deep breath but it chokes halfway through. "But don't leave."

"I don't think I could. I'm . . . it's intense for me, too. I . . . forgot."

I'M A LIGHT sleeper, but I don't wake once in the middle of the night. Not for water, not to go to the bathroom, not even to roll over and find a cool section of the sheets. When my eyes do open, the sun is high in the sky, and Finn and I are in exactly the same position we were in when we fell asleep.

He's not awake yet, but his body is. It takes about a hundred promises to myself—new shoes, ice cream for breakfast, lunch and dinner, an afternoon swim—to get out of bed and not roll him onto his back and take him inside my body just to see if he'll look at me again the way he did last night.

I do get out of bed, though, because it terrifies me that the first thought I have isn't about my mother, or whether she still needs me to drive her to her appointment later today, or how she slept last night. But it *should* be. Not forever, but *God,* for at least the first few weeks when my family—my center, my universe—needs me.

I have coffee brewing and am pacing the kitchen when Finn pads in, wearing the boxers he must have retrieved from the living room floor. I haven't even peeked around that corner, not sure I can handle seeing the loop of bungee cord discarded so casually on the carpet.

He rubs his eyes, walks over to me, and kisses my neck.

Because I'm trying not to melt, I stiffen instead and I can feel his little laugh against my skin.

"I'm freaking out a little, too," he admits.

"It's just that I have . . ." I start explaining. He pulls back and looks at me, those complicated eyes growing unreadable as he listens. "It's one thing to want distraction, but I don't need another obsession."

Way too honest, Harlow.

But he's already nodding. He even looks a little relieved. "I can respect that," he says, pulling his hands from my hips and stepping away. This is exactly how I needed this conversation to go, and yet . . . it stings a little. Finn softens it by adding, "I'm in the same boat, so to speak. And last night, you stopped being an easy fuck."

I pour us both a cup of coffee and smile over the rim as I take a sip. Lying to us both, I say, "We'll have no problem falling back into our antagonistic ex-spouse routine."

His eyebrow twitches. "Right."

Chapter SIX

Finn

ANY DOUBTS I had whether Oliver's shop would be a success—that maybe the constant stream of people on opening day was a fluke—are put to rest as soon as I walk in Friday afternoon.

Apparently there are a lot of nerds in San Diego.

The little bell over the door jingles as I step inside, and I'm stopped in my tracks, eyes wide at the crowd filling the small store. And not just kids, or hipster geeks like Oliver, but suits and soccer moms, people spanning pretty much every age bracket there is.

"Wow."

"Right?" I turn to the voice on my right to see Not-Joe standing at the register. He flicks his blond hair out of his face before he reaches for a box cutter, using it to open one of the many cardboard boxes behind him. "Work at a comic book store. Thought I'd get to hang out all day, read a little. Maybe sneak out back for a blunt." He shakes his head as I eye him and continues carefully pulling the contents out of one open box before breaking it down and moving onto another. "But dude, this place? Doesn't slow down."

"I can see that," I say, impressed. "Doesn't leave much time to browse the merchandise, does it?"

"Me?" he says, then shakes his head again. "I don't read comic books. This might sound weird, but they kind of confuse me."

I take in his blond dreadlocked mohawk, the constant, half-stoned glazed look, the white T-shirt he clearly washed with something red at one point. I mean, this is the guy that pierced his own cock. Not sure I'm surprised the comic books overwhelm him. "Not much of a reader?"

"Fiction, mostly," he admits. "Some biographies. Philosophy, if I have the time. Travel books. A little romance here and there," he adds.

I spy a worn paperback tucked just below the counter and feel my eyebrows disappear into my hair. I'm pretty sure it isn't Oliver's. "Wally Lamb?" I ask. "That's *yours?*"

Not-Joe laughs. "Yeah, best book I've ever read about overcoming self-loathing and forgiveness. *Finding yourself.*"

Okay. "I'm . . . wow."

Not-Joe shrugs before reaching for another pile of comics. "Plus, it was an Oprah Book Club pick, so you know. What Oprah says . . ."

"Right," I say. "So where's Oliver?"

"Last I saw him, he was in the back. Want me to go grab him for you?"

"No, no. I'm good." I look around for a moment, debating whether I should let Oliver know I'm here, or just head out and try to catch up with him later. What I should do is go back to the house and get my head straight; at the very least I should call my brothers. Most of the wiring should be replaced by now, but there's a sinking feeling in my stomach that that will be the least of our problems once they start taking panels off and looking deeper into the boat.

My meeting with the L.A. guys is in just a few days, and I've barely thought about what questions I need to ask, or even whether we have another choice but to say yes. This inability to focus on the entire purpose of this trip is exactly why Harlow was right and why we need to take a step back and cool . . . whatever it is we're doing.

Fuck. Harlow.

With a sigh, I drop down into the couch Oliver has set up near the front of the store. Being with her doesn't feel like our comfortable *arrangement* anymore. Even if Harlow hadn't been the one to step up and say something about reining this in, I'd have had to. I watched her fall apart in my arms last night; even the most oblivious person could have seen there was nothing casual about it for either of us.

God, she was so fucking perfect. I've never met anyone like her, as strong-willed as me and yet, just handing me everything, letting me take her apart one touch at a time.

Pulling out my phone, I see that I have one unread message, but my finger stops and hovers over the text bubble. I should read it, I know this. And I'm such an epic hypocrite for suggesting that Harlow was at a stage in her life where she hadn't figured things out yet. When here I am, thirty-two years old and feeling just as confused and unsure of the future as she is.

"Looks like you're thinking pretty hard there, Hercules. Don't sprain something."

I jump at the sound of her voice and my heart takes off in excitement. "I didn't see you come in."

She takes a minute to step behind the counter and plug her phone in to charge. Then she plops down on the couch next to me, her thigh pressed right to mine.

"Are you on your way into work?" I ask her.

"When you asked me that," she says, looking at me with a cute little smile, "did you use mental air quotes for the word 'work'?"

"Yeah."

"In fact yes, I am headed into"—she holds her fingers up and twitches them—"*work*." She lifts my arm, looks at my watch. "I have half an hour before I need to be there to deliver a tray of mini muffins to a meeting and send some faxes."

And so why are you here? I want to ask her, but I bite my tongue, knowing if the answer is anything other than "Because I was hoping to see you, dumbass" I'll be disappointed.

It's sort of strange to see this version of Harlow: prim and proper and dressed in her slim black skirt, heels, and bright orange silk blouse, long hair brushed and smoothed down her back. She's funny and charming, composed, and so different than the Harlow I see in bed, the one who begs me to spank her, begs for *harder* and *more*. And though it might seem like I'm the one calling all the shots, she's clearly been using *me*, using my body to forget herself and get off. It's a little worrisome just how much I like the idea that I'm the only one right now who gets to see the secret, unraveled version of this golden, beautiful girl.

"Since we're doing the just-friends thing," I say, "I can tell you that you look really fucking pretty today, Ginger Snap."

She blinks at me, surprised for a moment before she grins. "Thanks."

"Because the last time I saw you this early, you looked like you'd just rolled out of someone else's bed," I say, completely bypassing the fact that I saw her just this morning. She doesn't correct me and . . . well, good. I think we both know that particular conversation is a land mine, one definitely better left alone.

"Not one of my finer moments, so I'm going to breeze past that and agree with you. Definitely no more Toby Amslers in my future. I'm running out of fingers, so it's time for me to be more selective in the screening process."

"Running out of . . . fingers?"

"Fingers," she says, holding up both hands and wiggling all ten fingers in front of my face. "This is an incredibly personal decision, and one that can be approached in so many different ways, but I always said I didn't want to have sex with more guys than I could count on two hands. Eight fingers are accounted for, so I don't have room for any more mistakes."

It takes me a second to understand that this means Harlow has only had sex with eight guys.

Or rather, Harlow has had sex with seven guys that aren't me.

And . . . I'm conflicted. On the one hand, I'm sort of surprised. It's not that I had some sort of preconceived notion about any of this, but rather that Harlow herself seems to go out of her way to make people think her sex life is something it's clearly not.

On the other hand, I think of myself as a pretty progressive guy, and as long as you're not cheating or hurting anyone, you should be able to love or marry or *fuck* whoever you want. Still, as hypocritical as it is, there's something about listening to Harlow talk about the others guys she's been with that's making it hard to just sit here and nod.

And Harlow, who for whatever reason seems to pick up on every little thing I do, notices.

"Hey. Whoa, whoa-*whoa*. What's happening here?" She brings a finger up to tap my forehead, hard. "You're all frowny and scrunched up. Are you making a *judgey* face at me?"

"What?" I say. "I am *not* making a face." I'm actually glad I'm not because the face *she's* making is a little terrifying.

"You totally are. Are you trying to slut-shame me, Mr. Good with Rope and Ridiculous Oral Skills?"

"Absolutely not. I would never call anyone—"

"Don't think that just because I let you put your dick in me, that you get to pass judgment on what I may or may not have done. I like sex, just like you. And I'll fuck whoever or however many people I want, ten-finger rule be damned. Just because society would prefer that I—"

"Harlow. I wasn't saying that. Ten fingers. It's all good."

"Oh." She searches my face and seems to realize I'm being sincere. Her forehead relaxes. "Good."

"Good," I repeat.

"Then what about you?" she asks.

"What about me?"

"How many fingers do you have left?"

I sit forward and look around, indicating that we are in fact sitting in the middle of a crowded store. "I don't think this is the best place to have this conversation, Snap."

"Well, what else are we going to do? I have twenty minutes to kill, and since we're no longer banging . . ."

"Yeah," I say, and lean my head back against the couch. "That plan seemed to make a lot more sense right after we'd actually had sex. I was a little less tense then."

"*Right?*" Harlow shifts on the couch, lifting her long bare legs and draping them across my lap. "And speaking of, sorry I sort of melted down on you last night," she says, and I feel something tighten in my chest.

Harlow might have been tied up in bungee cords last night, but it was like watching her *bloom*, and I don't really want to hear her apologize for it. I'm not sure I've ever seen anything so *real*. In a matter of hours, things went from an easy, uncomplicated way to burn off some steam, to anything but simple. I *like* Harlow. Deciding we're not going to sleep together anymore? Fucking sucks.

"You don't have to apologize," I say, and without realizing it, I place my hand on her knee, squeezing it. Her skin is warm beneath my palm and my fingers ache to move, to smooth up and over her thigh, distract us both again.

Fuck.

I move to pull away but she reaches out, taking my hand in hers while she casually studies it.

"No," she murmurs. "Just saying I'm sorry if I made things weird."

"You didn't," I assure her.

She looks at me and seems to be biting back a laugh. "Thanks. You're so effusive."

I nod magnanimously. "That's what friends are for, right?"

"Is that what we are, then?" she asks. "Friends?"

"Definitely friends, maybe more? I don't know, we were married once, after all."

"The best twelve hours of my life, to be honest," she says in her best Scarlett O'Hara impersonation, and straightens her legs across me, her thighs shaking slightly as her muscles stretch beneath my hands. "The days since have been nothing but a pale impersonation."

Oliver walks in from the back, carrying a tall stack of books. "G'day. Nice to see you, mate."

It occurs to me that I'm still sitting with Harlow's legs in my lap, my hand resting a little too comfortably on her thigh. I blink back up and meet Oliver's gaze. He gives me a knowing smirk, so apparently it hasn't escaped his notice, either.

"Dude," Not-Joe says, emerging from the bathroom with a stack of comic books in his hands. He holds them up for Oliver to see, and the two of them exchange a look. "Look what I found."

Oliver groans, but I notice he doesn't actually *take* the books. "Not again."

"Again," Not-Joe confirms.

My eyes follow Not-Joe as he gingerly puts the comics on the glass counter. "Are those Wonder Woman?"

"Yeah. Every fucking time I clean the bathroom. It's *always* Wonder Woman."

Harlow stands and I immediately feel the loss of her warm skin under my palm. When Oliver nods, she says, "You mean people go in there and . . ."

Oliver nods again, picking up an empty box and using a stapler to slide the sullied stack inside. "Bloody oath. Is nothing sacred?"

Harlow leans over, peering into the box. "Well. I mean . . . can you blame them?"

She looks up to three sets of saucer eyes, all of us staring, slack-jawed at her.

"Can we blame them for . . . ?" Not-Joe begins, and lets his question hang meaningfully in the air.

"Oh, come on." She reaches over and plucks a pristine, plastic-wrapped copy of *Wonder Woman* from the shelf. On the cover of this particular issue, Wonder Woman is astride a giant seahorse, her lasso of truth suspended in the air above her, while a man in some sort of watercraft attempts to fire a weapon at her. All of this is supposedly happening underwater, though I don't bother to argue the logistics of how one would lasso a person mere feet above the ocean floor, or how a laser—or whatever it's supposed to be—would work in this scenario in the first place.

"Look at her!" Harlow says. "Even I'd have a little alone time with Princess Diana."

"You *knew* her real name was Princess Diana?" Oliver asks, and I swear to God he looks like a dog whose owner has just beckoned him to the porch for dinner.

She shrugs. "Of course I did."

Looking at me with fire in his eyes, Oliver says, "Finn, if you don't marry this woman again, I just might."

HARLOW HEADS OUT a few minutes later, kissing each of us on the cheek before she leaves and I pretend I don't hate that all three of us got the same treatment. Eventually I leave, too, making plans to meet up with Oliver later that night. I take the long way back to the house, deciding a drive along the harbor might do me some good, and then I remember the unread text still sitting in my phone. The missed call from Colton. Apparently Harlow is an excellent distraction even when we're not having sex.

In the end, I spend the rest of the afternoon driving up and back down the coast, pulling up to the house after sunset and only about thirty minutes before Oliver. I search the fridge and cupboards, pulling out a box of pasta and a handful of vegetables from the crisper. My phone stares at me from where it lies on the counter.

I do everything I can to avoid looking at it. I start dinner and unload the dishwasher. I watch a little TV, and even walk out to grab Oliver's mail, hoping the fresh air will clear my head. It doesn't.

Edgy and unable to handle it anymore, I toss the envelopes to the table and reach for my phone, deciding it's time to man up and face the music. It could be good news, I reason. My brother would have called and *kept* calling if it had been something really bad. Right?

I check my email first. There's a notice from the bank, some sort of stupid forwarded video from Ansel, and an email confirming my meeting in L.A. on Monday at 10 a.m. That last one does nothing to ease the sour feeling in my gut.

Finally I move to the messages, opening the single new text from Colton.

We are screwed, it says. We are absolutely royally FUCKED. I'm getting drunk.

———

THE KITCHEN IS filling with steam from a pot of overboiling pasta on the stove, when the sound of a door closing carries down the hall. "Honey! I'm home!"

I'm pacing between the counter and island, my stomach having bottomed out somewhere near my feet, when I hear Oliver drop his keys and kick his shoes off near the door.

Colton didn't answer when I tried to call him back, but Levi did. Just like his message said, Colton is off somewhere getting plastered—and most likely fucked senseless by one of his many regular bed-bunnies—which would explain why he didn't try to call me again.

According to Levi, engine one has thrown a rod, and the damage is so severe it's actually penetrated the motor casing and rendered it unsalvageable. Worse than that, because of the extra strain being put on engine two, the oil sample came back full of metal shavings, meaning we are only weeks from its complete failure. A few days ago we knew we were in rough shape but assumed we could limp through another season. Now we know we are, just as Colton said, *royally fucked.* We've all put nearly every penny we make back into the family business, and without income, have barely enough left over to cover our living expenses for the next six months. We can't take the boat out on the water until we fix it, and I have no idea how we're going to afford to do that.

Oliver crosses the room, turning down the stove before walking to the sink to wash his hands. "You all right, mate?" he says, watching me with concern.

"Yeah. Just ruining dinner." The next words are just sitting on my tongue: *I'm fucked. My future and the future of my entire family has just gone up in smoke—and oh, by the way, how's the store?*

I can't do that. But I know I need to talk, to hear myself say what's going on and hear someone else tell me it's not as bad as it seems, that everything will work out eventually.

Basically, I need someone to lie to me.

Normally, Ansel would be the best person for this job. He's stupidly optimistic, and has this way of making every doom-and-gloom situation sound like a perfectly timed stroke of luck. Unfortunately, he's not even in the same country right now, and there's no way I'm calling him and taking up what little free time he has to burden him with my problems. He's out.

Perry would be the next obvious choice, because she's bored and has historically been a good listener. But, Jesus Christ, I can't. I know I shouldn't take sides but even *I'm* mad at her for what she did to Ansel and Mia, and none of us are really talking to her right now anyway. She's out, too.

Oliver has enough going on, with the store opening and his long days on his feet. The last thing he needs is for me to unload how my business is ending just as his is taking off.

And if I'm honest, I don't really *want* to tell any of them. It's not that I don't think they'd be concerned, it's that I don't want them to worry. I don't want them to know how dire it all is.

Oblivious to my mental breakdown, Oliver crosses the kitchen and pulls a cutting board out of a drawer. "So you and Harlow," he says, reaching for a knife.

"Harlow?" I say, distracted, her name coming out a bit sharper than I intend. "There's nothing between me and Harlow."

"Course there's not. Just noticed how cozy the two of you seemed today."

Even with everything going on, I still manage to roll my eyes. "She's a pain in the ass," I tell him, and it's such a lie. With most women, the novelty of a pretty face would have worn off and I'd be ready to move on. But with Harlow, I find myself liking her more and more with each conversation.

"You sure you're okay?"

I turn to see Oliver watching me closely. "Yeah, why wouldn't I be?"

He shrugs, looks like he wants to throttle me, but then he blinks and the expression has vanished, and I wonder if it was ever there. "Don't know, really. Just . . . you never did tell me what you were doing out here. Everything good at home?"

"Great. Just here to meet with a few investors. Thinking about making some improvements during the off-season."

I can see a flash of relief on his face. "Finn, that's great. Look at us, look at our lives. Everything fucking coming up roses, mate."

Right.

I blink away, looking out the window. There's really only one person I want to talk to right now.

"Listen," I say, shutting off the stove. "I just remembered I promised my dad I'd give him a call tonight. You're okay eating without me?"

If Oliver is suspicious, he's a good enough friend to not call me on my bullshit. "Yeah, of course. Think I'll call Lola and see if she wants to hang out. You think you'll be back?"

I reach for my wallet on the kitchen table and push it into my back pocket. "Not sure. Just save me a plate and I'll heat it up when I get back. I just really need to make this call."

Oliver is already nodding, dishing up his plate before he waves me off.

My hand is wrapped around my phone before I'm even out the door.

Chapter SEVEN

I'M MOPPING THE floor. Why, when the house cleaner was at my parents' house today, am I mopping their floor?

Because I can't seem to focus on even the smallest task, and dropped an entire casserole dish of enchiladas on the tile.

Dad walks in, looks at me in my ripped jeans and his old flannel shirt, and then at the stained-red mop and the smear of sauce on the white tile, and doesn't even say anything. He just walks to the fridge, opens it, grabs a yogurt for Mom, and kisses my head on the way back out.

I make a couple of decisions in the next twenty seconds. First, I need another job.

There's a tiny chance I'll be offered a full-time, paid internship at NBC starting in January, but just talking about my current situation with Finn briefly made me realize I'm just spinning my wheels. I'm useless there and no self-respecting woman of the twenty-first century with no other earthly responsibilities works *twelve* hours a week.

Second, I can't bang Finn, but I also can't spend every free second at my parents' house. The reality of illness is it's a fairly miserable, isolating business. Mom doesn't want us hovering, and if she wants anyone, it's Dad. It's time to cut the apron strings.

Third, and maybe most important, I need to figure out what I'm doing for dinner now that I've shattered Plan A all over the kitchen.

When I'm on my hands and knees, scrubbing the last of the stain from the grout between the tiles, my phone dings on the counter with a number I don't recognize.

You up for getting a beer or two?

I squint at the screen in the darkening kitchen, typing back, Who is this?

The guy you were just fantasizing about.

Colonel Sanders?

The reply comes immediately. Try again.

I giggle as I type, Ethan? I hit send and quickly type, No! Jake, I'm so sorry!

Finn's reply comes up after about a minute: Funny.

Finn and I exchanged numbers in Vegas nearly three months ago and I'm strangely tickled that we've never used them until now. Are we going to a lumberjack bar? I ask.

I think the word you want is fisherman.

Whatever, I'm just impressed you're doing the texting. I type back. I look down at my outfit and cringe, before deciding—*fuck it*. And this is perfect, I'm dressed like you.

I'll be there in twenty.

I run upstairs, kiss my parents goodbye, and head out of the house, diving into my car and hoping to beat Finn back to my place. I don't want him to know I wasn't home. I don't know *why*, but maybe it's because right now—and shockingly—Finn Roberts is my happy place; just being around him makes me feel better, and part of it has to be that he never asks me, "How are you *feeling*? How is your mom? Hanging in there?"

She's such a fighter.

She's so beautiful.

So young.

I can't imagine how this must be for you.

Strangely, Finn is the one who probably *could* imagine how this is for us, and it's a relief to not have to face it when I'm with him.

I get home in record time; the traffic light gods were smiling upon me. I could change out of my grungy clothes, but don't bother. If we aren't banging, I'm not primping.

He's such a gentleman that he texts from the curb that he's here, and I meet him at his truck and jump in.

"I forget how to get to Fred's," he says by way of greeting.

"*Hello.*" After buckling my seat belt, I tell him, "Hang a right on Prospect and then a left on Draper."

"Oh, yeah." He maneuvers out of the spot and then follows my direction. "I think I'll remember from there."

"Especially given that it's *on Draper*," I say with a cheeky grin.

But he doesn't smile back. In fact, Finn seems lost in thought. He fiddles with the radio and settles on NPR, so instead of conversation, we have a rerun of Terry Gross interviewing Joaquin Phoenix to keep us company. He drums his fingers on the steering wheel at a red light, looking out his window away from me.

"This not-having-sex thing sure is way more stimulating! I'm super glad we're still cool just hanging out." I lean forward to get a better look at his face, but I don't even get a flicker of a grin.

"Just wanted to get out for a bit," he mumbles cryptically. Oliver lives a block from the beach. Finn could easily "get out" and do about a hundred different things other than taking me to Fred's, where we just went just a few nights ago.

He parks in front of the bar and meets me on the sidewalk, as usual gesturing that I lead the way. Mr. Furley calls out to me when we enter, telling Kyle to kick some "ratty-ass kids out of Harlow's booth."

"How dare they?" I hiss playfully to him.

"Kids these days," he says, wiping down the bar. "Buncha little assholes. How's Madeline?"

"She's hanging in there." I stretch across the bar and kiss his stubbly cheek before hopping down and grabbing the two bottles of beer he hands me. I give him my best Bogart: "Tanks, *schweetheaaart.*"

Handing one to Finn, I gesture for him to follow me to our corner, wiping a few stray peanut shells off the table as I slide into our booth.

"You sure have him wrapped around your finger," Finn says as he climbs in after me, looking back at Mr. Furley behind the bar.

"Yep. He's the best." I take a long pull on my beer, watching Finn swallow as he does the same. God, I love his neck. It's tanned, and defined, and dark stubble just barely shadows it, from his cheek . . . down his jaw . . .

I clear my throat. *No sex.* "So what's up?"

Finn shrugs, and stares at the television nearest us, currently playing a Padres game.

At first the silence is comfortable: I have my beer, he has his beer. He has the Padres, I have a couple of adorably dorky senior citizens cutting a rug on the dance floor. But when they go sit down at their table, I feel the weight of the silence at ours. I don't have the sense that Finn asked me to come out so he could sit and watch baseball alone.

"So, is Oliver working tonight?"

He doesn't seem to hear me.

"Do you want me to order us some food? I'm starving."

Again, he seems completely lost in thought. The music is pretty loud, but it's not like I'm whispering. Hello, I never whisper.

"I think I'm going to go over to the music booth and see if Kyle wants to get freaky on the dance floor with me." Nothing. "Maybe bang him on the bar. Or maybe a little action in the back room." I lean toward him. "And obviously 'back room' is a euphemism."

"Hey now," Finn says, pulling his eyes from the television. Finally, a reaction.

"Okay, so what's going on?" I ask him. "If you wanted a quiet beer session you could have brought Oliver."

"I just wanted to think."

"And that you could do alone, or on a run on the beach. So clearly you need to talk. Do you need a sounding board, or a brick wall?"

Finn looks at me like he has no idea what I'm talking about.

"Do you need me to help you think something through," I clarify, "or do you just want to talk it out without interruption?"

"Are you capable of that?"

My face right now. "In fact, I am."

Finn rises from the table, holding out his hand when I start to protest. "I'm going to explain. I want to talk it out, no interruption. I just need another beer first. Or three."

He starts to walk away so I call out, "Have Mr. Furley bring me some tater tots, too."

FINN IS ALMOST half done with his second beer when he finally starts talking. "When I said I was here on business, I was telling the truth. I know it sounds weird, because our entire tiny business is centered up on Vancouver Island."

I nod, inexplicably giddy to learn why he's staying in San Diego for so long. I feel sort of special that he's talking to me about this, but I absolutely don't let that show. I am poker-facing it like a champ.

"But it's not an easy business, and it's one of those things where if you have a bad year, okay, you can pull it out the next. But if you have two bad years, it gets harder. A couple bad years, a big commercial firm comes in . . . then the boats need fixing . . ." He runs a palm down his face and then takes a deep drink of his beer, finishing it and then grumbling a quiet, "Yeah, so."

I'm suddenly not quite as giddy anymore.

I can tell he's not going to lay the specifics of his business troubles on me and really, it's fine because I suspect I would be only marginally more helpful than Kyle the DJ would be in this situation. But I stay quiet, not only because of my inexpertise, but because I know he isn't done. I still have no idea why he's *here*.

"So about, I don't know, maybe a month ago, some people called up, said they had an idea for . . ." He cuts off and looks at me for a long pause. "For a show."

"Like a fishing expo?" I ask.

Laughing, he says, "No. Like a *television* show."

Oh.

Oh.

I lean forward, my elbows on the table. "And by 'some people' you mean . . ."

He blinks away. "The Adventure Channel."

I feel my eyes go wide. "Holy *shit*, Finn. They want to make a show out of your family business?"

"Me, Dad, Colt, and Levi. All four Roberts boys."

"And you're here to start negotiations?" I'm reeling. The Adventure Channel is huge. Finn definitely has a face and body for television, but . . . he's not exactly warm and fuzzy.

He shakes his head, saying, "No. See, one of our smaller boats was fucked a while ago, but before our main boat, the *Linda*, broke, I wasn't really considering it that seriously. I came down here because both my brothers want to do it, and I don't feel right making a unilateral decision about it without at least weighing the options." He rubs his face again. "But I found out about an hour ago that the *Linda* is fucked, too. I mean, *fucked*. We have maybe five thousand in the bank, and are looking at a repair that'll cost a hundred grand. Maybe two." Looking over at me, he says, "Now I have to consider this show, or bowing out of the industry completely. I don't want this, Harlow. It'd be a circus."

"Have you talked to the network since you've been here?"

"Only a couple of emails. I came down early because of Oliver's opening, and Colton was worried I was going to have a heart attack like Dad and wanted me out of town." He glances at me. "I'm meeting with them soon in person. They've been sending me promo materials."

My stomach bottomed out at the mention of Finn having a heart attack, but at his playfully hesitating look and the mention of promo materials, I can't help my smile. "'Promo materials,' you say? *This* I need to see."

With a grimace, he reaches into his back pocket and pulls out his wallet, fishing out a folded glossy 8x10 of the family sitting on a boat docked in the water. "Here's one thing they've sent." He hands it to me. "They've also made a logo and T-shirts."

"Wow," I say staring down at the picture. The lighting is professional, the colors rich. Each man in the photo is the perfect balance of rugged and polished. "This is the extreme fisherman version of a JCPenney glamour shot."

He snatches it from my hand. "Okay, and you're done."

I manage to snag it back before he can return it to his wallet. "So these are your brothers, huh?"

"Yeah."

Finn is in the middle, with his father and the youngest brother, Levi, on one side, and the middle brother, Colton, on the other. It's clear they've received some direction: Finn's dad looks welcoming, laid-back. Levi is beaming, an open book, whereas Colton is making sex eyes at the camera. Finn looks no-nonsense and world-weary. All four men in the picture are completely, ridiculously good-looking.

"Well, thanks for this. I might need to go home and masturbate for the rest of the evening."

"You know, if a guy said that, it would be super creepy."

"Oh, I'm sorry, Poodle. Does the sexual double standard make you grumpy?"

He laughs dryly. "You're a pain in the ass, Ginger Snap."

"So, the Adventure Channel wants you basically for a dating show."

"No. It's meant to be a gritty peek into our lives as *fishermen* and—"

"Does it say that on the back of the Glamour Shot?" I flip it over, pretending to look.

"Harlow."

"*Finn*." I turn the picture back over and point to it. "Look at you guys. You're, what? Thirty-two?"

"Yeah."

"And Colton is how old?"

"Twenty-nine."

"And Levi?"

He sighs. He's bagging what I'm raking, clearly. "Twenty-four."

"I bet there's a clause in the contract they showed you that you can't be in a committed relationship when filming begins."

His eyes go wide. "How would you know that?"

"Are you kidding? My mom has been offered a spot on a reality show a few times. They always have something in there about relationships. So you don't think this show is really about filming your bulging biceps on the boat and then getting you shirtless and hooking up with coeds?"

"You aren't helping. I already don't want to do this." He steals a few of my tater tots. "But my brothers think it will be a trip. It's like they don't really understand how it will change their lives. Colt is always sleeping with someone different. Levi . . . I swear I think he's a virgin."

I look at the sandy-haired hottie in the picture. "Okay, you're high. If this guy isn't putting out left and right, there is no God, Santa, or Easter Bunny."

He waves me off. "Whatever. I just don't think we'd make very good television." His argument is so weak, even he can tell. He winces at my gaping shock, looking away.

"You're kidding, right?" I ask him. "A manwhore hottie,

a virgin hottie, and the hottest older brother who's clearly too busy for love? This is a television producer's wet dream. This show practically writes itself."

As if relenting, he says quietly, "They're laying it on pretty thick. Two-season commitment to start, they bought my truck just as a good-faith gesture, and they'll repair our main two boats and get us a new one."

I let out a low whistle. "Wow. So you're upset because a huge television studio wants to give you oodles of money? Poor baby. Why aren't you jumping on this?"

He looks at me, and it's his turn to be incredulous. "I *like* my life, Harlow. It isn't cushy, and we're always sort of scraping by, but I chose this for a reason. I like my little house on the water, and working on the boat and cracking jokes with my brothers and those days where we get an unreal haul. Those days make all of the slow ones totally insignificant." He looks away, running his thumbnail down a groove in the table. "The idea of a crew coming on and filming us twenty-four hours a day for three days a week makes me nauseous."

"What do Oliver and Ansel think about it?" I ask.

"They don't know."

"I know something they don't?" I crow.

He shrugs. "It's hard to discuss this choice with my best friends. I'm in the middle of this crazy decision, but in two years I may look back and think, *Why did I even consider this?* I don't want to mull it over with people who will be in my life every day if I realize only later how pathetic it all seems. Does that make sense?"

So he's not expecting me to be in his life in two years? Okay. This one stings and I tilt my beer to my lips, looking away. "Makes total sense."

"Shit," he whispers, seeming to register how that sounded. "You know what I mean."

And in all honesty, I do. I haven't told him about my mom, either. I don't need Finn's support, and I like that being with him is just an easy place for me to inhabit. Maybe he likes that, in the long run, my opinion doesn't matter much.

I mentally shake off my minor offense and smile at him. "I know it probably sounds like a complete one-eighty from your life right now, but it could bring opportunities you've never considered. It would give your company name a brand, and—"

"Or make us a joke."

"And," I say, ignoring him, "they're giving you a boat? I know less than nothing about commercial fishing but I bet those cost as much as a house in La Jolla."

"Not too far off," he agrees. "I don't know. I'm not even sure the boat they buy for us would ever feel *mine,* either. It is, literally, selling out. But you haven't run away laughing, so I guess it's not insane for me to be putting some thought into it."

"I think you would be insane if you hadn't."

He nods, and turns his attention back to the game. This time, I'm pretty sure he's done talking.

Chapter EIGHT

Finn

I CHECK THE ADDRESS Harlow gave us as we turn off the street. The restaurant is packed, and I blow out an exaggerated breath as I circle the lot.

"Looks like it might not be our night," I tell Oliver, pretty sure that if my shifty eyes don't give me away, my horrible acting will. "Guess we better just head back to the house. Try this another time."

I turn the truck toward the exit but his hand on my forearm stops me. "Everyone's already here so just keep a lookout. Too late for a change of plans anyway," he says, peering out the passenger window before he adds, "No thanks to you."

"What's that supposed to mean?"

"It means that it took over an hour to get you out of the house, and you look like you're being dragged to the dentist, rather than a night of dinner and questionable humor with your best mates."

"That is absolutely not true." It's completely true.

"Ansel flew back to surprise Mia again and wants to see us. And despite what you said last night, you've been bodgy all week."

"I'm fine. It's just weird to be gone while so much is going on at home," I say, and offer a casual shrug for good measure. *Keep it cool, Finn. Don't fidget. Don't avoid eye contact.* "Not used to having so much free time is all."

The radio plays some random pop song in the background and Oliver reaches over, shutting it off. The click of the dial seems to reverberate around the cab and I make a show of squinting out the front windshield, still in search of a parking spot.

I don't like the way he's looking at me. Oliver knows me too well and would rip off my arms and beat me with them if he found out I talked to Harlow about all this before him.

"I'm your best mate, Finnigan. Wouldn't lie to me, would ya?"

I start to answer but he's immediately distracted by a spot opening up just ahead of us. "Oh, hey . . . right there, right there."

I pull into the spot, shutting off the engine with a heavy sigh. So I guess we'll be going in.

I AM PRETTY sure I have never looked guiltier than I do in this moment. Ever. Like a criminal just casually strolling by the house he's robbed.

As expected, Harlow gave me epic amounts of shit, and did what I've come to know as her *thing:* cracking jokes and using sarcasm to make light of the situation. But the look on her face when I explained why I couldn't tell Ansel or Perry or even Oliver hit me like a punch to the chest.

I'd managed to put it out of my mind until later, with Oliver snoring down the hall and me still wide awake and staring up at the dark ceiling, thinking, *Should* I tell them? Was it wrong to keep my closest friends in the dark and open up so easily to Harlow? Up until that point, I hadn't put much thought into Harlow and me. She's been a lot of things—a wild story, a distraction, and eventually a friend—but now none of that seemed enough.

And fuck, I do not want to face her tonight. Because not only do I have no idea where we stand or how I feel or how we should even interact, but now she has this giant secret. One I couldn't even tell my best friends.

I should have manned up and told Oliver.

I should never, *ever* have told busybody Harlow.

What if they can tell I'm keeping something from them?

What if she lets something slip?

Fuck.

Inside the restaurant it's dark and loud, so loud in fact that I wonder if I could sneak away at some point, disappear without anyone noticing.

Despite the number of bodies and booths crowding the small space, it's a good twenty degrees cooler inside than out. Which means it's only then I realize I'm sweating, the frigid air prickling at the damp skin along my forehead and down the back of my neck. *Jesus Christ, Finn. Get yourself together.*

We hear them before we see them. Even above the din of voices and music and clinking silverware, Harlow's distinct laughter carries all the way to the door. Harlow is never quiet.

"That is the best thing I've ever heard," Ansel yells, dissolving into a fit of giggles. You wouldn't think a twenty-eight-year-old lawyer would giggle, but this is Ansel and, well, you'd be wrong. Insecurity hums along the edges of my nerves as their voices get closer, and I feel my mouth pinch down into a frown.

"Sounds like they started without us!" Oliver shouts over his shoulder, and I can only nod, following him across the room and toward the table while trying to look like I'm not about to throw up.

They're all seated at a large booth near the back. Ansel is on one end, his long arms splayed across the back of the seat, and he leans forward, grinning while he listens across the table. Mia is next to him, Lola sits on Mia's right and—not for the first time since I met her—is lost in something she's doodling on a napkin. Harlow is on the edge, eyes wide and expressive as she relays some story to Ansel, who laughs. Again.

"Having a good time?" Oliver asks, stopping at the other side of the table. "Could hear you lot clear outside." Everyone's eyes snap up to him—and then me—before they call out in greeting.

Everyone except Harlow.

Her gaze locks on mine for the longest five seconds of my life before she blinks away, addressing Oliver. "Finally," she says, smile a little too bright. Nervous, maybe? *Guilty?*

"Did you—" she starts to say, but I interrupt.

"What was so funny?" I snap, and immediately want to smack myself.

Everyone turns to me, each of them with varying expressions of *What the fuck?*

Lola looks up, and I register that while she might not look like she's paying attention, she hears every single word. "Harlow was just telling the story of the time we locked ourselves out while skinny-dipping and we decided she was the one who had to climb through the upstairs window. Naked."

"Oh," I say, too horrified by my own reaction to linger over the mental image of Harlow, naked, scaling a wall, a window . . . anything.

Harlow watches me through narrowed eyes, and Ansel is looking at me like I've just shown up with my underwear on the outside of my pants.

"Right," Oliver says. "Gonna find the toilet, order me a burger if they come around, would ya?"

With Oliver gone my only options are to stand here like an idiot, or take the seat next to Harlow.

With a sigh, I steel myself and slide into the booth, careful to keep at least a few inches between us. Lola and Mia start talking about . . . something, and Harlow leans in.

"Take it down a notch there, Finnick," she whispers. Any other moment and I'd tell her exactly where she can put her cute little nicknames. But right now, I'll settle for just keeping my shit together.

"What?" I ask, trying to look confused. "I was curious."

"Curious? You looked like you were ready to flee the scene of a crime there for a second. You're all fidgety and . . ." Her eyes make a circuit of my entire face. "Jesus. Are you *sweating?*"

"I'm fine," I say. I wipe my palms across the denim on my thighs and exhale as I lean back. "Just, you know. Feeling a little weirded out by all this."

"By what? You didn't think I said something, did you?" She actually looks a little offended and so I answer quickly.

"What?" Probably too quickly. "No. Absolutely not. Just worried that, you know, maybe you don't have the best poker face."

"A poker . . . what the fuck are you talking about?"

"You're always meddling and shit. I thought maybe you'd slip."

Before she can answer—or, you know, elbow me in the balls—Oliver makes his way back to the table and refills every-one's glass, before dropping into the seat at the end of the booth, jostling me toward Harlow.

I straighten and mumble an apology but she shakes her head and laughs, leaning close and whispering so quietly I have to close my eyes to focus on her words: "I got news for you, Finn. I faked orgasms for six years before you and have more secrets than you could fit in that giant empty head of yours, so if one of us is gonna give away your big dating show secret, it's not going to be me."

"It's not a da—" I pause, and take another deep breath before reaching for my beer. "Never mind."

I know I'm being ridiculous, and yet, I don't relax. Because now, not only am I waiting for Harlow to slip up, but I'm watching her so closely I notice everything. I'm sure I'm staring at her like some kind of a serial killer, but the thing is, she's not looking back. At all.

A waitress appears at some point and takes everyone's order, and I'm so lost in my head that I have no idea what I've asked for until she returns, setting a giant salad in front of me. Wonderful.

Not-Joe stops by and helps himself to a beer, even crawling under the table to pop up next to Harlow, wedging his way against her side.

"Have a seat," she tells him with a laugh, and scoots over. Her thigh is pressed against mine and I have to force myself to keep my hands where everyone can see them, and far, *far* away from where they're currently itching to go.

"Watching your figure there?" Not-Joe asks, pointing to my plate with a giant fry he's snatched from Lola.

"He's not as young as he used to be," Harlow says.

And she's *still* not looking at me.

Instead she nods to Oliver. "So, how's the Wonder Woman situation?" she says, grinning while she cuts into her steak. *I* wanted a steak. "Any improvement?"

Oliver shakes his head and drains the last of his beer. "Don't ask."

Ansel, who up until this point has had some part of his face latched onto Mia, suddenly speaks up. "What Wonder Woman situation?"

"Jesus Christ," Lola says. "Got a little thing for Princess Diana, do you?"

Harlow breaks into giggles and Ansel blushes clear to the tips of his ears. "I . . . uh . . ."

"I've got to hand it to her," Harlow says, reaching for an onion ring. "Wonder Woman just keeps proving she's got it."

"I'm completely confused," Mia says.

"That's because Ansel's over there trying to suck your soul out through your mouth like some sort of Dementor," Harlow says, and then whispers in my direction, "It's a Harry Potter reference, Sunshine. Keep up."

Oliver explains the situation and if possible, Ansel's face is even redder.

"I wonder if anyone's had sex in there," Lola says, and we all turn to her. "*What?* I'm just saying, a little voyeuristic rendezvous surrounded by nerd porn?" She offers a small shrug. "I get it."

"Of course you do," Harlow deadpans.

"Well, *I'm* not having sex in that bathroom," Not-Joe says. "The couch? Maybe."

"Nobody is having sex in my store!" Oliver shouts, and then almost as an afterthought adds, "And don't get any ideas, because that includes all of you."

"Thank God there aren't any cameras back there," Not-Joe adds. "Can you even imagine the terrifying things you'd catch on film? The coolest, weirdest people come in there, it would make the sickest reality show."

I choke on my beer, coughing like I'm losing a lung.

The entire table jumps, arms go flying and cups falling over like dominoes, beer and foam soaking everything in sight.

"Oh my God, are you okay?" Mia asks.

I cough again, and feel Harlow's hand on my back, patting and moving in small circles.

"Pull yourself together, man," she mumbles, and I nod, reaching for a napkin to wipe off the front of my shirt. "He's fine," she tells the rest of the table, "just went down the wrong pipe."

When I finally get myself together, I sit back, carefully sipping my beer and trying not to make eye contact with anyone. Like a psychopath.

I focus on the feel of Harlow pressed to the side of my body, and how natural it seems. I keep waiting for her to give me shit, or make some joke at my expense, but she's completely poker-faced—cool and steady—barely sparing a glance in my direction. I'm trying to decide if it's intentional or not; is she really not looking at me, or is she just not looking at me as much as she normally does?

I manage to "accidentally" bump her arm once or twice, tap my knee against hers. I even manage to sneak over and fork a piece of her steak. Nothing.

And the more I watch her, the more I want her to look at me, talk to me, pick me out of all these other assholes. I like how she talks to everyone, always focused on that one person without overdoing it or having it ever come across as flirting.

And why would she? She's easily the most beautiful person in this place. She doesn't need to chase anything.

But . . . she did chase me, I remind myself. In Vegas, all the way to British Columbia and here, too. Fuck, I want to brag about that to *someone*.

And I want her to flirt with me, maybe just a little.

Not-Joe's phone vibrates across the table, and he climbs out of the booth, insisting he needs to go. Everyone else follows soon after. I note that Harlow hasn't checked her phone for close to an hour, but when she does, there's a visible change in her posture. Her shoulders stiffen and I'm pretty sure I watch the color slip from her cheeks.

Harlow has barely had anything to drink, but as the others head for their cars or start making the walk home, she hangs back.

"Want a ride?" I say.

She lifts a brow and I laugh. "That's not what I mean," I say. "Olls and I came together; would you like a lift back to your apartment?"

"Actually, yeah. That'd be great."

Her entire demeanor has changed, but I don't ask any questions. She hitches her bag over her shoulder and follows us out to the truck, insisting on climbing into the backseat and letting Oliver have the front.

The drive is quiet, and my eyes instinctively flicker to her reflection in the rearview mirror. I can't see much of her, only the briefest flash of light and shadow as we pass beneath the city streetlights, or she looks at her phone, but she's just so fucking beautiful. I blink up once to find her watching me and it's all I can do to look away, focus on the traffic, and not kill us all.

I have no idea how it happened, but I *like* Harlow Vega. A lot. I respect her. I want to get to know her. I want to fuck her for reasons that have nothing to do with distraction or my instinctive need to release semen.

I am so royally fucked.

We pull up to her building too soon and I jump out, opening her door and helping her climb down.

"Thanks," she says.

I nod. "And thank you," I tell her. "For listening and . . . for keeping it between the two of us."

"No problem. I'll catch you around, okay?" she says, before adding, "Bye, Oliver!" over her shoulder.

He peeks his head out the window and says his own goodbye, and then she's gone, making her way up the winding path and to the glowing building.

Harlow Vega walking away, still one of my favorite views. And definitely the image I'm going to use when I get home.

OLIVER AND I get back to the house and after a quick good night we each head in the direction of our rooms. I don't waste any time, clearing the hall in just a few long strides and closing the door behind me. I don't even think, can't manage to walk to the bed, or even do the respectable thing and make it to the shower, before I straighten against the wood and reach for my belt. My brain is fuzzy, my muscles tense as I fumble with my fly and push my jeans down just enough to get to my cock.

The relief is so instantaneous that I hiss through my teeth and have to still my hand, remind myself that Oliver is at the other end of the house and the walls here are paper-thin.

If I close my eyes I can still feel the press of Harlow's thigh against mine, the heat that radiated through the denim, the brush of her hair when she reached across me. I fill my lungs and huff out a breath, letting my mind go and conjuring up every dirty, lewd thought I've been trying to tamp down since we decided to just be friends.

I imagine things having gone a little differently tonight. That I went to the bar to get a drink and she followed, telling me to meet her in the bathroom. Maybe I fucked her in the stall, from behind with her legs spread wide, both her hands trapped in one of mine. I could spank her like that, just enough to see my handprint bloom across her skin and make her so wet it gets all over her, all over me.

Sweat pricks at my forehead and down my back. My shirt clings to my skin and so I pull it off, dropping it at my feet. The sound of my hand on my cock is obscene, the frantic clink of my belt in the otherwise still house. Somehow, it makes me harder, pre-come dribbling from the tip to help with the drag, leaving my hand slick.

I think of the last time we fucked and how amazing she looked all tied up, how much she *wanted* it. Did the cords leave a mark, a gentle abrasion on her skin that was there even after I was gone? I wonder if she'd press on them, make it hurt just enough to remind her of what we did, how it felt to be bound and just knowing that I would take care of her.

I'm almost blindsided when it happens, and I come with a choked-off sound, biting my lip to stay quiet as a Novocain numbness spreads heavy over my body. I work through the last of my orgasm, skin slippery as I slide over it in slow, lazy strokes. I manage to reach for my shirt and wipe off my hand before I cross the last three steps and fall, face-first, onto the bed.

I don't open my eyes again until morning.

Chapter NINE

Harlow

I'M IN A bad way, hard up, losing my mind—and I'm not even bothering with denial. Being near Finn—even when he's being a complete jackass like he was at dinner tonight—obliterates any other worry, and being trapped with him in that truck made me nearly lose my mind. I could smell his soap, the clean smell of his sweat. I could feel his eyes on me the entire drive, flickering up again and again in the rearview mirror.

After he drops me off, I get *myself* off on my couch, thinking about our night together in this very spot, before falling asleep half dressed. After all, there is no Finn here to carry me in a boneless heap to my bed and spoon me all night like a champ.

In the morning, I break routine for the second time in two weeks and head to the Starbucks where I ran into Finn his first day back in town. Spoiler alert: he's not there.

And now, I'm standing outside Downtown Graffick, hoping Finn is spending the morning here with Oliver. Unfortunately, through the front windows, I can see Oliver at the counter, but no Finn. *Dammit.* I should have just gone to their house in Pacific Beach to see him since I'm clearly past the point of pride. But what am I expecting? That somehow between last week and now, our situation has become convenient for a relationship? He lives in Canada. I'm in San Diego. My mother is undergoing aggressive cancer treatment and his family business is going under unless he signs on for a glossy reality television show that stipulates he can't have a girlfriend.

But all of the *other* obstacles—the ones I thought were meaningful only weeks ago, including our tendency to bicker and his bossy male act—don't seem that relevant anymore. We've softened together, found some sort of easy peace. Plus, I like his kinky little rope thing. I like the fact that working with his hands, and rope, is so ingrained in his history that it makes him wild to pull me into that world, too, literally wrapping me up in it.

Oliver looks out the window and spots me, waving for me to come inside. Now I'll have to go in and pretend I'm really looking for Lorelei because why else would I be at a comic book store? I've been friends with Lola long enough to hold my own with basic pop culture references, but Oliver knows the only reason I can differentiate Hellboy from Abe Sapien is because of Lola's T-shirt collection. I take a deep, confidence-building breath: if I'm here, I'm *obviously* here looking for her.

The little bell rings when I push through the door. "There you are, Lola!"

Lola looks up from where she's reading in the front nook, and just laughs. Oliver hands a customer some change and thanks them, before looking up at me. "He's in L.A. today."

"Grah," I mutter. "Busted." My pulse accelerates thinking about Finn going alone to Los Angeles to meet with the big television executives. He's got better life instincts than most people I know, but I feel a halfhearted spike of irritation that he didn't ask me to come along for moral support.

Ugh, I'm in a bad way. Hard up.

Losing my mind.

"Don't you work today?" Lola asks.

"No," I tell her, slumping down on the chair next to hers. "I changed my schedule because Mom starts chemo today, but then Dad told me to come see her tomorrow instead."

"What do you even *do*, Chandler Bing?" Oliver asks, laughing.

I look up, startled. I didn't realize he could hear us, and for a beat I'm panicked because I mentioned Mom's chemo. But Oliver doesn't look even a little surprised. Either he didn't hear that part, or Lola's already told him and he knows he's not allowed to ask me about it.

I wonder if he's told Finn. But if he has, wouldn't Finn ask me about it?

"Statistical analysis and data reconfiguration," I lie, playing along. "What's Finn doing in L.A. anyway?"

"Dunno," he says, and I love the way his accent puts an "r" sound at the end of every word ending in a vowel. He frowns. "He's not really talking about what he's doing here at all. Finn's always been that mysterious broody type, but I don't know. Quite secretive, really."

I nearly high-five myself, knowing now that I know something Oliver doesn't. Oliver knows Finn better than almost anyone. We've talked about his job and his family a little, but Bedroom Finn's history is an absolute mystery to me, and the more I want to see him, the more I hate the idea of him with hordes of girls, doing what we did at Oliver's house, and on my couch . . . acts that had left me feeling like my view of sex and intimacy had been wiped clean of a cloudy film I hadn't even known was there.

And now here we are, alone in the store without the man himself. No way am I going to miss this opportunity to dig.

"So you don't know what Finn is up to down here for a few weeks"—I decide to start slowly, keeping it about *professional* things—"but it seems like he's the one basically in charge of his entire family business?"

Oliver nods. "His mum died when he was twelve, right? Then a few years later his dad had a heart attack and a stroke, so Finn's running the ship. Literally."

"That must make it pretty hard to date." *Oops.* My slow-and-subtle plan crashes and burns.

Lola snorts next to me, flipping the page in her comic book without looking up, and Oliver gives me a dubious glance.

"I know Finn would tell me anything," I assure him. "If I asked."

Oliver studies me for a moment, running his finger under his lower lip. "So just ask *him*, then."

"I don't want him to know I want to know," I say, wearing my Captain Obvious expression. "Duh, Oliver."

Laughing, he says, "You two are messed up."

"Oh, because we are the only ones with secrets?" I tilt my gaze to Lola, still reading obliviously beside me.

Oliver gives me the touché face, and says, "Fair enough."

He's all but admitted out loud he has a thing for Lola! *I—am—giddy!*

"Besides," I tell him, coiling my hair into a bun on top of my head, "I may not know him like you do, of course, but we all know he's a fisherman who works all the time so basically only has time to bang skanky Canadian hockey muffs that he meets at the local Moose N' Brew."

"He doesn't bang *hockey muffs*," Oliver says, mildly offended.

Bingo.

"So just a parade of regulars down at the docks, then?"

Oliver scowls.

I lace my fingers behind my head, grinning at him. "You're making this so easy."

He starts to organize some receipts. "I can't believe you married him for twelve hours, knobbed him at his place in Canada, and have been fooling around for almost two weeks here, yet haven't discussed any of this."

"We aren't fooling around anymore," I tell him. When he looks up, surprised, I say, "We were too good at it. It was a little *too* distracting."

And here is where I know Lola has talked to Oliver about my mom: His eyes go a little sympathetic, a little soft. "Right. Sorry, Harlow."

"Gah, don't. She's going to be fine."

"Knowing your mum, yeah, she is." He bends to pick something up from behind the counter and it's all I can do to not hurl myself across the glass to hug him for sounding so confident. He's met my mom three times since he's moved to San Diego—at a barbecue, at Mia's official welcome-home party, and at a birthday party for Lola's dad, Greg—and I could tell Mom and Oliver have one of those unspoken über-calm-person bonds where they just automatically *clicked*.

"I haven't talked about it with anyone but the girls," I tell him meaningfully. He stands back up and nods, making the *zips-lips* gesture. "Anyway," I say, "tell me more about Finn's steady girlfriend."

Laughing, Oliver says, "You're relentless. He doesn't *have* a girlfriend. Though I will tell you that the steady act is far more his speed than the wild trench-coat-surprise act you prefer."

I let this settle in for a minute. *Is* that my preference? Trench coat flings and date-count maximums of two? It has been, I guess. My longest relationship was the four months I dated Jackson Ford in college. It never really got off the ground, though, in part because it spanned the summer I was off with Dad filming in Greece, and because spending time with Jackson was about as interesting as reading the back of a shampoo bottle. I've always thought of myself as *wanting* to be in a relationship. But most guys fail to measure up almost as soon as they start speaking.

Lola nudges me with her elbow. "Why are you trying to find a reason that you guys can't be together?"

"Because he's horrible?" I lie.

She snorts out a laugh. "He's built like a man who works with his hands, has a sense of humor drier than the Sahara, and the thing that gets him off more than anything in the world is giving you orgasms. What a *nightmare*."

My voice of reason is always Lola. "You're a jackass."

"You only say that when I'm being your voice of reason."

"Out of my head, witch. And don't piss me off," I tell her. "I'll buy you underwear one size too small for Christmas and make you hate life."

"Come to think of it," Oliver cuts in, walking around the cashwrap and leaning back against it to face us, "you aren't really Finn's type, so it's probably for the best that you guys stopped messing around."

"What?" I say, dropping my nonchalance to the side in favor of knee-jerk offense. "Why?"

"Well, you're a bit of an unnecessary ballbuster." I open my mouth but Lola elbows me again, sharper this time. "Plus, Finn doesn't just mess around, as I've mentioned. I only met one of his ex-girlfriends, Melody, and—"

"Sorry," I interrupt, holding up a hand. *"Melody?"*

He raises his eyebrows as if I'm proving one of his points and I bite my lips to keep from saying anything else.

"They were together for a few years before and just after Bike and Build. She was nice, just really quiet . . ." He tilts his head and winces, nonverbally suggesting maybe I'm not so quiet.

"But they aren't together anymore," I remind him.

"Nope."

"So maybe he doesn't *like* quiet. Maybe he likes chatty half-Irish, half-Spanish feisty gingers who call him on his bossy shit."

"Well, I thought it didn't matter anyway," Oliver says with a little smile.

———

REGAL BEAGLE TONIGHT, I text Finn once I'm home. Lola, Oliver, me, Not-Joe. You coming?

I stare at my phone for at least a minute, waiting for him to reply, but nothing. Ordinarily, Finn strikes me as the kind of guy who will forget he even has a phone until he empties his pockets at the end of the day, but lately he's been checking it nearly constantly, so I expect him to reply quickly.

But an hour later, he still hasn't.

I text, How did it go? I can't wait to hear about it.

Still no reply. Maybe he's driving. Maybe the meeting went long. Maybe he's sitting at a huge desk, signing contracts.

Lola and Oliver pick me up in his beater Nissan and I stare at the back of their heads as they jabber on and on about his store, her upcoming book launch, one of their favorite comics. How can they not see they're perfect together?

I want to shout it and hear it echo in the car, but the certainty of a beheading at Lola's hand keeps the words inside. When we get to the bar, I practically tear the car door off the hinges in an effort to launch myself onto the sidewalk, taking in a huge breath of air free of the Lola-Oliver-cuteness-overload.

But then my heart stops entirely, because parked behind us at the curb is Finn's truck. He's had it cleaned—probably before he drove up to L.A.—and it's empty. He must be inside already. And he didn't answer my texts.

I know I've been looking for him all day, but it's in this moment outside, staring at his giant beast of a truck and just charmed to death that he would wash it before driving to this meeting—that I realize I'm smitten. Really smitten. I knew I liked him, and that I liked sex with him, but I've never felt this way about a guy before: longing, fear, hope, and the tingly thrill of desire.

"What are you *wearing*?"

I turn to see Finn standing at the entrance to the bar, his mouth tilted in a smirk. His forehead is wrinkled, communicating mild concern, but even so, his inspection gives me goose bumps all down my arms. Lola and Oliver slip past him, walking inside.

I follow the path of his eyes and look down at my chest. I'm wearing a navy silk tank top, covered in small, colorful hand-embroidered birds and faded skinny jeans. I spent about an hour getting ready for tonight, though only under the pain of torture would he get me to admit that. "Excuse me, sir, this is a gorgeous shirt."

"It's covered in *birds*."

"You're going to lecture me about fashion? You wear the same dirty baseball cap every day and own two T-shirts," I say as I follow him inside and toward our booth at the back.

"At least they aren't covered in birds." He reaches the

table and hands me a glass of water before grabbing his own beer. He's already been here and he came to *our* booth? My inner girly girl squeals in delight. "Besides, if you haven't noticed, I'm not wearing a T-shirt today."

No, he is most definitely not. In my mind, I'm dirty dancing and perving all over this man, but outwardly I'm doing a calm inspection. He's wearing pressed black dress pants and a white button-up shirt with a small gray diamond print.

"You approve?" he asks quietly, teasing but also not.

"Can we focus on the more interesting topic of conversation, please?" I ask. "Such as *why* you are dressed like this?"

He looks over my shoulder to where Oliver and Not-Joe stand only about five feet away. "Not tonight."

"But did it go well?"

He tilts his beer to his lips, giving me a warning look.

"Nothing?" I hiss-whisper. "You're not going to say *anything*?"

"No."

I wish a dramatic-huff-and-stomp-away would work on Finn, but I know it wouldn't. And I still like the way he's staring at me. Although . . . now he's not inspecting my shirt, he's staring at my hairline.

"What?" I ask.

"Your hair looks . . . really red tonight."

"I put some temporary color powder in it," I admit, turning into the light so he can see better. "Do you like it?"

"I think you got some on your forehead."

I deflate, dunking my thumb in my glass of water and wiping at the spot he's pointing to. "Holy Moses, Finn Roberts, how you managed to date this Melody person for more than a week is beyond me." I ignore his raised eyebrows at this, and continue: "You're supposed to tell me I look pretty, and act like you're touching my beautiful face when really you're subtly wiping away my makeup mistakes."

"I'm not *supposed* to do anything." He gives me a dark grin. Leaning back against the side of our booth, he says, "I'm just a *friend* who likes to point out when you're ridiculous. Makeup for your hair, Harlow? Really?"

"Sometimes a girl feels like she needs a little extra something, okay?"

His expression straightens, and he blinks away, looking out over the small dance floor. "Not you. You look best first thing in the morning." I suck in a breath. I know exactly what morning he means; it's the only one we woke up to, together. In my bed, curled around each other. I can still feel how warm he was.

"Well, then I'm surprised you didn't make a comment about pillow creases on my face and morning breath."

"You did have pillow creases on your face, and your hair was a mess." His voice drops lower when he says, "But you looked perfect."

I'm too stunned to speak, continually swallowing around the lump in my throat. My heart feels like it's grown ten times its normal size.

He coughs and I know I've been quiet too long when he changes the subject. "Who told you about Melody?"

I sip my water, finally managing, "Oliver, but it was completely against his will. I brandished a musket."

Finn nods, taking another drink of his beer. Kyle turns the music up but even still, it feels like we're in our own little bubble, standing a few feet away from where our friends sit together in the booth.

"I only know her name and that she was quiet," I admit. "Will *you* tell me about her?"

"Why do you want to know this?"

"Probably for the same reason you asked if Toby Amsler went down on me."

He blinks over to me. "What do you want to know?"

"Does she still live near you?"

He nods. "We went to the same high school, started seeing each other a few months after we graduated. Her folks own the local bakery."

"Were you guys in love?"

He shrugs. "I was such a different person then. Right after we got together I left school to start fishing with my family." Seeming to consider the question more, he adds, "I loved her, sure."

"Still?"

"Nah. She's a sweet girl, though."

I know the question will burst out of me whether or not I really want to appear this interested in the topic. "A sweet girl who still gets to sleep—"

"No," he interrupts quietly. He looks back to me, his eyes making the slow circuit of my face. "Melody and I broke up five years ago; she's married with a kid now." At my expression, he murmurs, "There's no one back home, Harlow. I promise."

I swallow again, nodding.

"And if you remember," he says, voice stronger now, "*you* were with another man one night before you were with me."

Shit.

"Do you know how crazy that makes me feel?" he asks.

Honestly, I can't even imagine. He broke up with Melody five years ago and I still sort of want to scratch her face off. This situation is ridiculous. *I'm* being ridiculous.

"I know there's nothing between us, we're just friends," he says. "But it's not because the sex wasn't something really good, Harlow. Before you, in Vegas, it had been two years. I've been with four women other than you, and never in anything but a committed relationship, so this is weird for me. I'll tell you anything, okay? Since I know how it is to feel desperate to know every detail, I'll tell you. But ask *me*, don't ask my friends. I'd rather we find things out from each other, okay?"

What is this mad flurry of emotions? I'm relieved and guilty, swooning and overcome with the need to kiss his perfect mouth.

With a shrug, I tell him, "I just didn't want you to know that I wanted to know."

He laughs, tilting his beer to his lips and saying, "Socio-path," before taking a long drink.

"How many did you tie up?"

He swallows, and turns his eyes to me. I can tell with this question his pulse has exploded in his neck. I can see it throb with the rhythm. His voice comes out more hoarse than usual when he admits, "All of them."

My blood turns to mercury, swirling and toxic. "*All* of them?"

"Yeah, Harlow. I . . . *like* it." He ducks his head, touching the back of his neck as he looks at me through his eyelashes. "But I'm pretty sure most of them only did it because they wanted to be with me, not because it was their thing, too."

"Did any of *them* like it?"

He nods. "My first, maybe?"

"What was her name?" I can't help it. The questions are just falling out of my mouth before I have time to think bet-ter of them.

He steps a little bit farther away from the table, and I fol-low. "Emily."

"But you aren't sure she liked it?" It's so weird to be here, at Fred's and surrounded by our friends who are sitting in the booth only a few feet away and still having the most in-timate conversation we've ever had.

"Honestly," he says quietly, "I don't know. I mean, she was into it, sure, but I would love to know how she remem-bers that night now, looking back. She moved away after graduation, but we were together a little over a year before that. I just . . ." He blinks away. "The only place we could have any privacy was on my dad's little rowboat, down at the dock. The third time, we'd stolen beers from her dad. I just played around with her, and the rope, and it was . . ." He stops talking, finally just saying, "Yeah."

I nod, sipping my water. I think I know what he's telling me—that seeing his girlfriend like that did something good for him, and shaped what he likes now. But I don't really need to hear him talking about it anymore.

"That morning I saw you at Starbucks," he says.

I wait for him to continue, but he doesn't. "Yeah? What about it?"

He shrugs, giving me a *do-I-need-to-drag-it-from-you* look. "I know you hooked up, but you didn't look like you were particularly relaxed."

"Ah, right. The mother woke us up," I tell him. "In person. Second-worst lay of my life the night before."

He barks out a delighted laugh. "Who was the first?"

"*My* first. I realize now he was tiny, but it still hurt. I swear I look back on it now and see my virginity being taken by a baby carrot."

"What are you talking about over here?" Lola asks, appearing out of nowhere and sidling up to me.

Finn is barely recovered from his laughing fit. "Trust me, you don't want to know."

"Baby carrot," I tell her with a knowing grin.

Lola nods, smiling at him. "Awesome, right? Poor Jesse Sandoval."

"Our girl is a poet," Finn agrees.

Our girl. It eases somewhat the tiny twinge I still feel when I remember Finn told me about the television show because he didn't want to share it with more *permanent members* of his life.

Oliver steps out of the booth and joins our little circle. "So we're standing tonight? Usually Harlow likes to sit and throw things at me across the table."

I laugh because it's true. "You just have these creepy Crocodile Dundee reflexes."

"I'm a ninja." Oliver pushes his thick-rimmed glasses up his nose in a nerdy gesture that makes us all laugh. "And you know how much I love your limited Australian cultural knowledge."

"I try."

Behind him, Not-Joe is still sitting in the booth, high as a kite and dancing in his seat as he stares at a group of coeds out on the floor.

"Oliver, you and Not-Joe should go boogie down with those girls over there."

"Why not Finn?" Oliver asks with a knowing grin. "He's also single."

I shake my head. "He is, but look, he's all dressed up. It'd be like *A Night at the Roxbury* and everyone would be embarrassed for him." Not only will Finn refuse to dance, but if he's going to be out there, the cavewoman inside tells me he's going to be there for me and no one else. At least until he leaves.

Suddenly, I feel panic rise in my throat. Is Finn leaving tomorrow? He's had his meeting with the L.A. crowd; does that mean he'll go home?

Laughing, Oliver looks over at the dance floor, but not before taking a peek at Lola's reaction. "Those Sheilas are tiny."

"'Tiny' like young?" I ask, leaning to get a better look. The girls are definitely in their twenties. "Or short?"

"Very short."

"But look at you," Lola says, frowning. "You're over six three. Statistically speaking that means you're going to end up with someone under five three."

"That hurts me in my logic," Oliver says, smiling down at her.

"If you're not going to dance, then get me a beer," I tell him.

"I would but I'm paralyzed from my toes down."

I shove him playfully. "Take Lola, too. She needs another drink."

Lola protests that she doesn't, but follows him anyway, and I watch them as they go. She's tall, but he still looms over her, and seems to tilt in her direction as he walks, as if they're magnets. I wonder if Oliver realizes what it means that Lola has seamlessly made him one of Her People. It's a pretty exclusive club, including me, Mia, Lola's dad, my parents, and now Oliver.

"He'll never try it," Finn says beside me, and when I look at him I realize he means Oliver will never try to make something happen with Lola. "He's convinced she isn't interested."

"I'm not sure she is," I agree, "but it's mostly because Lola is clueless about guys, and all she thinks about is work."

He hums in response.

Turning to him fully, I say, "Okay, they're all the way over at the bar for a few minutes, Not-Joe is stoned out of his gourd and probably can't even hear the music in here. Can you relax? Tell me: How did it go?"

Finn swipes a hand down his face and exhales a long breath, glancing to make sure they really are out of earshot. "I liked them. I mean, there were a couple of idiots in the room who asked things about our love lives, and what kind of women we date"—he ignores the way I do a little victory moonwalk, and continues—"but the two guys who would be producing this show are pretty sharp. They've clearly done their homework on the industry, and . . ." He sighs. "I *liked* them. I liked their ideas. It didn't sound horrible."

"So why do you look so miserable?" My heart aches a little. I realize while I'm watching him struggle with this that I sincerely just want Finn to be happy.

When have I cared so much about his happiness versus my own orgasms? Lola isn't the only one who has seamlessly pulled one of these guys into her inner circle. Finn is officially one of My People.

"Because it's easier to feel strongly against it," he says. "This morning, I was convinced this was just a *going-through-the-motions* meeting. Now I see how this could work much more easily than the alternative. The alternative being we lose our family business and have nothing."

Not to put too dramatic a spin on it, but I'm really starting to think I know what drowning feels like. Mom has finished her first day of chemo—a treatment where the goal is to kill the cancer just slightly faster than killing the host—and all I have is a few texts from my dad saying she feels good. Finn is struggling with what is arguably the hardest decision of his life. I've just acknowledged that he's My Person, and now I'm powerless all over again to help either of them through this.

It sucks because I know that what would make us both feel better right now is some naked wrestling in my bed. But the more I realize I have genuine feelings for him, the more I know I couldn't just take him home tonight. Finn would be the first person I would have sex with who I might also love. Ugh.

He shrugs, sliding his hands into his pockets. "And that's pretty much it."

I'm feeling a little light-headed and have to force myself to breathe, to focus on the conversation at hand. I can lose my shit later. "When are you heading home?" I ask, going for casual, yet concerned.

He shrugs. "Couple of days."

A sharp spike drives into my chest. "Boo."

He smiles down at me, gaze hovering on my mouth. "Are you admitting that you're going to miss me, Ginger Snap?"

I give him the finger and don't answer.

Chapter TEN

Finn

*H*ARLOW SHOWS UP bright and early the next morning, balancing a tray with three Styrofoam cups on one flattened palm, a white paper bag clutched in her other fist.

"Good morning, Sunshine!" she chirps, pushing past me into the living room. "I brought breakfast."

"It's seven in the morning, Snap," I mumble after her, reaching up to scratch my jaw. I haven't shaved in two days, I'm not wearing a shirt . . . she's lucky I'm even wearing pants. "What are you doing here?"

"We're going to brainstorm." She walks into the kitchen and turns to whisper-hiss, "Is Oliver still home?"

The old house is still chilly. The floorboards are cold beneath my bare feet as I lag behind her.

"He's in the shower."

At least, I think he is. At home I'm up before sunrise, down at the docks. But this beach life has spoiled me and indulges my natural night owl tendencies. I don't think I've slept until seven in nearly twenty years. But I'm waiting until Oliver leaves to call my brothers and fill them in on my meeting with the producers.

Any thought of my brothers *at all* is wiped from my head when I turn the corner and get an eyeful of Harlow bent over the dishwasher, her perfect ass wrapped in a pair of skintight yoga pants.

Oblivious to my ogling, she straightens, and begins opening cupboard doors. "Plates?"

I cross the room and stop just behind her, reaching over her head to retrieve a stack of yellow plates from the shelf. Harlow freezes, fingers gripping the edge of the countertop before she seems to relax, and leans back against my chest.

"Here you go," I tell her, bending to say the words against her hair.

She smells so good and her ass is pressed against my dick, I have to step away before she can feel that I'm already half hard, worked up like a seventeen-year-old boy. Pushing back, I take a seat at the small island and weave my bare feet around the legs of the bar stool.

It takes a moment for her to collect herself, too, and I grin as she clumsily sets down the plates and opens the paper sack.

"You look a little breathless there, Snap."

She looks up, shoots daggers.

"So what is it we're brainstorming?" I ask, rolling an orange along the counter. My stomach growls on instinct when I see her reach inside the bag and pull out some of the biggest, gooiest, most frosting-coated cinnamon rolls I've ever seen.

"Your situation," she stage-whispers, and slaps my hand away when I try to sneak a fingertip of icing.

"My *situation* . . . ?"

"Dreamboats on the Pacific? Try to keep up, Finneus."

I roll my eyes. "You know that's not what it's called."

"Only because they never asked me for ideas."

"As much I love that you brought me food, couldn't we have talked later? You know, after the sun was up?"

"The sun *is* up."

"Barely."

Ignoring me, Harlow pulls one of the coffees from the tray and sets it and a cinnamon roll down in front of me. "I do my best thinking when I run," she says, and dishes up one for herself. "I have a million ideas for you."

I lean forward and take a bite of the warm, gooey pastry, and swear to God my eyes roll back in my head. "Jesus *fuck,* this is the best thing I've ever tasted." Without thinking, I stand and round the corner, placing a hand on either side of her face, before kissing her full on the mouth.

It's meant to be quick. It's meant to be a funny, dramatic little thank-you *between friends.* But Harlow's surprised gasp is quickly cut off by a soft moan, her palms moving up to rest on my bare stomach. Heat surges through my veins and I feel every point of contact between us: where her breasts press against my chest, her hands on my skin, her lips moving against mine.

I pull away with a shaky breath and Harlow clears her throat. "You taste like cinnamon," she murmurs, licking her lips.

"Well, g'day you, too."

Our heads snap to where Oliver leans against the doorway, arms folded across his chest. He scratches his cheek, giving me the smuggest fucking look I've ever seen.

I drop my hands to my sides and take a step back. "Just thanking Miss Harlow for breakfast."

"I'm offended, Finn. I made you *dinner* the other day and would've appreciated at the very least a sharp pat on the ass. I see how you are."

"Ha, yeah," I say, returning to my seat.

Oliver beelines toward the food and Harlow hands him his coffee, along with the now-closed white sack.

"I have to apologize up front, because no way could a man hope to follow up *that*," he says, nodding to me. "But thank you, pet." He bends and kisses Harlow's cheek.

"There's one in there for Not-Joe," she says, and I don't know what it is about watching the two of them like this, but it makes me feel like I'm being slowly, carefully uncoiled, like this is how my morning should be every damn day. "Tell him I expect a lap dance at Fred's later."

I groan, but Oliver only laughs. "Will do. Be good, kids."

We both watch Oliver disappear from the kitchen and sit in silence, listening as the front door closes, followed moments later by the sound of his Nissan roaring to life and heading down the street.

Harlow carries her own plate and coffee to the counter, sitting on the stool next to me, her foot tangling with mine. "You look like crap," she says, looking at my mouth like she wants to lick it.

"So do you." I look at her perfect tits, all perky and fuckable in her little running tank. "I'm almost embarrassed for you."

She tilts her head, exposing her long, tanned neck. "Hideous?"

"Revolting." I reach forward, wiping a tiny smear of frosting from her lower lip.

She stares as I stick my thumb in my mouth, sucking the frosting off, and I blink away, working to get my shit together. This isn't how we keep our clothes on and stay friends-only. This is how she ends up ass-up on the couch, getting spanked and fucked until dinnertime.

It's so strange being with her like this: eating in companionable silence and having it feel so . . . normal. This is what I have to remember: Sex with Harlow is amazing, but being friends with her isn't so bad, either.

"Thanks for breakfast," I say, wiping my mouth with a napkin.

"No problem. Like I said, I think better when I run, and unfortunately for my half-Latina ass, the bakery is right at the end of the best running trail in La Jolla. Now let's get back to the reason behind my visit: fixing your problem."

"I appreciate the thought, but I don't need you to—"

"Shut up. I have ideas."

It's obvious Harlow has made up her mind, so I decide to humor her. Instead of telling her not to bother, that I've probably thought of it all already, I reach over and tear off a chunk of the center of her cinnamon roll, popping it in my mouth.

She scowls at me. "That was the best bite. You're a menace."

"Mmm hmm," I hum around it.

She turns on her stool to face me. "What about tourists? Taking people out on your boat?"

I swallow, washing the bite down with a gulp of coffee. "No way."

"Why?"

"Commercial fishing boats are dangerous places, Snap. Things fall, lines get tangled, people trip. No way am I having a bunch of paying idiots wandering around my boats."

"Okay," she says. "What about investors?"

"You think I haven't thought about that?"

"There has to be someone who—"

"The only reason people loan money is to *make* money. The fishing industry isn't just going to recover overnight," I tell her. "Development, climate change, disease, it's all had an impact and as far as I can see, it won't get better anytime soon. I can't borrow money if I don't have the hope of paying it back."

I feel the truth of this reality sink like a weight in my chest. It will never be the way it was. My brothers and I will never know the life my dad knew, and his dad before him. There's something so utterly defeating in that. A smart man would walk away; he'd sell everything he could, split the money and make a new life somewhere else. But it's all the fucking history—what my family has fought for, sacrificed for, what Dad worked to keep after he lost Mom—that keeps me from just walking away.

"Right," she says. "I guess that makes sense. What about fishing other things, then?"

"We already do that. We do sockeye, pink and chum salmon, roe herring, halibut, invertebrates," I say, and then pause, seeing her face fall. I feel sort of guilty, she's clearly put some time into this and I'm just shooting down her ideas, one after another.

But in typical Harlow fashion, she seems undeterred. "So maybe we need to think outside the box."

"Outside the box, huh?"

"Yeah, let's see . . ." She leans forward, knees pressed to mine, her hand ghosting along the top of my thigh. I'm still shirtless, and swear I can feel the heat from her body, an *awareness* of having her near me. And I wonder if she has any idea how it feels, or if I'm the only one of the two of us who gets so wrapped up that I could accurately estimate the distance between us in millimeters.

"What about T-shirts?"

I blink. "T-shirts?"

"Yeah, like, your own clothing line. Imagine a glossy ad with you and your studly brothers. You're standing in the middle and wrapped in a tight T-shirt—"

"You're messing with me now, aren't you?"

"Maybe a little," she says, tapping my nose with her index finger. "Because you're so cute in the morning." Sitting up straighter, she continues, "So imagine this: you, muscles, and an arrow pointing straight down with the words ROBERTS BAIT AND TACKLE printed on the shirt."

"Pointing straight down," I clarify.

"Yes."

"To my cock."

"Yes."

I close my eyes and take a deep breath, counting to ten. "Ginger Snap. Honey," I say, and close the distance between us even more. "I promise I've spent more time on this than you can possibly imagine. I've considered everything."

"Everything?"

Nodding, I lift my coffee to my lips.

"How about selling sperm?"

Coughing, I splutter, "Pardon me?"

"Sperm. Jizz. Semen. Protein shakes. Love juice. Pecker spit. Face crea—"

"Harlow."

"What? You said *everything.*"

"Why . . ." I start, and shake my head. "Wait, were you starting to say *face cream?*"

She nods.

Shaking my head, I decide to move on from that visual. "Why on God's earth would I donate sperm?"

"I can't believe you have to ask that. Have you looked in a mirror lately? Have you seen your brothers? That is one hell of a gene pool. Hell, if I was a spinster living in an old Victorian on Golden Hill, I'd buy—"

And I kiss her. Again.

I don't mean to . . . actually, that's a lie. I do. But I don't mean for it to go on as long as it does. Harlow's words are lost in my mouth when I slide my lips across hers and her eyes close, the breath leaving her lungs in a soft sigh.

I slide off my stool and lean over her, one hand in her hair and the other on her jaw as I open my mouth, lick her tongue with mine. I hold her close, tight, in just the way I know she wants. My thumb moves down to press against her throat, not with intent, but just enough to let her know I have her.

Harlow's hands grip my hips and she stands, pressing herself fully along the length of my body. My skin is fiery where her fingertips brush over it, nails scratching and tracing the top of my pants. It's like the blood leaves my brain and surges downward, every thought suddenly of Harlow: where I can touch, what I can taste, if she'd mind if I laid her out right here on this counter, fucked her until neither of us could think anymore.

But I don't. And though I'm sure I'll hate myself later, when I'm alone and jacking off and wondering what the fuck I was thinking to pull away, I do. I take a step back and try to ignore the way she's invaded every one of my goddamn senses, how I can still feel the press of her body even though there's a few inches of space between us now.

"You still taste like cinnamon," she says, dragging in a rough breath.

"You taste perfect." I know I'm tempting fate, but I lean in the slightest bit, punctuating my words with another small kiss against the corner of her mouth, her jaw.

"I thought we weren't doing this anymore?" It comes out as a question, and I know it's because she's as confused about what the fuck we're doing as I am.

"We aren't." I confirm this with a short nod.

"Then why did you kiss me?"

"Had to," I say, and follow it up with another kiss to the tip of her nose. "Only way to get you to stop talking about my brothers as objects. It was offensive." I smile.

She bursts out laughing, closing the distance between us to rest her head on my shoulder. "Okay, no more Finn's-hot-brothers talk. I promise."

We stand there for a moment—her lips against my bare shoulder, my face in her hair—before Harlow seems to remember herself. She straightens and I feel the absence of her immediately. My arms fall to my sides and I watch as she turns back to the counter and gathers up our plates.

"So, I guess we're back to square one?"

I shove my hands in my pockets and rock back on my heels. "I guess so."

Harlow cleans the rest of the mess up before reaching for her keys.

"Don't you worry, Finnigan. I'm a genius and I'm not giving up yet. I'll figure this out."

"Harlow, I don't need you to—"

"Again, Finn?" she says sweetly. "Shut up. Stop being so stubborn and let someone else shoulder the worry for a few hours, okay?" I'm not sure how to respond, and so I stand dumbly as she stretches up onto her tiptoes, and presses the briefest kiss to my cheek. "I got you."

I USED TO think my dad was the most persistent person I knew. When I was eight, he was up and walking hours after major back surgery to fix two ruptured disks. When I was nine, he spent a winter fishing the shores off of Alaska, and lost the tips to three of his fingers when they were crushed between two steel crab pots. He went back again the next year. When we lost Mom, Dad buried himself in work, sometimes spending nearly eighteen hours straight on the boat. And when he had his heart attack the summer I turned nineteen, and the doctors told him to stay the hell off the boats, he insisted on showing up the day he was released from the hospital, just to make sure we weren't doing anything wrong.

I fear he has nothing on Harlow Vega.

Two days after cinnamon rolls and hearing the words *pecker spit* come from Harlow's mouth—I'm not sure I'll ever become unhorrified—my phone vibrates on the nightstand. It's hours from sunrise, and the little guest room in Oliver's house is still completely dark. I reach for my phone—managing to knock over a bottle of water and I have no idea what else in the process—and stare with bleary eyes. What if something's happened to Dad? Colton or Levi? The boat?

Make yourself pretty. I'll be there in thirty minutes.

Harlow.

A glance at the clock shows it's not even 5 a.m., and for a moment I consider texting her back, suggesting where exactly she should put her thirty minutes. I need to go back to sleep. I need to talk to Colton and Levi. I need to figure out what the fuck I'm doing with my life.

I drop my phone to the mattress and stare, blankly, up at

the ceiling. My heart is pounding in my chest and I rub a hand over my breastbone, feel the quickened beat just under my palm. My stomach feels both light and heavy at the same time, and even though the idea of shutting off my phone and sleeping for another three hours sounds amazing, I'm kidding myself if I think I might actually do it.

Harlow will be here to pick me up in thirty minutes, and regardless of what I *should* be doing this morning, something tells me we both know I'll be standing outside, waiting.

———

AND LIKE SOME boy with a school yard crush and no real responsibilities, I am. Harlow's car pulls into the driveway exactly twenty-nine minutes later, and I'm already sitting on the porch, two cups of steaming coffee in hand.

She steps out and crosses the damp grass toward me, dressed in jeans and a faded blue long-sleeved T-shirt, hair in a high ponytail, wearing a bright smile and not a trace of makeup.

I'm pretty sure she's never looked more beautiful.

"Ready?" she says, stopping just in front of the porch. She looks so much younger right now, innocent, and if the reappearance of that nosedive feeling in my stomach is any indication, I'm in way over my head.

"Not remotely." I glance down at her outfit again. She's gone pretty casual today. I lift an eyebrow. "Looks like for once I meet the dress code."

"You're perfect."

Steady, Finn.

I hand Harlow her coffee and she looks at me, brows raised. "Such a gentleman."

I ignore this, not wanting to obsess any more over the *five-minute* conversation I had with myself on whether it would be weird, or give Harlow some giant glimpse into my head if I made her a cup of fucking coffee. I am insane.

"So where are we going?" I say instead.

Harlow turns and leads us back to the car. "Fishing," she says, climbing in and starting the engine.

I look up from where I'm currently trying to wedge all six foot, three inches of me into the front seat of her sports car. "What?"

She checks her mirrors and backs out of the driveway, pulling out onto the street before she answers. "I figured we're here, and you've got to be so fucking tired of doing what everyone else wants to do. Plus I'm sure you miss home," she says. "So why not give you a little taste of home, here?"

She must misread my stunned silence, because she quickly adds, "I mean, I know it won't be the same for you, but trust me, Sunshine. It'll be fun."

And, okay. I'm sort of at a loss for words. Just when I think I have Harlow figured out, she does something to obliterate it. "Thanks," I manage, and quickly busy myself with my coffee.

"And maybe we'll see some trees you can cut down or something," she adds, and bites her bottom lip to keep from smiling.

"Do they even *have* trees by Barbie's dream yacht?"

With that, we're back to normal. The heaviness is gone from my chest, and this ever-evolving tension between us has settled back into its place.

"Have you ever been fishing before?" I ask her.

She hums to herself while turning on the blinker, and merges into the next lane. "A few times up north with my dad. River fishing, though, not ocean. I never really caught anything."

"That's because it's called fishing, not catching, Ginger Snap. Sometimes you're lucky and sometimes you're not."

"Right." She shifts in her seat and rests her elbow on the door, fingers twisting the ends of her ponytail. "Pretty sure this'll be different than your usual day of fishing, too. I assume you're not sacked out in lounge chairs while someone brings you sandwiches and beer."

"Uh, no."

"So tell me, Finn. What do you guys do? Do you just throw some lines in the water and wait?"

"Some do."

"But not you guys."

I shake my head. "*Linda* is a seiner, so we fish with nets."

"Nets, right." She pauses, looking over at me. "Wait, who's the captain of your boat?"

"That'd be me, Einstein."

She gives me a cheeky grin. "Can I call you Captain?"

"No."

"Can I be your first mate? Will you swab my decks?"

I laugh as she wiggles in her seat. "You've lost your damn mind."

"Just trying to speak your language, Huckleberry." She merges onto the freeway and spares me a tiny glance once we're settled in the fast lane. "Okay, we have a little drive before we get to Point Loma. It's time for you to school me in the art of Vancouver Island fishing."

I look out at the passing scenery: the blur of the freeway, the houses rushing by, the palm trees. The sky is just starting to lighten up at the edges and there's something so peaceful about being out here like this. And I'm realizing that I sort of do want to tell Harlow about life on the boat. I like talking to her, and the time we spend together is pretty much the only time I'm not worrying myself toward an ulcer.

"So first we have to be on the fish," I start, my thumb tracing the fancy emblem on the dashboard. "That means we locate a school in the water. Then we drop the nets and circle the school. When the fish are surrounded, we cinch up the bottom and the fish are trapped inside. Basic concept, but there's a ton to do besides that. When we aren't actually fishing, someone has to check the float line and floats, the lead lines, make sure there aren't any holes in the nets, as well as the power skiff and all the other electrical and hydraulic equipment. The skiff used to pull the nets up is run on equipment powered by the auxiliary engine. Which is why we have to have both engines in working order and why it's so devastating when one goes down." I pause and look at her again, certain she has to have zoned out. She hasn't. "You're still listening? That's a miracle."

"Well, it's not like twittering or shuffling papers at NBC," she teases. "But I am kind of fascinated by what you do all day. Feel free to add the little details, if you want, like how you guys do all of this with your shirts off and the ocean sprays your muscles so you glisten in the sun. Just to help with the visual a little."

"I'll keep that in mind."

"I assume your days are pretty long, huh?"

"Start working when it's light, stop when it's not. Normally I'm up before the sun, without an alarm, but I swear my internal clock is a mess here. Well," I say, smiling around my coffee cup, "unless you're on the porch at dawn to wake me up."

We go on like that for a while as the beautiful scenery zooms past us, and before I realize it Harlow's pulled into a parking lot and shut off the engine.

"Well, and look, the sun is here to greet us."

I look out the windshield and point to the forty-three-foot diesel docked in the harbor. "That the one we're on today?"

"That's right, Captain."

I give her a playfully reprimanding look and then say, "You ready to get schooled, Ginger Snap?"

She laughs and drops her keys into her bag. "I'm ready for whatever you've got, Sunshine."

Chapter ELEVEN

Harlow

*T*HE BOAT SEEMS *ginormous,* but Finn climbs aboard as if he's stepping onto a dinky rowboat. Is it my imagination, or does he seem taller on deck? I stare at him while he talks to the captain, absently rubbing my finger over my bottom lip, remembering the teasing slide of his teeth when he kissed me at Oliver's two days ago.

I swear my pulse hasn't calmed down since—because it wasn't just a kiss, it was a confession. That kiss told me I'm not the only one who's moved into Feelings Territory. Now my mind is a pile of unfamiliar thoughts: If we both feel something, are we going to try to make it into a relationship? Finn argued against every idea I had to rescue his business, but if he signs on for the Adventure Channel show, then according to the contract, we can't be together. And if he turns down the television show, he'll most likely lose his family business and not be in the best mood for a new relationship anyway.

As the engine chugs and pulls us away from the dock and into the open water, my brain is a mess, my body is on fire for this hot fisherman version of Finn (which—I giddily recall—is *everyday* Finn) . . . and I have no idea how to handle a rod and reel as big as the one he retrieves for me.

He hands it over silently, giving me a patronizing pat on the head, and we step closer to listen to the safety guidelines with the other dozen tourists gathered on the deck. I expected Finn to space out during this, or carefully slip away to go check out the boat, but he seems riveted. Whether he's seeing how sportfishing is handled on a professional level, or he's just *that* in love with fishing, I can't tell. But I love that he isn't acting like it's beneath him. He's excited, even for this little half-day trip.

When Captain Steve has finished his spiel, we find a spot at the back corner of the boat, and Finn works quietly with the wind whipping his fleece flush against his chest. He sets up our rods, adjusts my line and my reel, and then leaves, telling me to "hang on." A few minutes later, Finn returns with a pair of boots in one hand and a baseball cap with the boat's logo in the other.

"It gets messy," he says. He hands me the boots and puts the cap on my head, carefully feeding my ponytail through the back, whispering, "There," once it's situated. His hazel eyes dip down to my mouth, as if he's considering kissing me again, but when he blinks, the look is gone. "Ready?"

"Am I ready to kick your ass in fish counts?" I ask, pulling the cap lower over my eyes before stepping into the giant boots. "You betcha."

He laughs, shaking his head. "Okay, you heard the captain say all of this but I'm sure you were thinking about my naked body or buying new makeup for your hair, so I'm going to remind you: This boat fishes halibut, rockfish, and bass. The halibut can get pretty big, but don't worry"—he gives me a winning smile—"I'll help you pull them in."

"I'll have you know I am a regular at kickboxing class," I tell him, acting offended. "And I surf."

"Right, but you won't be pulling these fish up with your legs." He grabs my skinny arm and shakes it like a chicken wing before taking my rod from its stand and casting the line deep into the water. The fish bait on the end lands with a heavy plunk and Finn grins as he hands the rod over to me. "Put it in the stand. Your arms will get tired if you're fighting the water while we move."

I do as he says and watch him cast his line out. He looks so happy, and I'm torn between wanting every viewer in America to see *this* expression on *this* face on their giant HD televisions and wanting his private joy to stay that way.

"Do you think you would hate having a camera on you while you do this?" I ask.

He shrugs. "It's not that so much as the idea that the show wouldn't really be about fishing."

"But what if it was?" I ask. "What if that's your condition?"

He pulls his cap off his head and scratches his scalp with his little finger. "Yeah. I don't know."

I think neither of us wants to think about it after that, because we fall quiet, watching the water and the birds and, probably more than anything, each other.

———————————

ALMOST AS IF the fish sense that Finn will more quickly put them out of their misery than I will, he catches three before I've even had a bite: two rockfish and a huge halibut. If I said it bothered me that he's crushing it and I'm sucking, I'd be lying. Nothing is better than watching Finn reel a forty-pound fish up onto the deck.

That's not entirely true. Sex with Finn on this very deck might be better . . . but only slightly. The sun is warm out on the open water and he's taken off his fleece; the sight of his tanned forearms as he pulls and reels the line in . . . it . . . it might cause me to spontaneously orgasm.

"It's going to be weird to leave, even though it's only been a couple weeks," he says, oblivious to my leering, and casting his line back into the water. I blink, clearing the fog of my Finn Lust and wait to hear what he means. It seems to me, from watching him today, that he would want nothing more than to get back to his life on the water.

"Weird how?"

He surprises me, saying, "I don't think I'll like not being able to see you whenever I want."

This is not at all what I expected. I expected him to mean he's going to miss the Southern California weather or awesome burritos or hanging with Oliver and Ansel.

I want more than anything to reach up, cup his face in my hands, and kiss him like I've never kissed anyone before, out of relief that he's nearly perfect.

Instead I say, "I masturbated thinking about you last night."

He bends over, bursting out laughing when I say this. Finally he manages, "You did?"

"Absolutely."

When he straightens, I can see a hint of a blush on his face beneath the shadow of his baseball cap. That's new. "Me, too," he admits.

"Yeah?"

"Yeah."

"Was I awesome?"

He turns and looks at me. "You sucked dick like a champion, Ginger Snap."

"I would, too." I give him a proud lift of my chin.

He reels in his line a couple of feet. "You would."

I always expected to fall in love and feel jittery or hyperaware or overwhelmed. I never expected falling in love with someone would just make me feel even more comfortable in my own skin. I sort of want to tell him, "I think I love you," because I suspect he would make a soft sound of sympathy and agree that it's unfortunate timing.

I glance over at him, at his angled, stubbly jaw, his long tan neck and the arms that give me an odd sense of safety I never knew I craved. But didn't I? Isn't that who my father has always been until recently—not only my sounding board, but my rock, my guardian? I *did* know I always wanted any man in my life to live up to that expectation.

My chest hurts with how tight it's grown from recognizing that steady, passionate, loyal Finn is what I always hoped I'd find.

He looks out across the water, his eyes narrowing and I wonder what he's thinking. His chest lifts with a deep inhale and he closes his eyes as he exhales, his expression looking as torn as I feel.

I know I'm right when he opens his eyes and glances over at me. And this is terrifying, because if there's one thing I know about my heart, it's that it isn't fickle. Once someone gets inside, they burrow deep in there, permanently.

Just when I open my mouth to say something—and I have no idea what is going to come out, but sincere emotion has risen high in my throat—my rod jerks in front of me, the entire top half bowing sharply.

"Whoa, okay," Finn says, eyes lighting up with excitement as he steps forward and guides me closer to my rod. "You've got one."

Fishing with my dad in the rivers of Northern California when I was a kid in no way prepared me for the process of hauling a fish in from the ocean. When it's a nine-inch trout in a river, your bobber dunks underwater and your skinny twelve-year-old arms can easily reel that sucker in. Here it takes every muscle in my body to pit myself against this swimming beast. I tug the rod, turn the reel in mere centimeters, each one a victory. Beside me Finn shouts and whoops as if

I'm hauling in a great white shark. A couple of men gather behind us to watch, calling out their encouragements.

"Want me to take over?" Finn yells over the cheering.

"Fuck no!"

But now I know why he took his fleece off; I'm sweating, swearing, cursing the moment I decided deep-sea fishing was a good idea. But when I get the first glimpse of the halibut on my line—of the spikes along its spine, of the sheer *size* of it— I'm giddy.

"My fish is so much bigger than your fish!" I yell.

Finn steps behind me to help me pull, taking over the reel after about ten minutes, when my hand starts to shake and grow numb. With both of us holding the rod, we pull, and pull, and finally the halibut comes out of the water, glorious. It flops on the deck, and I hate that part a little, but then Finn holds it and does something so fast I can barely see, and it goes still. The fish is ice cold from the water when he hands it back to me, and with a little gesture he indicates that I hold it up by the gills so he can take a picture.

I need to use both hands, it's that huge. It's the biggest fish we've caught so far, and the feeling is amazing, though not nearly as good as when Finn looks at me as he lifts his phone.

"Hold it up, baby," he says quietly, eyes gleaming in pride. "Let me see that fish."

My arms are shaking under the weight but I hold it up for him to see. He snaps a picture and then moves to my side, taking the halibut and handing it to Steve to tag for us.

"We gonna talk about how you just called me 'baby'?" I ask as he ducks down, getting my line rebaited.

I feel more than hear his quiet laugh as he stands and kisses the top of my head. "No."

I do everything I can to tamp down the ridiculous smile that's tugging at my mouth. Like murder it with my bare hands tamp down. I am so giddy right now I could burst into an enthusiastic Disney medley right here on a boat full of salty old men.

WHEN WE GET back to the dock, I excuse myself to go to the bathroom, but really I need to call and check in on Mom. We've been gone all morning and into the afternoon, without cell service. It was both wonderful and terrifying. What if something happened?

Dad answers on the first ring, sounding relaxed and easy. "Hey, Tulip."

"Hey, dude. How's the queen?"

"Good," he says. "We're out for lunch."

"So nothing going on? No complications?"

Dad sighs on the other end of the line and I wince, knowing I'm sounding like a maniac. We've been told at least five times by her doctors that this first round of chemo should feel relatively easy for Mom. It's the later rounds that get hard.

"You have to pace yourself," Dad says, and I can tell he's smiling but I also know he's serious. "This is the long haul."

Sighing, I say, "I know, I know."

"How was fishing?"

"It was awesome. I'm smitten."

"With the sport, or with the guy?"

It's my turn to sigh. "Maybe both."

"Good. Bring Finn tonight. I've told Salvatore I'll be available when *Release Horizon* begins filming in April."

Tonight is a party hosted by Dad's colleague and good friend Salvatore to celebrate the launch of Sal's new production company. *Release Horizon* is their new Oscar-hopeful-baby, the sweeping drama Dad told me takes place on—drumroll—a ship. I honestly can't even imagine Finn at the party, but that knee-jerk reaction makes me feel surly and rebellious against my own instincts. If Finn is one of My People, then he belongs there, whether he knows anyone or not.

Besides, Dad signing on for a project that begins principal filming in just over six months makes my heart soar. It's so optimistic regarding Mom.

I return to the dock to find Finn snacking on a giant bag of chips. He offers some to me, and I grab a handful. I didn't realize how hungry I was until I got a whiff of the salty vinegar deliciousness.

"Want to go to a party tonight?" I ask around a mouthful.

He speaks through an equally huge mouth of food. "What kind of party?"

"Movie people. Fancy. Martinis and olives."

Shrugging, he says, "You're my date?"

I shove another handful in my mouth and nod.

He smiles, wiping some salt from my chin. "Sure thing, Snap."

———————

FINN IS DRESSED and waiting outside Oliver's when I pick him up at seven. He's wearing the same clothes he wore for his meeting in L.A., but tonight he manages to look infinitely *better*. He's more relaxed and has clearly been outdoors all day. Sun-kissed Finn is deadly.

He climbs into the passenger seat, grumbling about my tiny car, and then looks over at me.

"Whoa," he says. "Get out."

"What?" I panic, looking down at my dress to make sure I didn't spill OJ all over myself when I chugged it straight from the bottle just before sprinting out the door.

"I want to see you," he says, leaning across my lap to open my door from the inside. "Get out so I can see you."

"Oh." I climb out, smoothing my dress down my thighs, and walk to the front of the car. Finn doesn't follow me out, he only slumps back against the seat and stares at me through the windshield. I watch his mouth say, *"Jesus."*

"What?" I call.

Shaking his head, he says, "You look amazing."

I look down at my dress. It's sapphire blue—my best color—with a tight bodice and flared skirt that hits just above my knees. I'm wearing gold strappy heels, and around my throat is the simple gold arrow necklace my father bought me for my eighteenth birthday. To be honest, I barely focused on getting ready tonight, and it strikes me as a little funny that the night of the bar, when I wanted to look casually adorable, Finn teased me endlessly. Here, when I was distracted and chugging OJ like a hungover frat boy in my hurry to get back to him, he seems speechless.

When I climb back in the car, he immediately leans across the console, taking my face in his hands, and looks at me for a heavy, pounding heartbeat before he presses his mouth to mine. As soon as we touch, his lips part slightly and he exhales a quiet "Oh," and then leans closer, taking my bottom lip between his. When I feel the teasing slide of his tongue, it's done, I'm *done*.

My hands are in his hair, and I want so much more I'm nearly wild. I want to feel him along every inch of me. His sounds are so deep and quiet they're like vibrations that go straight to my bones, rattling me, turning me into nothing but individual pieces of a girl: hands that shake, and blood that rushes too strong in her veins, and legs that push her up off her seat and over onto him. He reaches to his side, flipping his seat back with ease, and I'm crashing over him, legs spread over his lap. He yanks me down, grinding up into me and I cry out when I feel the thick press of his cock between my legs.

When he groans, the sound pushes a button somewhere inside that unleashes the frenzy. I don't care that we're in the car in the middle of a street. It's quiet. It's dusk. We may as well be alone on an island somewhere for all I care about the setting.

Feel him, take him in your body and feel him. It's been too long.

He's one step ahead of me, reaching between us to unzip his pants and shove them down his hips and I feel his bare cock on my thigh; the skin is paradoxically warm and soft around something so inflexible. His fingers fumble with my underwear, pushing them aside, not even bothering to take them off, fingertips seeking and finding me wet and greedy, my unintelligible sounds telling him where I need him to be.

"We doing this?" he rasps.

I nod urgently and he holds himself for me to take in. It's all happening so fast, he's sinking deep inside, and we're gasping because it's so good.

It's so *good*.

His gaze catches mine and the relief in his expression makes me feel shaky and fragile, like blown glass. I've missed this, I need this.

I think I need *him*.

He sits up, kissing me wet and messy, groaning against my teeth when he's buried inside and grunts these tiny perfect sounds of approval every time I rock forward and back, whispering, *Like that,* and *Ah, so good,* and, *Jesus, baby, I can't . . .* He trails off, more kissing, more teeth grazing my lips, my jaw, my neck. More sounds of need. *Just please . . . I can't.*

He reaches between us, two fingers so gently petting where I need him. A ragged groan tears from his throat, and I hear the tiny hiccuping sounds I'm making, begging, *so close—*

"Oh, shit, I'm coming," he gasps right when I'm falling. And I throw my head back and scream—because it feels so different—and at the same time he cries out, arching from the seat and wildly shoving deeper into me, my body clutching and squeezing all around him. It feels like forever that I'm coming and kissing him and his hands are on my face and his sounds are pressed into my skin in my tiny car with no tint on the windows, at the peak of the sunset in Indian summer.

I love him.

I love him.

I crumple against his chest, on the verge of tears. It's a relief I can barely process—being with him like this again, even if it's in the front seat of my car with the skirt of my dress billowing around me. He feels so sturdy, his heart pounding against my ear.

Finn twitches inside me, his shaking breath ruffling my hair. "Harlow," he says quietly, exhaling in a tight burst.

"I know," I agree. "Holy shit that was amazing."

"No . . ." He pulls my shoulders so I'm sitting upright, and I feel the press of him, still hard, still inside me. "Baby, we didn't use anything." His face is so close to mine, his eyes searching and anxious. "I don't have a condom on."

I groan and start to climb off him but then stop, reconsidering our attire. I really don't want to Monica Lewinsky it into the party with this blue dress. "Can you grab me a tissue from the glove compartment?"

He nods, reaching around me, and somehow manages to retrieve one. It's such a *real* moment, and in such stark contrast to the wild fucking of a minute ago, that I feel a little light-headed. Just as I move to pull away, he reaches for me, touching two fingers to my jaw and whispering, "Shh, wait, wait, wait. Come here."

I lean in, closing my eyes and giving in to the sensation of melting into him as he groans, digging his hand into my hair to hold me close. His tongue slides against mine, gentler now. My heart is slamming into my breastbone from exertion, and from the teasing adrenaline of my impending panic.

"Are you okay?" he says against my mouth.

I nod. "I can't believe we did that."

"Me, either."

"I guess we should go clean up before the party."

We adjust our clothes and stumble out of the car. Back at the front door, he pulls his keys from his pocket, unable to meet my eyes when he quietly asks, "Are you on the pill?"

"No." I try to do the math to figure out where I am in my cycle—I think I'm supposed to get my period in a matter of days—but I don't want to linger on the potential implications of the unprotected sex we just had. I want to stay in the happy, jelly-limbed place of bliss and my newfound admission that I'm totally freaking in love with Finn Roberts.

"It'll be fine," I tell him, with absolutely no proof whatsoever. It just feels good to say it, and as soon as I do, I feel sure of it. It will be fine! Everything will be fine!

He nods and walks inside, leading me down the hall to the small bathroom next to the room he's been staying in. I turn and look through the open bedroom door as he stops and grabs a washcloth from the hall closet. His suitcase is open on the bed, filled with neatly folded clothes.

"You're leaving tomorrow?"

"Maybe," he says. And then, "Well, probably not. I don't know." He nods toward the bathroom, indicating I lead us inside.

Turning on the hot faucet, he holds his hand underneath until the water heats, and then wets the cloth. "Come here."

I watch him reach under my dress, and close my eyes as his hand glides up the inside of my thigh, around to my hip, and he slips my underwear down my legs to my knees. I gasp when he gently slides the warm cloth between my legs.

"Okay?" he asks.

"Yeah." *More than okay. Heaven.* "It feels nice."

He reaches under my dress with his other hand, wrapping his fingers around my hip and squeezing. "I mean, you. Are *you* okay?"

"Are *you* okay?" I volley back.

He looks up at me, smiles a genuine smile that crinkles the corners of his eyes. "Yeah, I'm okay."

"Even if I'm knocked up?"

"Yeah. We'll figure it out."

I swallow, nodding. "Then I'm okay, too."

His expression straightens and he blurts, "Tell me that wasn't just sex for you."

Reeling from this, I slide my hands into his hair and pull him into me. "It went way past 'just sex' a while ago. I think that's why I wanted to stop. There's too much else going on. For both of us," I add.

He tilts his chin to look up at me, resting it on my navel. "We gonna try to do this anyway? I mean"—he swallows nervously—"I really want you, but not just like this anymore."

I bite my lip, wanting to unload all of my angst about the last two weeks: worrying about my mother, using Finn for distraction, and then becoming so absorbed in him I feared I would want so much more than either of us could manage. And now he's telling me he wants it, too. I close my eyes, thinking about the television show, and the stipulation that he not be in a relationship, and the thinly veiled goal to find him an on-screen romance. Now the easiest path forward— signing on to the show—would make a relationship between us impossible. Even if he passed on the show and went home to try to salvage the business, we'd never see each other be- cause he would be working even more than he is now.

"I want it so bad I feel like I can't breathe," he says, squeezing his hand around the back of my thigh so I'll look down at him. "I've been trying to focus on everything going on back home, but I can't think about anything but this."

"I want this, too," I tell him. "I'm just not sure how it would work."

He stands, kissing my jaw and intentionally misunder- standing me when he says, "We could skip the party and I could show you."

I start to answer, "Absolutely," but then pause. Some- thing clicks, like a lock turning in my thoughts. There *is* one way to salvage his business without him having to do the show, and it's been right in front of me this entire time.

———

WE WALK INTO the party holding hands. Something has shifted between us, and it's so achingly tender that I want to launch myself at him every time he looks at me, or speaks to me, or puts his hand around my back and curls his fingers around my hip as if there's a hold there made just for him.

Dad, who came here alone without Mom tonight, sees us as we walk into the kitchen and excuses himself from the small group conversation he's engaged in to come greet us.

"You must be Finn," he says, holding out his hand. "I'm Harlow's father, Alexander Vega."

Only two boys I've dated have ever met my father, and they were stammering, anxious messes the entire time. In a way, it's understandable. For one, my father has won two Academy Awards, and is a fairly well-known name for a cinematographer. But he's also tall, and muscular, and perfectly capable of being intimidating when he wants to be.

But right now, I can tell he doesn't want to be. And it doesn't matter anyway, because Finn—who is admittedly enormous in comparison—greets him with a firm shake, a confident smile, and a "Thanks so much for inviting me along."

My father puts his arm around Finn's shoulders and leads him deeper into the room to be introduced to some people. Dad tilts his head to me, indicating I join them, of course, but I'd rather watch the two of them greet Dad's colleagues and do the guy-bonding thing I've never seen my father do with a guy I've so much as kissed.

This guy-bonding thing is exactly what I need to happen tonight.

I head into the kitchen to get a drink and say hi to Salvatore's daughters. They're six and eight years older than I am and still living with their parents; Valentina and Ekaterina Marìn are two of the most spoiled "children" I've ever met in the film industry, but it's easier to just be friendly than avoid them, because Dad and Sal work together on more than half of their projects.

I kiss each of them on the cheek and smile that this time, Valentina smells like Chanel, and Ekaterina smells like something new . . . Prada Infusion d'Iris, maybe. Their biggest fight two years ago caused them to not speak for three months and was over which sister could claim Chanel No. 5 as her signature scent.

This is what Finn used to think I was like.

"Your boyfriend sure is something," Valentina says, lifting her chin in Finn's direction.

I pour myself a glass of sparkling water. "He is."

"Rugged," she purrs.

"I *love* the blue-collar ones," Ekaterina adds.

Oh, here we go. I look back into the room at Finn and know exactly how they spot it even though he's wearing dress pants and a dress shirt: He just looks out of place here. He's muscular in a way that bucks the Hollywood slender trend, his hair is cut short, and he stands with his legs set shoulder-width apart, as if constantly steadying himself against an incoming wave.

"He owns a fishing business," I tell them.

"Ooooh," Ekaterina coos. *"Niche."*

I plaster on a smile that turns genuine when their father walks into the kitchen, and I tilt my head to him when he leans to kiss my cheek. His daughters may be unbearable, but Salvatore has been like a second father to Bellamy and me.

"And how is my darling girl?" he asks.

"I'm doing fantastic. Congratulations again on the new business, Fancypants. You must be excited."

"I am. I've also been gunning to get your father to come on board for *Release Horizon.*"

"It sounds like he's already there," I tell him.

"Now I just need to get you to come work for me and the world will be settled perfectly."

I take a deep breath and say, "Actually, Sal, I wanted to talk to you about that . . ."

FINN PRESSES ME against the wall outside my apartment, growling into my neck over how long it's taking me to find my keys. We nearly pulled over to the side of the road four times on the short drive back to my place, because his hand was in my dress, his mouth on my neck, his fingers guiding mine to his lap when he pulled his cock free, whispering for me to feel him.

You're getting me all fucking messy, Harlow. You gonna lick this clean when we get there?

He *was* messy and slick when I slid my hand all the way down his length. I'd stroked him until he'd lifted his hips from the seat, began grunting quietly with every stroke of my hand over the head of his cock as I steered with the other hand. I'd brought him to the edge—panting and rigid—and then parked in front of my building.

He groaned, stilling my hand. "Not in the car again."

The metallic ring of my keys echoes down the hall as I jangle them free of my purse, and, still smashed up against me, Finn grabs them from my hand, opening the door and pushing me inside. I'm on my back on the floor only a split second before the sound of the door slamming shut rings through the apartment.

Finn hovers over me like a predator, inspecting his hunt. I slide my hand down his body, gripping the thick, inflexible shape of him through his dress pants, intent on finishing what I'd started in the car. But he seems to have regained control, and reaches for my hand, moving it away.

"When I met you at the bar back in June," he says, gaze traveling from my lips to my hair to my neck, "you walked up to me and looked me up and down like I was put up for auction, and then sat down right next to me and said, 'I'd love a tequila gimlet.' It was like liquid slowly spilled out on that chair. You were so fucking beautiful."

"Like an oil spill?"

He wipes a hand across his face, eyes crinkling in my favorite Finn smile. "Exactly. I just knew I would never be able to clean you off." We both laugh and then his expression straightens. "I've never been able to be myself with anyone, not the way I am with you." He bends down, kisses me. "I just figured you only wanted fucking, and so it's the only place my mind went. I didn't think we fit this way."

"Me, either," I admit quietly. "I just assumed you were like every other guy and would disappoint quickly enough."

"That may still be true," he says, kissing along my jaw. "I might just take a little longer."

What he's doing feels so good, just his lips on my throat and his fingers slyly sliding my dress up over my hips. "Take all the time you need," I mumble.

He talks as he undresses me. "You liked watching me at that party tonight?"

One of my shoes, and then the other, hits the floor.

"Yeah." In fact, I loved it. He didn't seem completely in his element, but he was happy enough to try, for me. It's what we'll do for each other, I can tell. We'll try to find that common ground and live there.

"Did you refer to me as your boyfriend to the Kardashian look-alikes in the kitchen?"

His hands slide up under my dress, hands spread across my hips before he grabs and pulls my underwear down my legs. Way, way too slowly for my mood.

I push up into his touch. "I didn't refer to you that way, but your fangirls seemed disappointed that it might be true."

He rolls me slightly to reach behind me and unzip my dress. "Did you confirm I'm taken?"

"They knew," I say, arching so he can slide my dress down my body. When I'm completely naked, and he's staring at me like I'm Thanksgiving dinner and the Crown Jewels and a *Playboy* centerfold all rolled into one naked body, I add, "They could tell from the way you looked at me."

He snorts, unbuttoning his dress shirt. "The way I looked at you?"

"Yeah."

He shrugs out of his shirt and leans back over me, immense. "And how do I look at you?"

His arms strain against the cotton of his undershirt and it seems somehow to barely contain his biceps, the width of his chest. The way the T-shirt is smoothly tucked into the flat front of his black dress pants . . . *sweet Jesus.*

He runs a warm palm up my stomach and spreads his giant hand across my ribs. "Snap?"

"Shh, Poodle. I'm having a Johnny Castle, *Dirty Dancing* moment right now."

"Is this a good thing or a bad thing?" he asks, bending to lick up my neck.

"I carried a watermelon."

He pulls back and looks at me before ducking to sniff my breath. "How drunk are you?"

"For the love of God, man, I'm not drunk. Get naked or put that mouth between my legs."

I expect him to be a good boy and comply—he's been so good tonight—but he disappoints.

Standing, he reaches for my hand and pulls me up, wrapping his arms around my waist. "I'm not fucking you on the floor," he says.

"Then why did you put me there?"

"Impatient. Maybe clumsy."

I laugh. There is not a clumsy bone in Finn's body, but there are definitely 206 impatient ones.

He leads me down the hall to my bedroom, passing the hall closet without a second glance.

"You're not going to tie me up tonight?"

He shakes his head.

"But I *like* it."

I hear his quiet laugh. "I like it, too. I just don't want to do it every time we're together."

"I'll put my hands all over you," I say, as if it's a threat.

"That's the point." He turns, bending to kiss my neck and inhales slowly, smelling me.

Reaching down, I pull his shirt free from his pants. "So the rope isn't really for bondage, it's—"

"Sometimes it is," he admits quietly, sucking on my pulse point. "I like the freedom it gives me to touch you any way I want. I think we both know I'm a controlling type."

I laugh and it turns into a moan when he runs his hand down my shoulder and across my breast.

"But I also just like the evidence of it."

I bite my lip, grinning as I unbuckle his belt, unfasten his pants, and push them down his hips. "'The evidence?'"

He watches my mouth, stepping out of his clothes. "I like leaving marks. I like seeing you wet, and watching you walk differently in the morning because I fucked you so good your legs aren't working right." Finn swipes his tongue over my throat, making me shiver. "How you looked the morning I saw you at Starbucks? You'll never look like that after a night with me."

I exhale a jagged breath when he sucks hard against my shoulder, pulling a mark to the surface. "I like seeing what I do to you," he says, "especially *you,* because I can tell how much you trust me—and seeing how good I can make you feel makes me insane. Rope is just something I'm very, very . . ." He lifts his head from my neck and kisses my mouth, my jaw, my cheek, and hovers near my ear, whispering, "*Very* comfortable handling."

"*Oh.*" Oh sweet lord. I'm aching, my skin flushed. I swear if he touches me between my legs once I will go off like a bomb. "So possessive," I mumble, arching my neck to give him better access.

"Yeah," he agrees. "That's exactly it." Studying me, he guides me to lie on the bed and crawls over me. He's massive in the dark room, a planet looming over my bed. Slowly bending his head to my chest, he licks my nipple, sucking and playing with my breasts until the tips are swollen and aching, flushed and hot. "Like this," he whispers, bending to lick, and suck, and pull the peak between his lips some more until my skin glistens in the shadowed room. "I like these wet and hard . . ."

He bends again, biting just beneath my nipple. His teeth press in harder and sharper until the only sensation I'm aware of is the sharp line of them, the pressure and the delicious sting, sting, *sting*—

"Ah!" I cry out, and just before I think he'll draw blood he pulls back, running his tongue over the bite mark, kissing it sweetly.

"Feel good?" he purrs into my skin.

I'm about to answer, "Hell no," but the pain is gone and in its place is a feeling unlike anything I've experienced before: throbbing heat and intense pleasure commingle. His bite has created a tiny spot of insatiable hunger on my chest. I want his mouth back there, sucking and soothing and biting me more.

"More," I manage.

Finn's eyes seem to gleam with victory at my reaction— my hands pulling his face to my chest, back arched off the bed—and very carefully he bites deep grooves into an intricate pattern all over my breasts. Around my nipples and in the full curve below. Along the sides, and at the smooth slope of them just above the swollen peaks.

He kisses each spot, licking and sucking until my skin shines, and I'm on the verge of screaming. He drags my hand up so I can feel each small indentation. "Touch them," he says, dragging his teeth down over my shoulder, to my arm. "Tell me how it feels when I lick you."

The tiny grooves remind me of the rope marks, but are more intimate somehow. These red marks that tell the room and the sky and the swollen moon outside for only a tiny trip of time: I belong to him. My body is his.

I don't want them to disappear, and can tell he doesn't, either, returning to the first one, pushing his possession back into my skin.

I need his body pressed to mine, covering my breasts so the puff of his breath across the peaks won't make me cry out, and I want the wet, soothing slide of his tongue over the sensitive bite marks. I feel cracked open, devoured and hollowed out, filled with a desire so consuming and deep I can sense how warm and soft I am beneath him, ready to pull him down onto me. Into me.

He sucks at me while his hands are busy elsewhere and I hear the crinkle of a condom wrapper and the wet sound of its lubricant as he rolls the latex down his length.

"Tell me if it's too much," he says into my skin as he positions himself and then presses his chest to mine, sliding into me in a long, smooth stroke.

I might be screaming or cursing or begging—I don't know. My skin is aching for friction but terrified of it all the same. It's a divine torture. The bite marks pulse and heat, and my chest is so wet Finn slides across me, groaning as he moves in and out. *Oh God.* The drag of his skin across my breasts burns and aches, pleasures and soothes, and when he lifts his chest away I need it back. Pulling him down over me I beg for faster.

Please . . .

"Tell me how it feels," he rasps.

"It feels . . . it feels . . ." My breasts are pulsing with every heartbeat and so sensitive I'm sure he could drag his tongue across the peak and—

Finn bends and presses his flattened tongue just below my nipple and drags it up just as he shoves in deep and begins fucking me in these tiny perfect jabs. I cry out, clutching him.

It feels like I'm yours.

His tongue soothes the burn but makes me arch, makes me beg and beg for his hips to move faster and his mouth to make my breasts wetter and for him to *please*

please

please

please make me come.

He makes a noise against my skin right when I jerk beneath him, gasping. His sound is half laugh, half thrilled groan and in a flash he draws my hands up over my head, pinning me, working me with his hips and his mouth until I'm thrashing.

I'm filling with pressure, climbing, skin flushing hot and wet, and then I'm screaming his name, consumed by the silvery, pulsing of pleasure until I can't differentiate any particular touch. It's only Finn over me and the pleasure tearing through me and his soft hoarse sounds of encouragement: "That's it. That's it. Oh, fuck me, you're coming. *Oh fuck.*"

It's strange to lose one's mind, but it's what he does to me—in these moments of wild bliss, when I've just come and he's losing himself in me—everything else in the world disappears. The stars could fall, the ocean could take over the land, and I wouldn't even realize it until long after Finn slows his hips and runs his hand up my leg and along my side, until he reaches my jaw, cupping it and telling me he's never wanted anything the way he wants me.

———————

IN FACT, IF the world ended tonight, I suspect we wouldn't hear about it until morning. Finn gets out of bed only long enough to get rid of the condom and come back with a wet cloth, wiping the lubricant from my skin so he can do some of the most wicked things with his mouth between my legs.

His tongue laps at me, he grazes me with his teeth and growls like a wild animal, spreading my legs apart with one hand gripping my thigh, fingering me with the other. I feel the full depraved meaning of the phrase *eating her out*. He is *devouring*.

And then, with his eyes pinned up the length of my body, he slides his fingers lower and does something so unexpected, the only way he knows I like it is the way I scream when I come harder against his mouth than I think I ever have before.

Finn kisses my thigh, my hip, my navel, rasping, "Fucking hell."

And then he pulls me down the mattress, setting my feet on the floor so he can bend me over the bed.

"You sore yet, you dirty fucking girl?" he asks quietly, tearing a new condom packet open with his teeth.

I turn and look at him over my shoulder, lifting my chin in challenge. "No."

"Good."

Because when he positions himself and pushes in so deep I collapse against the bed, I know he's going to fuck me, dirty and hard.

It's Vegas all over again: rowdy, with his palm on my ass and his other hand digging so hard into my hip I look forward to the tiny bruises I know I'll find tomorrow. But I finally recognize Vegas for what it was: It wasn't his "usual" stranger fuck, Finn being domineering and rough. It was Finn unbound, Finn laid bare with *me,* his perfectly matched stranger. All at once I know with someone else he would have been careful that first night—slower-handed, softer words, easy, rolling hips—but with me he couldn't be.

He could only do rowdy because he felt what I felt: that whip-crack unleashing that comes when you meet the person who frees you.

Finn lowers us to the floor, running his hand down my sweat-slicked spine, and then I feel his own sweaty chest press into my back as he curls over me, entering me again and immediately riding me fast and smooth, his greedy hands cupping my breasts.

He's insatiable on the floor, against the wall, back up on the bed with my legs on his shoulders. It's like this, under the firm touch of his fingers, that I come apart with a scream and his teeth bared against my ankle. I can tell he's close to his own release but he slows his thrusts, humming into my leg.

"What do you want me to do?" I ask, running my hand down his sweaty chest and lowering my legs to his sides.

"It feels fucking *amazing,*" he says through heavy

breaths, bending to kiss me. "I want to come, but I also don't."

"There's no rush," I purr, pulling him down so his chest presses all along mine.

"I got a taste of you bare, earlier," he admits quietly. "Do you have any idea how good you feel without this fucking condom? I can't stop thinking about how warm and sweet you were."

How is it possible I'd forgotten what we'd done in the car? A mixture of longing and anxiety shadows my thoughts.

"It's like I'm trying to fuck this thing off." He laughs into my shoulder and begins moving again. I remember how warm he felt, how smooth.

I want to feel it, too.

I push on his chest so he pulls out of me and I reach for him, sliding the condom off.

"No, Harlow, I didn't mean—"

"Shh, I know," I say, reaching for the wet cloth on the bed and using it to wipe him off this time. "Come here."

I lay back, pulling his hips up higher, over my face. Of all the things he's done to me, he's never let himself finish this way.

With his knees on the mattress at my sides, he carefully slips between my lips, and into my mouth.

"Fuck." He groans, squeezing his eyes shut. "You're gonna ruin me."

He gives me tentative, short strokes at first until he's wet and hungry and so tight against my tongue that I can't help but make little desperate noises as he moves deeper. There is nothing in this world I want more right now than watching him slowly start to climb, his hands flat against the wall at the head of the bed, his chest shuddering with his jagged exhales. He chokes out a tight "Close."

I slide my hands up his thighs, and to the middle, circling his base and behind his balls with both hands.

"Keep doing that and I'm coming in your mouth," he warns.

I squeeze my hands, suck harder, and he arches his back, swelling against my tongue and coming with the hottest fucking groan I've ever heard in my life. He hovers over me, sweat dripping from his forehead onto the pillow beside my head, watching me with flared nostrils and savage eyes as I lick and kiss him.

Pulling slowly away, he sits back on his heels over me, catching his breath. "My God."

His cock rests heavily on my chest and I feel thoroughly wrecked, in the best way. I'm exhausted, boneless, sweaty, and probably the most satisfied woman in the history of sexual relations.

Scooting down my body, Finn seems far more serious. He does a careful inspection of my breasts in the dim light filtering in through the bedroom window. His fingers trail across the nearly vanished bite marks. "You okay?"

"Yeah."

He lowers himself, covering my chest in small, sucking kisses. "I needed this tonight."

"I needed it, too," I say in a burst, exhaling a huge breath. "It's scary how much."

"You good?" he asks, rising above me in the dark. "You need more?"

"I'm perfect." He could go *again*? Holy shit.

He bends and kisses the tip of my nose, as if he can see every one of my features in the dark. "Yeah."

For all his surly expressions and monosyllabic answers, Finn is a surprisingly generous lover. I'm sort of rocked by the realization that he gets off on my pleasure more than he does when I touch him.

"Has anyone ever told you you're kind of amazing?" I blame my post-multi-orgasm high for the way my voice comes out a little shaky.

But, predictably, he laughs, pressing a kiss between my breasts. "No." He gets up to walk across the room and into my bathroom, getting a drink of water.

"Well, for the record, you're amazing, Sunshine."

When he returns, the mattress dips and I feel the unbelievable heat of his body slide behind me beneath the covers. He's careful not to jostle me but curls along my spine, the thick band of his arm sliding around my waist, hand splayed across my stomach with a new, thrilling possession. Eventually my breathing evens out and I'm in that delicious space just before sleep, where everything in the entire world is perfect.

"It's you," he whispers, and then bends to kiss my hair.

It's you.

And suddenly, I'm on an epic mental bender, imagining all of the things he could have meant when he said it. It takes no time for him to clarify, though.

"I want to be good to you." He rolls me to face him, and kisses me once before admitting, "I'm just fucking wild for you."

"I think I spotted that just now," I whisper.

"I mean," he clarifies, "the *I love you* kind of wild."

I feel every drop of blood in my body collect in my chest, pressure and thrill building, and then it bursts into my limbs in a mad rush of adrenaline and relief and a love so enormous I feel light-headed.

"Yeah?" I ask through a smile so dopey I'm relieved he can't see me very well in the dark room.

But his laugh tells me I'm wrong, and he can see me just fine. "Yeah."

I manage to say it back, laughing into the firm press of his mouth over mine, hard and rowdy, all over again.

Chapter TWELVE

Finn

I'M GROWING FAMILIAR with this position: in bed, my mind going nonstop while I stare up at the ceiling.

But this view is new, and instead of the shadow of palm trees on the plaster above me, there's the shimmering night-reflection of a pool in the courtyard just outside. Harlow's neighborhood is quieter than Oliver's: There's no teenage band playing in the garage on the corner, no barking dog in the yard next door, fewer cars passing by at every hour of the night.

It's so peaceful—with only the soft, measured sound of her breathing right next to me—that I imagine if I try hard enough, I could hear the ocean a few blocks away. It's pitch-black out and she's been asleep for the last hour, her leg slung easily over my hip and practically every inch of her bare skin touching practically every inch of mine. And when she shifts in her sleep, tightening her grip on the sheet at my waist, it's almost enough to distract me from the silence, to tempt me into waking her up and wearing her out all over again.

Almost.

I've never been a huge talker. I've never had the inclina-tion to put into words all the things that are going on in my head. Never felt the need some people have to fill silence with pointless chatter. I get the feeling that's usually who Harlow is for people—she's the one who carries on the conversation and manages to pull sentences from even the least talkative person around—but she never really tries that with me. She can outtalk and outwit almost anyone I know, and yet when we're together, she's okay with my silence. She's okay letting me be me.

I thought I knew what we were for each other, but underneath the stress and anxiety of the last few weeks, something changed. It's a complication I wasn't expecting and now that it's here, I *want* it. Last night was the first time we really talked about what we are, but did we actually decide anything? I want her. That's all I really know.

Harlow mumbles something in her sleep and I shift to my side, brushing the hair from her face. When I'm this close to her it's easy to forget the stack of bills waiting on the boat, the broken-down equipment and the start of the next season that gets closer and closer every day.

But fuck, I need to go home. I've been putting it off as long as I can but I'm needed there. I belong there. But how do I leave now? One smile or smart-ass comment from her and all my thoughts sort of rearrange themselves, the inappropriate, usually pornographic ones sliding to the front, while the important ones like family and responsibility are shuffled to the back.

I've tried to ignore it. I've tried to downplay the way my heart jumps in my chest when I hear her name, done my best to explain away the times I find myself thinking about her, wondering what she's doing, worrying whether she's all right. But I can't anymore. I don't want to.

Jesus, I've never thought this much about a woman in my life.

"Finn?"

I look down to see her blinking awake. "I'm here," I tell her. I kiss her temple, her cheek, let my hand move down her body to rest at her hip.

"You stayed." It's not a question, and I feel the moment she really wakes up, realizes that I'm still here, with her. Harlow pushes herself up before she climbs on top of me. Her silhouette blocks the streetlights filtering in through the dark window and all I can make out is the shape of her body, the pink of her nipples against her skin.

"I stayed so I could fuck you again," I tell her and she laughs.

Actually, I'm as surprised as she is that I'm still here. I'd promised myself I'd wait until she was asleep, I'd make sure she was okay and then I'd head back to Oliver's. I'd come up with some sort of a plan. Clearly, I'm a liar.

Her hands move over my stomach, my cock already hard between her legs. She rocks her hips and I can feel where she's still wet, the way she slides over me.

"Done sleeping?" I ask, placing a hand on each of her hips.

She nods, slow and sleepy. "Dreamed about you."

I trace my thumbs in small circles over her hip bones and in, toward her navel. "What about?"

She rocks a bit more forcefully now, with intent. "This."

With every shift backward she brings the head of my cock closer, closer, so close to slipping inside. Bare.

"Careful," I warn, but it's halfhearted at best.

Harlow's head falls forward, the ends of her hair brushing my stomach, my chest. "Feels so good," she says, hitching in a breath. "Oh . . . God, it's so good."

I know I should take control, guide her away from where I'm hard and greedy, but I can't bring myself to do it.

One more time.

One more second.

"Wait," I start to say, and hiss in a breath when I feel the gentle rise of her clit, warm and slippery. "Let me get something, sweetheart."

"Just for a second?" she asks, grinding over me. "*Ahh* . . . right there. Right there."

"Yeah?" I say, propping the pillow behind my head and watching my cock disappear over and over again between her legs. "Fuck, this is so crazy. Baby, what are we doing?"

But even as I'm saying the words, I'm canting my hips off the bed, helping her slide over me. There's something about seeing her use me like this, use my body to get herself off, that leaves my brain fuzzy, trying to remember why we should *ever* stop. It's just enough friction and I'm sure I could come from this alone, the two of us rutting against each other like a couple of teenagers.

Harlow leans back, reaches to steady herself on my thighs, and it's that slight movement, the tiniest change of angle that opens her up, and lets the head of my cock slip inside.

"Oh *fuck*," I say, tightening my grip to keep her still. I feel hot all over, feverish and hungry, and know I should stop this but every instinct fights against it.

Harlow moans and sinks down a little farther. "Do you want me to stop?"

I nod my head but the word "no" comes out instead. Actually a whole lot of curse words come out but I'm not sure Harlow is paying attention to any of them.

"Fuck. Right," she says, voice pained. She straightens, and moves to climb off me but I reach for her waist, stopping her.

"God. Wait." I take a deep breath, suddenly aware of the sweat at my temples, the way the sheets are clinging to my back. Every muscle is strung too tight, like live wires ready to snap with the slightest pressure. Her body feels like it belongs to me now. "Just let me . . . feel you. Just for a second."

And I must be some kind of a masochist because why else would I torture myself?

Harlow's skin is sleep-warm and her limbs heavy where they rest against me. I'll never last more than a minute with her looking down at me—sleepy and needy—with nothing between us.

It takes me only a second to decide, to roll us both over and slip back between her thighs. Her legs fall open, knees bent and pressed to my sides. "I just want to feel you," I tell her again, trying to ignore the eager way she nods, how willingly she agrees with me. Her mouth is too tempting, lips wet and parted, and I lean in, tasting her. "And if you want . . . I could pull out?"

She pushes her words out between tiny, biting kisses: "Would you . . . come . . . *on* me?"

There have always been things I've been into—things that got me off in the privacy of my own head—sex acts that are hard to bring up in a new, more tentative relationship. I want to be messy, rough, a little dirty, a little taboo. I want to claim Harlow everywhere, try anything she wants, and see the mark of rope and teeth and my spankings on her skin.

I like that she wants this as much as I do.

"You want that?" I ask, slowly pressing inside and nearly growling from the pleasure of it. "You want to see it on your skin?"

Harlow throws her head back, fingers twisting in the sheets. Her tits move with each of my thrusts, the mattress squeaks in the darkness, and I'm only vaguely aware that there are neighbors next door, people both upstairs and down. But the only thing I care about is the way she grips me from the inside out, how her skin looks in the moonlight and the tiny sounds that escape her mouth with every thrust.

I'm too close and it's too fast but I don't think either of us even cares. A spark flashes hot and moves down my spine, heat that settles in my lower body. I feel myself get harder, my fingers grip her hips so tightly I'm actually afraid she'll be bruised tomorrow.

And then Harlow is coming, clenching around my cock

and I'm holding on by a thread, riding her through it with my jaw tight and my body so tense just to hold my own release at bay. She gasps, pushes up into me, claws at my chest until her arms slide down my torso, feeling where I'm moving in her. With a groan I pull out, hand moving over my length in a blur and my orgasm is there, so close that I can't hear anything but static in my ears. Her name is on my lips and I wish I'd thought ahead to turn on a lamp so I could see her face as I cover her stomach, her tits, her neck.

Harlow looks down at my come on her skin, runs a finger through it and around her nipple. The action is instinctive, and possessive . . . and I know in that moment that I am absolutely, thoroughly *fucked* over this girl.

I fall to the mattress in a heap of boneless limbs, my heart racing so hard that I actually have to work to breathe, to gain control of my arms and my legs.

"You'll stay the night?" Harlow asks, and I lift my head just long enough to look at her.

"Yeah, I have breakfast with the guys in the morning, though. I can't stay too late."

Harlow yawns, reaching for a discarded T-shirt to wipe the mess from her skin. "I have to pick my mom up, anyway," she says absently. "I'll wake you before I leave."

I nod, kissing Harlow's jaw and then her cheek, feeling the flush beneath her skin against my lips.

"Love you," she says, eyes already fluttering closed.

It has to be coming up on three in the morning, and I say, "I love you" back as I pull her close, molding my body to the shape of hers. I'm so tired, but alert enough to know that something doesn't sit right. I just wish I were awake enough to figure out what it is.

HARLOW LEAVES BRIGHT and early like she said she would. She wakes me with kisses and invites me to take a shower. I fuck her against the bathroom wall before we ever manage to get in.

San Diego smells like the ocean in the morning, like salt and wind and something sharp that wraps like an old blanket around everything. It smells so close to home some days, that if I close my eyes I can *almost* forget where I am, over a thousand miles and a lifetime away from where I'm supposed to be. It's a little unnerving.

Even scarier? How much it's starting to feel *right*, and how many times I've considered not leaving at all.

A call from Colton first thing out of the shower pops the Harlow bubble I've been floating in, and brings me crashing, face-first back into reality.

I'd texted him after the initial meeting with the Adventure Channel, with a brief "It was good, lots to talk about, I'll fill you in later." But I never did—not that night or the next morning—hoping I could put them off just long enough to decide what the fuck we should all do with the rest of our lives. I still have no idea. Of course when I call him back it goes straight to voicemail—because it's eight in the morning and they're actually working—and I promise to get back to him later that night, to explain everything.

Now I just have to decide what the hell I'm going to tell them.

On the one hand, I'm glad my brothers are clearly so busy they've barely had a moment to worry about the meeting, or even realize that I've been avoiding the discussion altogether. I've never been this irresponsible in my entire life.

Do we sign on for the show? Do we not? The terms they're offering are great, the money a godsend. But it will change everything: How we live, how people see us. How we see ourselves. And what about Harlow—how would that even work? Before recently the impact this would have on a potential relationship was the furthest thing from my mind. But now, it fucking *matters*. Unless I leave the business and my family, I can't see a time I'd ever be in California on a more permanent basis. And unless Harlow has an even bigger surprise up her sleeve, she won't be moving to Vancouver Island anytime soon.

Harlow on the deck of our run-down boat . . . now that's a sight I don't think I'll ever be prepared to see.

I'm positive I'd feel better if I talked to Ansel and Oliver, and am feeling more than a little guilty about not having told them what's going on. The truth is that I haven't seen as much as them as I'd like lately, which is why I find myself navigating the narrow streets of the Gaslamp Quarter, attempting to parallel park my giant truck to meet them both for breakfast.

The sidewalks are fairly empty this early in the morning, the streets littered with delivery trucks and a handful of ambitious healthy types out for a morning run. I spot Oliver's beat-up car as I turn up Fifth, walking toward Maryjane's.

I see the guys in a booth near the back, a set of stylized Mick Jagger prints hanging on the wall above them, and a TV tuned to a music channel just off to the side.

"Ladies," I say, and slide into the seat next to Ansel. "Gorgeous day outside."

"Finn," Ansel says. He reaches for the mug in front of me and fills it with hot coffee from a carafe left by the waitress. "We ordered for you. I got you the most manly thing on the menu."

I laugh. "Thank you."

Oliver is sitting directly across from me. "You seem decidedly less surly this morning. Anyone in particular we should thank?"

"Good morning to you, too, Olls."

Oliver leans forward, pushes his glasses up his nose before resting his forearms on the table. "You're right, where are my manners? Good morning, Finnigan. How are you?"

Ansel chuckles next to me.

"I'm excellent, thank you. And how are you, Oliver?"

"I'm good, I'm good," he says, nodding. "I did notice you didn't come home last night. In fact, you haven't been spending much time at home, at all lately. I was beginning to grow concerned. Young man, alone in a big, strange city, wandering the streets all night . . ."

"This sounds like a story I'd like to hear," Ansel agrees, taking a sip of his coffee.

But Oliver isn't done. "You've never really been a one-time-hookup kind of a guy, so I can't help but wonder who you're spending all your time with."

"I was at Harlow's," I admit. "We've been, um . . . seeing each other."

I'm saved from their interrogation when the waitress arrives with our breakfast. "Wow. This is certainly . . . manly." I study the towering sandwich made of toast, bacon, and fried eggs with bright yellow yolk oozing out onto the plate.

"Would it be possible for me to get more of this," Ansel asks her, holding up a small white bowl filled with some sort of brown sugar mix. "I have a . . ." He stops to tap a finger against his mouth, searching for the word. "A, um . . . *comment ce dire*? When you like sweet things?"

The waitress blinks at least three times, and even sways a little where she stands. I'm about to reach out and steady her when she finally shakes her head, eyes coming back into focus.

"A sweet tooth?" she asks.

"Yes! That's it, a sweet tooth! And I would love more of this."

Pink floods her cheeks and she nods, taking the bowl from him before wandering away from the table, in search of Ansel's brown sugar.

"Jesus Christ, Ansel," Oliver says.

"What?"

"I am totally telling Mia you did that," I say.

Ansel dumps a bowl of blackberries into his oatmeal and looks up at each of us, blinking innocently. "Did what?"

"Why didn't you just fuck her on the table?" I ask. "It would have been only slightly more awkward for us."

"She's probably pregnant now." Oliver points his knife in the direction of the kitchen. "Try explaining that to your wife."

Laughing, I say, "I bet she brings him every goddamn bowl of brown sugar they have in the place."

"You're both very funny," Ansel deadpans.

"How is Mia, anyway?" I ask.

Ansel looks up at me with the most goofy, dimpled smile I've ever seen. "Perfect."

"Ugh," Oliver says, setting his fork down. "Do not get him started. Lola says she's had to start warning them before she comes over. Last time she could hear them all the way down Julianne's driveway."

Ansel only shrugs, looking disgustingly pleased with himself. "What can I say? I am quite the vocal lover, and would never stifle the loud, satisfied cries of my wife during what is possibly the best sex anyone has ever had." He leans in, looks us both in the eye in turn, and repeats, *"Ever."*

Both Oliver and I burst out laughing when we realize that, at some point during this monologue, our waitress has materialized at the table and placed a giant bowl of brown sugar in front of Ansel. I'm not sure how much she just heard, but judging by the blush creeping up her neck and flashing hotly across her face, I'm guessing it was enough.

"Merci," Ansel says again, smiling widely.

The poor girl mumbles "You're welcome," before she turns and heads back to the kitchen.

"I hate you," Oliver says.

"You wouldn't hate anyone if you were getting a little yourself."

"He's got a point," I agree.

Oliver takes a bite of his breakfast, shrugging.

"Come on. You're a good-looking, successful guy," Ansel says. "Why aren't you seeing someone?"

"Are we really doing the *Sex and the City* thing right now? In case you haven't noticed, *Carrie,* I just opened the store. When would I have the time to meet anyone?"

"Who's Carrie?" I ask.

Ignoring me, Ansel says, "Are you kidding me? I've only been there a few times and it's crawling with weird hot chicks."

"Eh. I'm not really looking."

Ansel narrows his eyes. "*Not looking?* That doesn't make any sense. You have a penis."

Oliver laughs. "I do."

"You've never had a problem getting laid and yet I haven't seen you with anyone but Lola since I got—" Ansel stops, his mouth forming the word for a few beats before he says, "Ohhhh. I get it."

"'Oh'?" I repeat, glancing between them. "Get what?"

"You like *Lola.*"

Oliver is already shaking his head. "No, no, I don't. We're just friends."

"'Friends,'" Ansel and I repeat in unison.

"Honestly. I like her. But not *like* her like her. She's smart and fun to hang out with, that's it."

Jesus Christ, he is a terrible liar.

"You two were *married*," I remind him.

"Yeah, but unlike you two, I never even kissed her."

Ansel is already shaking his head. "We *all* kissed them. I even have the photo somewhere. She's the hottest nerd girl alive."

"Just because you got married doesn't mean everyone else needs to settle down. Look at Finn."

"Me?"

"Sure. I can only assume—and don't try and deny it—you've been fucking Harlow the entire time you've been here and you're not ready to propose."

"Um," I say, picking up my knife and digging into my food with renewed interest. "I mean, we're . . . it might not be strictly *just friends* anymore."

Ansel lifts his hand and cups it around his ear as if he didn't hear me correctly. *"Comment?"* he says in French. *What?*

"I like her." I bring my fork to my lips and hold it there, adding, "*More* than like her."

"Don't hurt yourself," Ansel says, and I snort, taking the bite.

"Holy shit. Finn," Oliver says. "Seriously?"

"Yeah, seriously."

"But, wait. You're leaving," he adds. "Aren't you? I mean I know you haven't really told me what you're doing here, but I was never under the impression it was anything permanent."

"It's not. I've been looking into some business things, but I have to go back soon. I'm not really sure what Harlow and I are going to do."

The table is silent and we each pretend to be interested in our food, everyone trying to process the giant admission I've just dropped like a bomb in front of us.

"You guys are good, though, right?" I ask Ansel. "You and Mia? Being apart." Mia and Ansel have been doing the long-distance thing for a few months now, and if anything, they seem even more infatuated with each other than they did in Vegas.

Ansel leans against the back of the bench and exhales, this deep, long breath. It's the kind of breath you take when you're so full of something you feel like you might explode if you don't let it out.

"Things are going . . ." He swipes his hand down his face. "I'm just so *happy*. The days when we're apart are hard, of course. But when we're together, it's like I don't even remember. None of that matters."

Oliver swallows, points his fork at me. "You two are thinking about doing the long-distance thing?"

"I don't know," I admit. "I don't know what the fuck we're doing yet."

"You like it here, yeah?" Oliver asks. "In San Diego?"

"Yeah, of course. But I have to go back eventually." My food sits, practically untouched in front of me, and I push it around with my fork. I suddenly have no desire to eat. "I mean, not *eventually*, but probably in the next day or two."

"You'll make it work," Ansel says. "Harlow's not going to leave her mom right now, but—"

My head snaps up and I blink over to him, the same sense of unease I felt last night in bed flares in my chest. "Why wouldn't she leave her mom?"

"Well, how she's . . ." Ansel's words trail off and he glances nervously over to Oliver. "Shit."

Oliver is a rock, usually completely unreadable, but I know him better than almost anyone. The way he shifts in his seat, he's definitely uncomfortable. And then it all clicks, and before either of them have even said anything, I know.

Harlow mentioning that her mother wasn't feeling well. Mr. Furley asking after Madeline. Harlow's flashes of desperation and need for escape.

Harlow's mom is *sick* sick. Not just with the flu, or a lingering cold.

"Jesus Christ," I groan, pressing my hands to my face.

"Breast cancer," Oliver says quietly. "I think . . . stage . . . advanced? She had surgery a couple of weeks ago, and is between rounds of chemo."

"Stage three?" I guess.

He nods. "That sounds right. From what I hear she's doing all right, for now."

I can't do anything but stare down at my plate, a familiar ache pulsing fresh in my chest. I'm not sure who I'm madder at: Harlow for keeping this from me, for telling everyone *but* me, or at everyone else for keeping her secret. I told her *everything* and she couldn't even tell me this? The one thing I would have understood. The *only* thing I could have offered her.

I drop my fork and the sound rings through the restaurant, louder than the shitty rock song playing on the TV overhead, louder than the other customers. What little I've eaten sits heavy, leaden in my stomach, and I'm not sure if I want to throw it up or get the fuck out of here.

"Finn," Oliver says, reaching out to grip my arm. "Look, I don't know why she didn't tell you, okay? But it wasn't my secret to tell. I swear to God."

"I know."

"She had to have had her reasons," Ansel says quietly.

"Yeah, thanks. That's super comforting."

"Think about this before you do anything crazy, okay? I fucked up so bad with Mia . . . just, hear her out."

I stand, pulling out my wallet and tossing a twenty to the table.

"Where are you going?" Oliver says.

I shake my head. I can feel my pulse pounding inside my ribs, hear the rush of blood in my head. My heart hurts for her, but I'm frustrated and confused about why she didn't just tell me. My face feels hot and I'm not sure if I want to find Harlow and ask what the fuck is going on . . . or if I just want to hit the road and drive.

"I've got some calls to make," I say instead. "I haven't been the best captain or brother lately and I need to catch up. They're doing some repairs and I need to check in on a few things. I'll talk to you guys later."

Chapter THIRTEEN

Harlow

*O*NLY ONE HOUR into my five hour shift at NBC and I get a call from Salvatore, telling me he's agreed to my proposal. He loved my idea, and also? He is going to find a place for me on the staff of his new production company.

"No way in hell you should still be shuffling papers at that place," he'd said. "You've got places to be, kiddo." And for the first time, I agreed.

I'm ready.

I can barely concentrate on the giant stacks of folders I need to file, what copies I'm making or whose coffee I'm pouring. Finally, I think we might have a solution that works for everyone: It could save Finn's family business . . . and it could allow me to be closer to him far more often.

The first thing I do Monday afternoon when I get out of work is text Finn: You at Oliver's?

I see him begin to type, and then stop. And then I'm in the elevator, and leaving the building, and walking to my car, staring at my phone and nearly walking into a telephone pole and getting hit by a bicycle because I'm not watching where I'm going.

I'm already almost home by the time his text appears: Yep.

OK, headed there, I reply, laughing over how long it took him to write one word.

It also takes him forever to answer the door, even though his truck is parked out front. And when he does, he looks . . . bad.

Sour, even.

"Hey," I say, stepping close and stretching to kiss him. I can tell he's just showered, but he didn't shave. He's scratchy and smells like soap and coffee. But he doesn't bend to me, and instead offers the stubbly angle of his jaw.

"Hey." He steps back, avoiding eye contact, and letting me walk past him into the house.

"You're awfully . . . surly," I mumble, sitting down on Oliver's couch. Unease bubbles in my belly, and I study his expression, mentally rifling through everything I've said or done in the past twenty-four hours that might make him act this way. "Did I do something?"

He hums, shrugging, and then asks, "So what's up?"

I pause for a beat; he didn't answer my question at all. But the good news I have pushes forward in my thoughts. Whatever his foul mood may be, I have the power to cheer him up. "I came over because I wanted to tell you something. Something really good, actually."

"Something good?" he says, looking at my face. His expression turns from dark into hopeful. "Is it good news about your mom?"

I freeze, not sure I heard him right. "What did you just say?"

"Your mom," he repeats. "Is it good news about her?"

"How . . . ?" I pause, closing my eyes as my heart drops in my chest. I haven't told Finn yet, which means he heard it from someone else. "No. I . . . how did . . . ?" I trip around, trying to find my footing. Who told him and what does he know? My stomach sinks. Now I understand his mood. "Finn, I was going to tell you about that, but that isn't what—"

His face is tight again, jaw clenched. "You realize your mother has the same thing that killed my mom? I thought maybe you would want to confide in me since, of anyone in your life right now, I understand what you're probably feeling. Also, you know, because you love me."

I pull back, anger rising like steam in my chest. "You're giving me shit for not sharing this *immediately*?"

He closes his eyes, pressing his fingers to his forehead. "I've been all over the map about this today, Snap. I get why you wouldn't want to talk to me about that at first, I do. But then later . . ." He shakes his head. "I felt like my shit was falling apart and it really helped me to have you there. *You,* specifically. It's part of what helped me let myself see this thing between us as more than just physical. But apparently you didn't need the same thing from me."

I start to interrupt, but he holds up his hand to stop me. "And even after it was clear it was more—even *before* we said it concretely that it was more between us, we *knew* it was— you didn't tell me about all of this. I know what your family is to you, Harlow. I know how close you are. I get why you were such a desperate mess early on and probably didn't want to think about it when we were together. I get that. What I don't get is why last night, or all of the other times it was just you and me understanding each other perfectly, you couldn't just . . ." He trails off, running his hand down his face and lowering himself into a chair across from me.

"I just haven't really been talking—"

"Don't say that," he interrupts, angry now. "Everyone else knew. Ansel, Oliver, Lola, Mia. They all fucking knew. I'm the one in your bed, I'm the one you're looking at like I'm someone, and I'm the only person who doesn't know what's eating you up inside so bad that you came looking for me in the first place."

I want to get up and go over to him, but his body language is so unfamiliar: shoulders hunched, elbows on his knees, cap pulled so low over his brow I can't even see his eyes. It's like seeing the Finn from weeks ago. When he was just some stranger I'd married. "Finn, I'm sorry. I didn't keep it from you because of you. I just . . ."

He shakes his head, sighing. Finally, after what feels like forever he says, "I . . . understand what you're feeling—how hard it is to go through this. How protective you feel of your family. And . . . I don't know, thinking it over, I realize I might have done the same thing if this was all happening to me now. All this, it just surprised me, that's all."

"I'm sure."

"I mean," he starts, looking up at me, his expression anxious. "Are you *okay*?"

"Yes and no."

Silence fills the room for a long, painful minute. I don't

know what else to say. It seems like it would be a good time to finally talk about what *is* going on with my mom, to update him on everything, but the mood is all wrong. I don't want to force him to be tender with me right now, and I certainly don't feel like talking about it if he's going to continue to be distant and silent.

I slip from the couch and crawl across the floor, letting an unsure smile appear on my lips.

"Hey," I say, putting my hands on his knees.

He watches me for a moment, swallowing thickly.

"Hey, baby," he whispers finally, spreading his legs to make room for me. I slide my hands up his thighs, his stomach, his chest, pulling myself up his body until I can press a little kiss to his frowning mouth.

"I don't like that this is a thing between us," I tell him and follow it with another kiss. "I was planning on talking to you about it soon, probably even today, but last night I just wanted it to be us."

He nods. "I know."

Slowly, under my tiny, sucking kisses he starts to unwind, and I feel his hands move up my sides and down my back.

"It's just a thing for me, okay? What you're going through with your mom was a big thing in my life. Easily the biggest. If we're doing this . . ."

After I realize he's just going to leave the sentence like that, I say, "I promise I'll talk to you. I need someone to talk to."

"Okay."

Our kisses are short and soft; Finn gives me only the tiniest tip of his tongue to wet my lips against his. His hand slides back around to my front and down between my legs, cupping me over my denim cutoffs.

I wince a little, shying away from his firm grip.

"You hurt?" he asks, pulling back to look at me.

"Just a little sore. You rode me like a rodeo horse."

Laughing into another series of soft, brief kisses he whispers, "Want me to kiss it and make it better?"

The vision of Finn's head between my legs and memories of his warm suction and growling vibrations, of the things he did to me last night, make me hungry for different kisses, deeper ones that give me his tongue and his sounds.

His other hand comes up to grip the back of my head and he gives me exactly what I want: the deep, demanding kisses of a man about to throw me down and satisfy me.

His cock presses into my stomach and it's a presence I can't ignore. Kissing down his neck I push his shirt up with my hands, nibbling and sucking on his warm chest, stomach, hip bones. He lifts up once I have his fly unbuttoned, helping me pull his jeans down his thighs.

I love the honesty between us, how he watches, eyes steady and lids growing heavy when I draw my tongue up his length from base to tip, sucking away the sweetness.

"Fuck that's good," he whispers.

Playing, I lick around the base and up his entire length, making him wet all over so I can take him in my mouth as deep as I can, sucking up and down as he stares, eyes dark and lips parted.

Sliding back up, I release him with a smile. "I like how serious you look when I'm giving you head."

"It's something I take pretty fucking seriously." His thumb comes up to rub across my lips.

I lick his thumb, lick the head of his cock, taking both between my lips, playing with them with my tongue. Beneath my flattened palm, his stomach muscles spasm and tense.

"Let's go to the bed," he says, voice tight. "I wanna lick you while you do this."

I pull back and stand, and when he gets up, he pulls his jeans back up over his hips and bends to me. "Come here."

His kiss is so sweet, so searching it literally makes my legs wobbly. The band of his arms around my waist and back, the curl of his huge body over mine . . . I feel like I'm climbing him, clawing my way up so I can wrap all around him.

"Was that our first fight?" he asks against my lips, smiling.

"I guess," I say. "Not too bad."

"Hey," he says, pulling back to look at me. "Tell me your good news before we get naked and forget the world."

Oh, right.

I swallow, taking a deep breath. I don't know why I'm so nervous—*this is a good thing*—but this is a big deal for both of us and I want it so much I can taste it. "I think I have a way to save your business."

A short laugh escapes his lips, and he steps a little farther back before asking, "Oh yeah? Hit me."

God, this is hard to do when his slight edge has returned. Pushing forward, I say, "I had an idea at Salvatore's the other night, but didn't want to mention it to you until I got a sense from him whether it would work."

Finn's eyes narrow.

"See, Salvatore's new production company—along with my dad—is starting filming on this really huge movie in April. Much of it takes place out on the water, on a large boat."

He continues to stare at me, no reaction at all. My stomach twists.

"I thought maybe he could fix your boats as payment for using them as a set in the spring. And I accepted a job with him, at the production company, so I could be up there with you a lot."

He nods slowly, studying me. "I'm not sure I'm following what you're telling me."

"I'm saying I've connected you with Salvatore, and he wants to pay to use your boats for a movie that would film for a few months. But the best thing is they would need weird hours, like middle of the night, so I thought you could still fish during the morning and—"

"You offered my family's boats to a film crew without talking to me?"

My skin goes cold, panic rising in my chest. "Not *offered*, I just wanted to see if it could be an option—"

"But obviously it had to go up enough channels internally for Salvatore to call you personally and give his approval. And all this happened without even talking to me." He reaches down, buttoning his pants. "I just want to make sure I'm understanding here."

"Finn, I—"

He lets out a short, pissed-off laugh. "Do they even know how much it will cost to fix these boats?"

"Well, they'll first fix the *Linda* to use, but then at least it's a leg up for you, right? I mean, it's a few hundred thousand dollars or more that you can use to get back on your feet."

"You've already discussed which boats? And *money?*" Finn's eyes are so wide it makes me see for the first time how green they can be. "Harlow, you've never seen my fucking boats. Are you even serious right now?"

This whole conversation feels like whiplash. I can still feel the warmth and shape of him in my mouth. My hands are shaking, my eyes stinging with the threat of tears. "Finn, there's only been a couple of conversations so far. They know you need to fix your boats." His face turns red, his jaw tightens, and I hasten to add, "They're really excited to work with you on this."

"A shit ton of decisions can be made in a couple small conversations. Are they counting on this?"

I feel my stomach drop out. "I think they're ready to move forward on their end, yeah."

His expression grows thunderous. "Why couldn't you have talked to me before you ever approached Salvatore?" he asks, turning and pacing the room. "Why did you think it was a good idea to meddle in *this?* This is *my* business, Harlow, this is my life. My family. How do you even know if this could work for us? You're here shuffling papers and getting donuts for NBC executives downtown while I'm trying to save an entire business my grandpa started when he was *eighteen, for fuck's sake*. My dad and brothers and I depend on this! I don't even know what you told these guys!"

"I can tell you everything," I say, following him and putting a hand on his arm. "When I talked to Salvatore at his place—"

"Aw fuck, Snap," he interrupts, not hearing me and starting to pace again. He pulls his hat off, rubs both hands over his scalp and down his face. "This is a fucking *mess*."

This whole conversation has me feeling unsteady on my feet, struggling to figure out what to say to make it all clear that it's a *good thing*. "This is money that allows you to fix your main boat," I remind him, trying to keep my voice steady. "And to use it *exactly* as you've been using it before it broke. You wouldn't have to do the reality show to keep your boats. This would allow your business to stay solvent, to work with your brothers and get in front of—"

"Do you have any idea how naïve you sound right now?"

I gape at him. I can actually feel my pulse in my neck, that's how hard my heart is pounding. "You know what? Why don't you call me later and we can talk about this. You're being an *epic* asshole."

He turns to look at me, flabbergasted. "*I'm* being an—?" Closing his eyes, he takes a deep breath and then exhales, opening his eyes again. "Yeah, it's probably best if you go."

––––––––

MIA PULLS THE third mug of coffee out of my shaking hands. "I don't think you need any more caffeine, sweetie."

She's taken precious time away from Ansel to come see me in my crisis mode. I drop my head onto my arms on the table, groaning. "Am I a jerk? Is *he* a jerk?"

Lola picks at her blueberry muffin. "Both, I think."

"Can someone please explain the male brain to me? First he was mad about Mom, then I was about to give him the head of his lifetime, and then I'm trying to save his business, and then he goes and throws a huge mantrum." I feel the threat of tears returning. "What the hell just *happened*?"

"Well," Lola begins, "you basically aired all his dirty laundry to a potential business partner for him and offered something you aren't sure he can deliver."

I groan. "God, when you put it like that I sound like an idiot."

Lola makes the *Well?* face and winces sympathetically.

"This thing with Salvatore could be amazing, Lola. Yes it was risky but it could work out if he only stopped with the caveman chest thumping and thought about it!" Looking at each of them in turn, I say, "By the way? You can't tell Oliver or Ansel any of this. Finn hasn't told them yet."

Lola nods immediately but Mia squirms a little in her seat. Finally she says, "Okay. But I really hope he tells them soon because secrets with me and Ansel? Historically not a good thing."

"I know, Sugarcube, and I'm sorry I put you in this position." I lean across the table to put my hand on her arm. "But lest we forget, it was your chatty husband who spilled the cancer details to Finn before I had a chance to, so you guys kind of owe me."

"I'll only put out once tonight to punish him," she jokes. I laugh. "Troll."

"Seriously, though. Ansel is half Adonis, half puppy. You want me to be mad at him for worrying about you and forgetting he wasn't supposed to talk about your mom?" Her mildly raised eyebrow tells me she knows the answer.

I drop my head back onto my arms again. "No. He's adorable and sweet and I'm an idiot for meddling in someone else's business, per usual." Sighing, I say, "Usually it works out so well."

"What I don't fully understand is, what was going on with you two?" Mia asks. "I thought you were just sleeping together, and then you weren't, and now it's got you like this? I hate to point out the obvious, Harlow, but you've never called an emergency conference over a boy before."

Lola nods. "I was pretty sure you were the first woman in history to make it to twenty-two without a guy crisis."

"We said the *I love you*'s last night," I admit in a whisper.

"What?" they yell in unison. A few café customers nearby turn to stare at us.

"God, take it down a notch, psychos," I say, laughing in spite of myself. They're enjoying this *way* too much. "At first he was this fun distraction from what was going on with Mom and my complete lack of a good job and all those quarter-life crisis things no self-respecting person over thirty has any sympathy for."

I pick up a paper napkin and start tearing it into little strips. "Then I started thinking about Finn more than I was thinking about anything else, and he had this boat thing going on—though I didn't know the details until later—so we sort of agreed to cool it."

"And?" Mia asks.

"*And* . . . then I was having fun trying to figure out how to fix his problem, and we were spending a lot of time together because you assholes were busy with work or husbands or totally oblivious to the men who are blatantly in love with you."

"Wait. What?" Lola asks.

Ignoring her, I continue quietly: "Finn is sweet, and funny and stoic in this way that is totally foreign to me but I actually really appreciate, coming from the Family That Discusses Everything. And he's *hot*. Dear Lord, you guys. Finn in bed is *no joke*. And he's not a whiny La Jolla mama's boy, he's a *man* who was raised to get shit done, and not cry over hangnails. Finn could break your vagina and be just handy enough to put it back together." I pick at the sleeve of my sweater, dropping my voice even more. "He looks at me like he adores me, but then he'll make fun of me—which I like, turns out—and he started to feel like *my* guy, you know?" I don't even care that I'm babbling now; I'm just letting it all out. "He looks at me like we have this little secret, and we *do*. My secret is that I fucking *love* him. And he was a jerk today."

Mia puts her hand on my arm and slides it down, weaving her fingers with mine. "Harlow?"

I look up at her. Mia and Ansel have been married since June, but only a little over two months ago they had a huge fight, something so huge and hurtful between them that I could see on her face she was worried she might have lost the thing she wanted more than anything in the world—even more than to erase the accident that shattered her dream of dancing for a living: her marriage.

So I know what she's going to say before she even opens her mouth.

"You just have to go fix it," she says simply. "He's mad, you're hurt. But as clichéd as it sounds, none of that really matters in the long run. Just go talk to him."

I LIFT THE R2-D2 knocker and drop it down against Oliver's front door, but my stomach is already gone, dissolved away from my body and leaving in its place a hollow, aching pit. Finn's truck isn't at the curb.

Oliver answers the door shirtless, in lounge pants that hang way too low and expose way too much muscular hip for a guy I'd like to firmly and forever keep in the friend zone. He's clearly just got out of the shower; his hair is wet and messy, his glasses a little foggy. Even with the panic rising in my throat, I can still take a second to appreciate how cute he would be with Lola if he would just man up and ask her out for real.

"Expecting a booty call?" I ask, keeping my eyes on his face.

He takes an enormous bite of apple and chews it with a wry grin on his face. Finally swallowing, he says, "I think we both know I'm not." He lifts the apple to his mouth and says behind it, "Just dressed as if I'm hanging out in my house alone, as you do."

"Alone," I repeat. "Because Finn is gone?"

"Left 'bout an hour ago."

"Left as in . . ."

Oliver points north. "Canada." His Aussie accent turns the word into *kin-ih-duh* and even though, logically, I know what he's said, it still takes my stubborn brain a second to let the confirmation sink in that Finn left town without saying goodbye to me.

He left town, and didn't kiss me goodbye, or wait to make sure I'm not knocked up with his spontaneous car-sex love child, or even come *find* me. What a dick.

I'm suddenly so angry I want to take Oliver's fucking apple and throw it at the wall. "I told him I loved him last night," I tell Oliver, as if it's his business. As if he needs to know. But it feels so fucking good to explain the storm pounding in my veins, the hurt and fire making me want to scream. I want confirmation that Finn is as epic a dick as he seems to me right now. "The best part? *He* said it *first*. And now he's fucking left without *saying goodbye?*"

If any of this surprises Oliver, he hides it remarkably well. This is his superpower, I think. The comic geek always has one, and Oliver's is a poker face that would leave even the Holy Trinity guessing what he's thinking. Too bad Lola's superpower is never needing to dig for information that hasn't been offered. They're going to *Remains of the Day* this thing until the end of time.

"You want to come in?" he asks.

I shake my head, hugging my arms around my shoulders. It's almost seventy degrees out but I'm freezing. Is this what heartbreak feels like? Like a hot skewer in my chest and I'm too cold and can't take a deep breath and want to cry all over Oliver's awkwardly naked shoulder?

Heartbroken sucks. I want to kick it in the nuts.

"Look, Harlow," he starts, before pulling me in for a hug. "Aw, pet, you're shaking."

"I'm freaking out," I admit, leaning into him. How could Finn just leave town? "Oliver . . . what the fuck?"

He pulls back and looks down at me. *Way* down at me. Holy shit Oliver is tall. "I've known Finn for a long time," he says slowly. "It takes a lot to get him upset, and even more before he shows it." He winces a little and then says, "I can tell you're upset, too, but he basically grunted out a few words, said we'd talk soon, and then walked out to his truck. I dunno what's going on with him, or why he left or . . . anything, really, that might help you feel better. You sure you don't want to come in?"

I shake my head again. "He didn't tell you what happened?"

Oliver laughs a little. "Finn rarely tells us much of anything. He usually tells us things after he's got them all figured out. If there's something going on with him, and he confided in you, then he wasn't lying when he said it first."

"Said what—oh," I say. He's talking about the *I love you.* Ugh. Punch to the gut.

He bends, catching my eyes. "Call him, yeah?"

Chapter FOURTEEN

Finn

𝓘 DID A LOT of things in San Diego that weren't stereotypical Finn Roberts: sleeping in, watching TV, buying Starbucks coffee, not working a steady fifteen hours a day. But this—driving away as the sun sets over the water—is the first familiar feeling I've had in a long time.

Oliver came home while I was packing and watched me warily from the doorway. "You want some coffee for the road?" he'd asked.

"Yeah, that'd be good."

Things had been the slightest bit tense between us, and I knew there were probably a hundred questions Oliver would ask if given the chance. In turn, he knew there were about a hundred reasons why I wouldn't answer any of them, and so once my bag was closed, we walked to the kitchen, stood over the Keurig in silence, both of us watching the final drip drip drip of coffee into the cup below.

"You can't have this one," he said, turning away from me to spoon in more sugar than any human should probably consume in one sitting.

"Of course I can't. It's your Aqua Man mug, you think I want to lose an eye?"

He glanced up at me, smiling weakly. "No, you can't take that one because yours will take a few minutes to brew and I wanted the chance to talk to you before you left."

"Ah."

"I know you have some stuff going on." He let the sentence hang for a moment, suspended in the air while he walked to the fridge and retrieved a carton of half-and-half.

I felt a flash of panic, worried that Harlow had decided to get even with me after all, and told him everything. But she hadn't; I knew this even without hearing what else he had to say. Harlow may be a lot of things—meddling, naïve, impulsive—but disloyal is absolutely not one of them.

He returned to the counter and opened up the carton, checking the date before continuing without missing a beat. Like we were just having a casual conversation after work, like he wasn't giving me yet another chance to open up. Which of course, I didn't.

"Just know that you can talk to me."

"I know," I said, grateful that Oliver never seemed to push. "Thanks."

And that was it. He handed me my coffee, gave me a long hug that would have bordered on awkward even for Ansel, and I left.

I pulled out of his neighborhood and headed straight for the I-5, not glancing even once at the road behind me.

THIRTY-THREE HOURS AND one horrible, sleepless hotel night later, I'm home. I pull into my driveway—the sound of gravel crunching beneath my tires is like a lullaby—and see my house for the first time in weeks. It weird to be home and see how small and alien everything familiar looks after I've been out in the wide-open world for what feels like forever.

It's in these moments I realize just how different my world is from Harlow's. How much quieter. Instead of buildings crowding overhead, my view here is nothing but towering evergreens, crystal blue water and sky; color in stretches that seem to go on forever. I'm almost completely surrounded by forest, so much so that even the smell of the water on the back side of the house is eclipsed by the heavy scent of decaying trees and foliage out front. There's no traffic, no noise, and it's entirely possible to just start walking and go days without ever seeing another person.

The air feels wet—*everything* feels wet—and my boots squelch in the grass that needs mowing along the drive. After weeks in the California sun, the temperature takes me by surprise. By next month the storm season will be here, and in just the few weeks since I've been away, the leaves have started to change, the ground is littered with spikes of orange and red and brown. I climb up the porch and fish out my key, kicking away even more leaves that have gathered in little clumps around the mat. The lock opens easily and the door swings wide, the screen door closing with a creak and a groan at my back.

My house is a tiny two-bedroom, but it's clean and comfortable, and just a few steps out the back door puts you right on the water. I managed to buy it in one of our better years, and I'm grateful now to Sensible Finn who thought ahead and bought a house, rather than dumbass Colton who bought a gas-guzzling Mustang and a condo all the way in Victoria.

It's stale and musty inside, and so I set down my bag and walk from room to room, opening the windows to air the place out. It brings in the chill, but it's worth it and almost instantly the house is filled with the scent of salt and pine. A set of glass doors along the back wall leads out onto a deck where the only view is miles of blue and green, the tree line so thick in some places it stretches clear down the bank to the water's edge.

I leave the doors open and force myself to the kitchen to find something to eat, and quickly realize the mistake I made not grabbing something on my way through town. The fridge is practically empty but I manage to scrounge up a can of soup and some peaches I find in the pantry, and stave off starvation until I can make it to the store tomorrow.

Hours on the road, a head full of jumbled thoughts, and not enough sleep have taken their toll, and it's almost more than I can do to make it into my room. Without closing the windows, I strip off my clothes and pull back the blankets, and for the first time in ages, climb gratefully into my own bed.

THE HOUSE IS freezing when I wake up. But it's good—it's life here, and the sharp air is exactly what I needed to get me back into the mindset of a day spent on the boat.

A full night of sleep gave my brain time to reboot after all the thinking I did on the drive up. I get out of bed and get ready, feeling good about where I've landed on the question of what to do about the business. It's a relief to have made a decision, even if my stomach remains a little sour with nerves. I trust myself and my brothers enough to know we'll land on our feet no matter what.

I just hope I'm not about to ruin our lives.

I'm on the dock before five. Salt air fills my lungs and my body moves on autopilot, my muscles remembering exactly what to do.

The boys have been busy. Planks of new decking have been laid where they replaced the wiring, and the controls in the engine room seem to be working just like they should. No equipment has been left out, nets have been repaired, and I feel a swell of pride for my brothers.

"Finn?" I hear, and turn to see my youngest brother, Levi, climbing on board.

"In here," I call out.

He follows my voice and steps inside, cradling a steaming mug of coffee in his hands. He's dressed in a heavy plaid jacket, a beanie pulled down over his curly hair. "Well, fuck," he says, setting his cup down and pulling me into a giant hug. "Nice to have you back, stranger."

Apparently, I've become a softie in San Diego, because I find myself pulling him back in when he pulls away, hugging him tighter. "Thanks," I tell him. "Thanks for taking care of the boats. You guys did good." I pull away but not before I snatch his cap off his head, messing up his pretty-boy blond hair.

His characteristic grin is in place. Levi has always been the smiling brother, the jokester, and he doesn't let me down. "Colt's just behind me but we could totally sneak off to paint each other's nails if you're feeling needy."

"Fuck you," I tell him, laughing as I toss his hat back in his direction.

Colton is there next, giant paper bag holding his lunch in one hand, an apple in the other. "Look who it is," he says. He hugs me with every bit of force Levi did and it's just like it always is, the Roberts boys on the boat, ready to start a new day. Except this day will start very differently.

"So, hey," I begin, pulling off my baseball hat and rubbing my forehead. "I think we should stay docked today."

Colton studies me for a moment. "Why?"

Looking down the dock, I still don't see Dad heading down to the boat. "Dad still at home?"

"Probably be down later," Colton says. "Especially since he knows you're back."

"What's up, Finn?" Levi asks. "We're not tossing nets today?"

I decide to go ahead and tell them, with or without our dad here. I slip my hat back on and look at each of my brothers in turn. "I think I've come around."

Levi takes a step closer. "Meaning what?"

"Meaning, I think we should sign on." I look over at Levi and laugh at his hopeful expression. "For the show."

My brothers both let out enthusiastic whoops, and high-five each other before hugging me again.

"Fuck *yes!*" Colton yells, and his voice echoes down across the water. "Oh, this is good, Finn. I'm fucking stoked."

"Can you imagine what people are going to say?" Levi asks, though his grin tells me he isn't particularly worried. "They're going to give us epic shit, I'm sure."

"Yeah, well, they can give us all the shit they want," I tell him. "You can wave at them from the water because our engines are working."

"I'll blow them a fucking kiss wearing nothing but my bank statement," Colton adds.

Levi laughs. "I'm sure you would."

There's a moment where I just watch the two of them, measuring this Levi and Colton against the ones I left the day I headed to Oliver's. Things were looking *bad*, and maybe I didn't realize how bad they were until right now, seeing the contrast in them. They're smiling and happy, young. Hopeful for the first time in years. Money can't buy you happiness, but happiness sure is a hell of a lot easier to find when you're not worried about where your next meal is coming from.

"Come on," I tell them, reaching for a clipboard that hangs on a nail near the door, and thumb through the daily logs. "I need to take stock of everything so when we call, I can tell them what's gotta be fixed."

Levi follows me up into the wheelhouse. "So, tell us about California."

"What he means is tell us about the pussy," Colton interrupts.

"Check yourself, Colt," I chide him quietly.

Colton looks at me with the most comical look of feigned innocence I've ever seen.

"It was good. Great to see Oliver and Ansel. See the new store." I scribble a few notes on the charts, add today's date, and start a list of repairs needed in order of priority. "I saw Harlow," I add, and regret it almost immediately.

"Harlow," Levi repeats with glee evident in his voice. "Harlow of the trench coat?" Of course Levi would remember that. Because karma has an incredible sense of humor, Levi just so happened to be pulling up to my house as Harlow climbed into her cab. He definitely enjoyed sharing that piece of information with my entire family.

I glare at him over the top of the clipboard. "Yes. That Harlow."

"Well, damn, son. I wouldn't have answered my phone calls, either."

"Yeah, about that," I say, but Levi is already shaking his head.

"We're big boys, Finn, we can handle the load for a while. You deserved a break, man."

"This," Colton echos.

"Okay, well," I say, a little overwhelmed and not exactly sure how to respond. "We have an engine to pull apart before we can make the big call, so let's get to it."

IT'S LIKE I never left. I work from sunup to sundown—taking a break only at lunch to call the producers with my brothers and my dad and tell them, finally, that we're in—and it feels so damn good to wear myself out and work until I can hardly stand, too tired to worry or even *think*.

It's only the middle of the night that the mental clarity goes to shit. I wake from a dream that was too real. It was Harlow, over me, laughing at something I said. Her bare skin was only half visible in the moonlight, and waking without that sight sends a spike right through my gut.

It's easier to lie in bed and stare at the ceiling than risk going back to sleep, where I might dream about her again. I'm not sure whether Harlow cemented the impossibility of a relationship when she went behind my back to talk to Salvatore Marìn, or whether I did just today when I agreed to do this show, but however it happened, I have to accept the fact that there's no future for us.

Despite what I thought, I know now that I've never loved someone before and I'm beginning to realize that I have no idea how to get over it. It's terrifying to wonder if I'll always have this carved-out feeling beneath my ribs, like I left something vital behind in California.

IT'S BEEN FOUR days since I've seen her, and anyone who says it gets easier with time can go fuck themselves. I'm not sleeping well, I'm not eating enough, and I'm working myself into the ground.

I've tied up the loose ends with Salvatore and put our smallest boat up for sale so we can focus on the two larger boats. The show is sending a crew of mechanics to get to work on the *Linda* in a week or so, but it's impossible for me to be still and not try to tackle some of it on my own while I can. I'm the first one at the dock every morning and the last one to leave. By Wednesday, we've torn apart the entire engine and finally come to the conclusion that this particular problem is too big for us to handle on our own.

Colton spends the afternoon on the phone with the producers scheduling the repairs while I help Levi check the pulleys for wear. Dad is checking the nets and commenting on each and every repair, when I hear a familiar voice.

"Permission to board, Captain Wanker."

I look over the side to see Oliver, smiling up at me.

"Holy shit," I say. I wave him up and around the boat, watching as he climbs on board. "What the hell are you doing here?" My first reaction is joy, elation at seeing my friend, that he came all this way to see me.

A second, more physical emotion is fear. I came and left without giving him any reason, and never bothered to check in once I arrived back home. And now I've made a pretty monumental decision about our family business and still haven't told my two best friends anything. "Is something wrong? Ansel? Harlow?"

He's already shaking his head. "They're fine," he says. "I

just wanted to talk to you." He pulls me into a hug before stepping back, taking a minute to look around. "Never thought I'd step foot on one of these again," he says. "Smells like fucking fish."

"Well, I'll be damned."

We both turn to see a grinning Colton making his way toward us.

"Colton," Oliver says, shaking my brother's hand. Oliver glances from me to Colton and back again. "Looks like you're going to be as ugly as this one here, you poor bastard. How are you?"

"Good. Great, actually. Did you hear about the show?"

Fuck.

"The . . . show."

"Yeah, the Adventure Channel show," Colton barrels on obliviously. "Two fucking seasons, Olls. Can you believe—"

"Colt," I interrupt him, holding up a hand. "I was hoping to tell Oliver about this myself."

Oliver turns his smile on me and I've known him long enough to know that this is not an *I'm-so-happy-for-you* smile. This is the condescending smile he gives to someone who confuses *Star Trek* with *Buck Rogers,* or doesn't understand the dynamic behind the Wolverine-Jean Grey-Cyclops love triangle. "Good plan, Finn. I like hearing things directly from the source."

I reach up to scratch the back of my neck, waiting while Colton and Oliver catch up. I only tune back in when I hear Colton ask how long he'll be here.

"Heading back tomorrow morning."

Colton groans. "Why such a short trip? We could use your help next week when the mechanics descend and Finn is banned from the boats."

"Very funny."

"Listen, I gotta get back to the engine room; make time for a beer tonight, yeah?" Colton asks, walking backward.

Oliver nods. "Definitely."

"Cool. Good to see you, man, we'll talk tonight."

We watch Colton round the corner and disappear out of sight. Oliver is the first to speak. "I like your brothers," he says.

"They're good guys. Really held things together while I was gone."

"You know who I don't like right now?"

"Ansel?" I guess.

He laughs. "Walk with me, Finn."

Oliver steps back onto the dock and after a moment of hesitation when I wonder whether I could actually swim back to my house, I follow. On the surface, Oliver is about as laid-back as anyone I've ever met. He's one of those people who keeps everything in, letting their emotions out in small, measured pieces. The fact that he flew up here to check on me without even knowing about the show . . . I think I'm in for a world of hurt.

Despite the sun high overhead, there's a distinct bite to the air. The wind whips through the boats and it gets even chillier the farther we walk. A ship's horn cuts through the silence and Oliver turns to me.

"I'm assuming this whole show thing has something to do with why you left? And with what was bothering you the entire time?"

I pull my cap off and run a hand through my hair. "Harlow tell you anything?" There's a part of me that almost wishes she had. If Harlow's already told him then there's no need for me to, no reason to spill my guts out and onto the dock.

I am not that lucky.

"No, actually she said it was your story to tell. And I agree."

The sound of the water, small waves breaking against the base of the pier carry up to us, amplifying my silence. I should have told him. I should have told Ansel.

"Finn, I know you're not a big sharer. I get that. Hell, after spending time with chatterbox Ansel, I even appreciate it at times. But I love you, you're my best mate and I wouldn't have given you so bloody many chances to confide in me if I didn't actually care what was happening in your life. Talk to me."

"I don't like discussing things until I know what I'm going to do."

"I get that," Oliver says, nodding. "But seeing as how I came up here to make sure you were okay, and I find out just now from your *brother* that you've *already* signed on to do a *television show* . . ." He waves his hand forward, indicating he doesn't really need to finish making his point.

I point to a bench at the end of the dock, and we walk

there in stiff silence. We sit down, and Oliver stretches his arms across the back of the bench as I lean forward, elbows on my knees, staring down. The dock is old and weather-worn, but I swear I could draw the pattern of grain in the wood from every plank from memory.

"The last few months, things haven't been good," I tell him. "Fish counts are down, the cost of fuel is at a premium. People are losing everything left and right. Dad was going to take a loan out on the house. I was pretty sure I was going to have to, too. And you've seen my house, Olls. You know we're not talking about a huge line of equity, okay? We were scraping the barrel."

"Shit," Oliver mumbles.

"So," I continue, "a month ago we got a visit from a couple of suits at the Adventure Channel. They wanted to film on the boat, document our lives and what we go through. Document *us*. My first reaction was that they were totally fucking with us. My second reaction, when I realized they were for real, was to say no, because it's clear that the goal of the show isn't about fishing, it's to show us and our lives."

"The lives of four eligible, brawny blokes up in Canada, you mean."

"Exactly," I say, rubbing my face. "But the guys—my brothers and my dad—they thought we should hear them out. They're tired of fighting so hard, you know?"

Beside me, Oliver nods.

"We talked, and it was decided that since I was the only

holdout—and believe me, I was dead set against it—I'd be the one to go out to L.A. and meet with the production company, get all the details, and come back. We'd decide together."

"Okay," Oliver says. "Hence the visit."

"The more I thought about it, the more I knew I didn't want to do the show. Even as I was driving down to San Diego, I knew. I didn't want to make light of what people are going through up here. I didn't want us to be some kind of a joke. But then I got to California and . . . one of the engines threw a rod and it was one thing after another and pretty soon, it was either that or lose it all. No way would any loan help us dig out of the mess."

"But you didn't tell me. You didn't tell Ansel."

I shake my head. "I didn't."

"You *did* tell Harlow."

I take a deep breath and look out over the horizon. A seagull circles overhead before it swoops down, dipping its beak into the ocean. "Yeah," I say finally.

"Should I be mad that you told her but not me? You were in a relationship with her for, what, twelve hours?" Oliver says. "We've been friends for over six years."

"You're right. But you and Ansel, you're a permanent part of my life. Harlow was temporary." Oliver lifts a brow and I quickly add, "At first."

"And that made it easier to talk to her? Someone you barely knew, rather than someone you've known most of your adult life?"

"You don't think that makes sense? I didn't want you to know what was happening until *I* knew what was happening. I didn't want it to change how you saw me."

"You are a stubborn, prideful idiot, Finn Roberts."

I adjust my hat on my head. "I've heard that before."

"So what I'm hearing is, you left when you found out Harlow was doing basically the same thing."

I pull my brows together, not understanding.

"She didn't want to talk about her mother with you, you didn't want to talk about your boat problems with us. You both wanted to keep things separate."

"No," I say, shaking my head. Realization sinks in. He thinks I split town because Harlow didn't tell me about her mother. *Jesus.* Do I really come off as that callous? "I didn't leave town because Harlow didn't tell me about her *mom*, Oliver. For fuck's sake. That stung because of *my* mom, and because I told Harlow everything about my problems, and the night before we'd basically confessed our undying love. But if that was the only thing that happened I wouldn't have just bailed."

"Okay, clearly there is a lot more going on, and Harlow is just as tight-lipped as you are."

I rub a hand over my eyes. "I left town because I had to get back here. And . . ." I pause, looking up at him. "I left town because I was pissed at Harlow for trying to find a way to save my business without talking to me."

Oliver pulls back, shaking his head to tell me he doesn't understand. "What?"

I explain to him how Harlow approached Salvatore Marìn without talking to me first. How she discussed details about my life that weren't hers to share. How she offered something—access to my boats for months—when she wasn't even sure I could deliver.

"So she didn't tell you because she wasn't sure it would work out, right?" Oliver asks, and his voice is gentle and curious as if he simply *wants to know*, but I can feel his laser-sharp point lurking just behind. "She didn't want to share it with you before it was a real possibility?"

"Yeah," I say, wary. "That's probably what she'd say."

"Just like you didn't want to tell us about what was happening with the television show before it was a real possibility?"

I see the point he's making, but it just doesn't add up. "Oliver, the whole situation is messed up. Yes, I should have told you out of courtesy because you're my friend. But Harlow should have told me out of necessity because it's *my fucking livelihood*. These two aren't the same."

He looks out at the water and seems to consider this for a long, quiet beat. "Yeah, I get that."

There's nothing else for me to say. "Let's go get a fucking beer. I can fill you in on the details of the show."

He nods, standing beside me and following me as I walk down the dock toward my truck. "Are you happy up here without her?" he asks. "You feel pretty good going home alone every night?"

Laughing humorlessly, I tell him, "Not so much."

"You think she must be a real asshole, I guess, to try to ruin your business. What a *twat*."

"Jesus, Olls, she wasn't trying to *ruin* it," I say, instinctively protective. "She was probably just trying to find a way for us—"

I stop, turning to look at Oliver's giant shit-eating grin.

Groaning, I say, "Go fuck yourself, Aussie."

Chapter FIFTEEN

Harlow

I WAKE UP TUESDAY and immediately know I've gotten my period, which of course brings a huge wave of relief . . . which of course makes me pissed-off all over again that Finn just hopped in his truck and drove north, leaving the mess between us behind.

One of the things I appreciated most about Finn was the plain assumption he seemed to always have that he sees things through with work, friends, and family. Apparently, that didn't apply to the fight he had with the girl he'd married for twelve hours, loved for a day, and potentially knocked up.

But remembering that makes it clear why I appreciated that about him: because it's the way I was raised, too. Take care of your own. Don't leave loose strings. Clean up your messes. And, as my father has told me countless times, "Worrying is not preparation."

So I drive to my parents' house at the break of dawn to

check in, reconnect, or, as Dad would probably say, be a meddling worrywart.

Dad is already up, eating cereal and staring out the window in his typical pre-coffee zombie zone, so I jog upstairs and crawl into bed with Mom. I don't want to get so wrapped up in my own internal drama that I forget what she's going through and that, at the end of the day every day, she's still a mom who needs cuddles.

She hasn't lost her hair yet, but I already mourn it. I inherited my father's olive skin, but my mother's auburn hair, and hers spills out over her pillowcase, just as long and full as it was when I was little. Mom's trademark during the peak of her career was her hair. Once she even did a shampoo commercial, which Bellamy and I love to give her endless shit about because there was a lot of shine and hair flipping.

"Morning, Tulip," she sleepy-mumbles.

"Morning, Pantene."

She giggles, rolling to press her face into her pillow. "You're never going to let me live that down."

"Nope."

"That commercial paid for the—"

"The camera that Dad used to film *Caged*," I finish for her. "Which got him lined up at Universal for *Willow Rush,* for which he won his first Oscar. I know. I'm just being a menace."

But there's the rub. Mom's work paid for Dad's work, which moved our family forward, and nowhere in there did pride come into play, even though Dad is one of the most prideful men I've ever known. Mom came from a rich family in Pasadena. Dad came from a poor single-mother household in Spain. He never cared that his career took off because of the money and connections Madeline Vega made first. Once he'd convinced the love of his life to marry him, only three things mattered to my dad: that my mother took his name, that he could make her happy, and that they both got to do what they loved for a living.

"Why are boys so stupid?" I ask.

She laughs. "I've literally never heard you sound upset over a guy. I was worried."

"Worried I was into girls?"

"No," she says, laughing harder now. "That would have been fine. I was worried you were a cold-blooded man-eater."

"Dad's a tough act to follow," I explain, pressing my face into her hair. Beneath the scent of her shampoo and face cream, she smells the slightest bit different—not bad, but . . . different—a result of the chemo and all the other things they're currently doing to her body. It's not like I go even an hour without thinking about it, but it hits me in this moment like a physical blow, this reminder that my mom is sick and my world is different than it was just two months ago. It makes me miss Finn and the strength he provided so acutely, that for a flash, I can't breathe. "It was hard to take anyone seriously before now."

"Before Finn, you mean?"

"Yeah."

She rolls to face me. "What happened?"

I tell her—vaguely—about the hooking up, about my need for distraction, about how he was *too* distracting. I tell her about the real feelings, the *I love you*'s. She already knows about the potential deal with Salvatore, but apparently she doesn't know how it unfolded.

"Sweetie," she says, putting her warm hand on my cheek. "Your heart is always in the right place. But a partnership always starts at the beginning. I did the commercial to help Dad, but we decided that I would do that together."

"I understand that Finn was upset that I didn't loop him in," I say, "but I still don't understand why he couldn't have stepped back and realized it was a good thing, or at least had a discussion with me about it. It isn't like there's a contract with Sal that has been drafted. He's just *interested*. Finn flew off the handle."

"What do you think Dad would have done if I'd come home from the Pantene shoot and handed him a check, saying, 'Go get your camera, babe'?"

I roll my face into the pillow and groan. "Dammit."

"What are we '*dammit*ing'?" Dad asks from the doorway, lifting his mug to his lips to sip his coffee.

"Your daughter is learning relationship rules," Mom says.

He snorts. "Finally."

"Are you two done giving me crap?" I ask, climbing out of bed in a half-feigned huff. "I am very busy and have important things to do."

"You work today?" Dad calls to me as I stomp down the stairs. I can hear from his tone he doesn't think I am.

I pause on the third step, shooting Dad a dirty look he can't see. "No!" I yell back.

"Call Finn!" Dad shouts at me down the stairs. "I like him!"

THE PROBLEM IS, I don't *want* to call Finn. I want to drive to Canada, kick him in the nuts, and then drive home. He's acting like a giant baby, and leaving town the way he did showed his ass. I'm tempted to mail him a care package with a plastic halibut, a copy of Salvatore's latest film on DVD, and a box of tampons.

I officially leave my internship at NBC, and I swear no one will even notice I'm gone, or if they do, the narrative will be *Hollywood Child Can't Hack Being Coffee Girl*. Salvatore sets up an office for me in his Del Mar building, and when I promise him I'll be the best coffee girl he's ever had, he laughs and tells me that's great, but I'll probably be up at the Los Angeles offices with him at least three days a week so someone else can handle coffee duty.

This news is dropped like a bomb full of glitter and puppies in my lap: Not only has he given me a job, but he's made me his primary assistant. I went from NBC coffee-pourer to the right-hand woman of one of Hollywood's biggest producers. My dad doesn't even blink when I tell him the news.

"Knew it was just a matter of time," he tells me instead, and gives me that smile that makes me feel like I'm the brightest, most beautiful star in the entire sky.

But even with this big change on the horizon and a week

full of phone calls and contracts and picking out office furniture . . . a whole week without Finn around is weird. I almost call him about a thousand times, just to tell him what I did all day, or share my excitement with him about the job with Sal.

But as soon as I pull my phone from my purse and notice the complete lack of texts, calls, or emails from him, I manage to fight the urge to let him back in.

Salvatore mentions him at lunch, just over a week after Finn split town. "Your boyfriend is quite—"

I point my fork at him. "Finn is *not* my boyfriend."

Sal holds up his hands in surrender. "Fine, fine, your *friend*, Finn—is that better?—is a class act. He worried the damage on his boat might cost more than the value of using it for the set and said he was unable to work with us at this time, but he did suggest some great options up in the area and agreed to be our primary consultant for *Release Horizon*."

"Oh?" I can't tell if the maniacal drumming of my heart means I'm elated that Finn will be involved in some way and has taken the professional initiative to call Salvatore, or if I'm terrified that I am going to completely lose my shit when I inevitably see him at some point.

"We'll head up there next week to check out some boats." Salvatore looks up when my fork clangs loudly on my plate.

"Next *week*? But filming doesn't start until April."

"You work for me *now*, Tulip," Salvatore reminds me, using my family's pet name for me to take the edge off his gentle chastisement. "I need you up there. Is coming along to Canada a problem for you?"

"Obviously what's going on with me and Finn has nothing to do with any of this. Sorry, Sal. I just had a moment. I'm fine."

He pushes his chin out, doing his best Godfather. "You want I should break his face?"

"No, I'd be devastated if you took the opportunity from me."

I take a bite of sandwich, chew, and swallow. I leave out the part where I actually like Finn's face.

"God, I hope you're not making a mistake bringing me on for all this," I say. "I know the business, but are you sure you wouldn't like someone with more—"

"I've got enough experience for the both of us," he says, shrugging as he spears a green bean. "You know how these things work, and I get to train you to be exactly what I need you to be. I like your backbone and I'll get you up to speed. It's hard to find people with your combination of loyal, smart, and ballsy."

I take a second to stare adoringly at Sal. "I love you, you know that?"

"Yeah, yeah." He takes a sip of his iced tea. "So what happened with Finn?"

Sighing, I drop my napkin on the table. "I didn't exactly tell him I was talking to you about using his boats to film a huge multimillion-dollar Hollywood production. He was angry. Blah blah."

His eyes lift back to me, half amused, half incredulous. "You're kidding."

"Before you say anything else, please note that I've heard from everyone that I'm wrong here. I feel like an idiot, actually."

His face relaxes and he gives a little shrug before taking a bite of his salad.

"And then he just *left*," I tell him. "That's why *I'm* angry. It felt . . ."

He swallows, and then finishes the sentence for me: "Shitty?"

"Yeah."

"Well, you can tell him all about how you feel next week. We're taking him out to lunch." Sal meets my eyes and bats his lashes innocently.

Fuck.

"SERIOUSLY, ANSEL," I say, slipping into the booth at Great Maple for Saturday breakfast with the crew. "How much are you paying to fly here practically every week?"

"A lot," he admits with a laugh and his obscene dimple poking into his cheek. "But actually I'm here this weekend because we are house hunting."

"Uh, pardon?" I ask, leaning forward to stare at Mia.

"Say *what*?" Lola adds.

"The lawsuit from hell settled this week!" Mia squeals, and she's beaming so enormously I could count every single one of her teeth. "Ansel is officially free to look for jobs here and he already has an interview at UCSD!"

"Holy crap, that's amazing!" I jump out of the booth and make Oliver get up so I can tackle Mia on the other side. "I am so happy for you guys!"

Lola joins the girl pile and I hear Ansel say something about getting a video camera and maple syrup.

I climb off the tangle and smack Ansel's arm before straightening my shirt. "I can't believe it. It's like we're all going to be together!"

"Well. Almost," Lola says, making a *this-is-awkward* face.

"Right. Except for Finn," I say, and everyone kind of looks over at me like I'm made of glued-together eggshells and am rolling toward the edge of the table. I laugh, too loudly, sounding completely mental. The effect is to make it even more awkward. "Obviously I realize he's not here any-more." And then I add for no reason other than my mouth is still moving and no one else is coming to my rescue: "He left without saying goodbye."

Lola snorts, petting my shoulder. "Shh, crazypants."

I bite back a laugh. "That came out a little Glenn Close, didn't it?"

"A little," Ansel agrees, laughing.

"I went and saw him last weekend," Oliver says, and I swear the sound of screeching brakes tears through my head.

"You saw *Finn?*"

"Yeah. I flew up to see what the hell was going on with him since no one here told me anything." He gives me a pointed look, but then winks.

And see? This is what I mean by Oliver's poker face. I'd

never have known from his reaction nearly two weeks ago that he was so concerned over why Finn left that he would leave his new store in Not-Joe's questionably capable hands and fly up to Canada just to check in.

I want to say something to show I'm not completely consumed with pain at the thought of someone else flying up and checking on Finn. And by the way they're all looking at me, I can tell they expect me to make some quip and lighten the mood . . . but I can't.

I'm done being mad. Trying to stay mad is exhausting, and I've never been good at it. I fucking *miss* Finn, I miss My Person, and I can feel my jealousy that Oliver got to see him for a weekend climbing in a hot flush up my neck.

"You okay over there?" Lola asks gently.

"Not really," I admit. "I have to go up there next week to look at boats with Sal and we're taking Finn to lunch to thank him for coming on as a consultant. I already know it will be awkward and hard to see him because he's so good at being distant and professional. This whole thing is making me sad."

God, I hate how honest I get when I'm feeling devastated. It's like I've been trained under some Pavlovian trigger by my parents to talk it all out as soon as I have feelings too big to stuff into a sarcasm cannoli.

"If it helps," Oliver says, "he looked just like you do now when I told him you stopped by the house, looking for him the day he split town."

"Did you tell him the part about how I was mad, or the

part about how I was sad?" I ask. "Because I want him to imagine me with a chain saw and ass-kicking boots."

Oliver laughs, shaking his head and returning to his waffle.

"Did he tell you why he was mad?"

"A bit," Oliver says around a bite.

"So it's at least a little bit of an overreaction, right?" I can hear in my own voice that not even I am convinced.

Ansel pokes at his breakfast and asks, "Did he ever tell you why he dropped out of college?"

"Yeah, briefly. I mean we never really talked about it, but I know he left to start fishing with the family business."

"Not exactly," he says, putting down his fork. "He dropped out to *run* the family business."

"Wait," I say, holding up my hand. "In college he did? I thought he took over after Bike and Build?"

"No," Oliver says. "When he was nineteen his dad had the heart attack and then a stroke a year later. Colton was sixteen. Levi was like eleven? There was literally no other choice for Finn but to take over."

"His father is better now," Ansel continues. "But there's a lot he still can't do, and Finn has basically run the entire thing since he was a kid. He took the summer off one year for Bike and Build when Colton was old enough to give Finn a break, and he came to Vegas, but other than that, this trip to San Diego was his only time away from the water."

I nod, lifting my water glass with a shaky hand. I want to see him *now*, want to kiss him and help him and fix all of this.

"I actually like what you tried to do," Ansel says. "When I talked to him a couple of nights ago he told me about it."

"Did he use lots of four-letter words?"

"None, actually."

I raise my eyebrows, impressed.

I look over at Oliver. "When you saw him this weekend, did he tell you what he's going to do about the business?"

Oliver tilts his head, blinking. *"Harlow."*

So he's not going to tell me. Fine. I go for broke; I have no more pride: "Did he even mention me?"

Oliver shrugs. "Not much. But remember this is Finn we're talking about here. He usually says the least about the things he's thinking about the most."

I laugh. *Well played, Aussie.*

————————

OUR FLIGHT TO Victoria on Monday lands at four in the afternoon, and Sal and I ride to the Magnolia Hotel together in a cab, discussing the plans for the next two days: meetings, boat visits, and more meetings. The air here smells like ocean, but so different from home. It's heavier, saltier somehow, and the winds feel more substantial, making me think of San Diego as a sweet, docile beach town. This place is on the edge of the ocean frontier.

I'm so nervous to be here, so close to Finn again that even in the October sun, I feel chilled. The last time I came here, I had nothing but the champagne bubbles of excitement, effervescent in my stomach and giving me a secret smile the entire trip. I barely noticed the wilderness, the space between houses, and how much water there is, everywhere.

This time, I notice *everything*. Even as we discuss work, and names I need to know and what kinds of notes Sal needs me to gather on this trip, I notice it all.

Finn lives here, I can't stop thinking it. He lives here, in this otherworld, this alternate life surrounded by green and the sapphire-blue of the ocean. Fred's bar and Starbucks and Downtown Graffick feel so far away from all of this. Finn must have felt like he was stepping into Tokyo when he came and stayed with Oliver. Into a video game.

I can't even imagine how he felt about Vegas.

We check in, and as we wait for the elevator, Sal looks down at his phone and makes a little *hm* sound in the back of his throat.

"What?"

He smiles, handing me his iPhone open to *Variety* and I begin reading as we step into the elevator.

Adventure Channel Signs Roberts Brothers
for "The Fisher Men"

The Adventure Channel has signed on for an unprecedented two full seasons of a new reality series following a family of four men—three single brothers and their father—as they navigate the fishing industry off Vancouver Island's west coast.

The program, featuring Stephen, Finn, Colton, and Levi Roberts, will be an "exploration of family responsibility and the complex dynamics binding these men by love and the business they run together. The story of each son's quest to both save the family business and build a life off the water in the often-brutal Pacific Northwest fishing industry is what drew the Adventure Channel to this show," according to the co-executive producer, Matt Stevenson-John.

Along with Stevenson-John, Giles Manchego is on board to produce. The deal was finalized on Friday, according to an Adventure Channel spokesperson. "The Fisher Men" is slated to begin filming in the spring when the salmon season begins, with episodes premiering July 1.

"Wow." I feel every particle of air evacuate my chest in a gust with that single word. Handing Sal back his phone, I say in a tight voice, "They signed on."

"Looks like it."

I'd told Sal there was a possibility, so he's clearly not surprised by any of this, but I don't know what to feel. I don't know what to *say*. I don't know why *I'm* surprised, but seeing it like this—in the crisp digital font accompanied by one of the promo shots Finn hated so much—I'm unprepared for the way it hits me like a physical blow to the center of my chest.

I'm not entirely sure my legs will keep me upright and I lean against the wall of the elevator.

"You all right over there?"

"I just . . ." I close my eyes, take three deep breaths the way my father always told me to when I felt overwhelmed. Oliver and Ansel probably knew, and didn't tell me. Finn didn't call me. I feel so . . . insignificant. "I didn't expect him to do this."

But didn't I? Didn't I sense he was leaning this way, knowing it's what his family wanted? If he didn't take Sal's offer, what else could he have done?

"It's a great move, if you ask me," Sal says, and I know him well enough to know that he's choosing to act oblivious to my internal meltdown. "From what I hear, the AC is putting a huge amount of money into this one. Finn's family will get up-front costs, of course. But a cut of the merchandise, too."

I nod numbly. It is a good thing. It's an *amazing* thing. I repeat this thought over and over.

We arrive at my floor and Sal tells me to meet him at eight the next morning in the hotel executive lounge. "I'm sure you'll find something to do," he says, as I step out and he remains in the elevator because he's staying on the Fancy Ass People floor.

"We don't have plans tonight?" To be honest, with this new information, I want nothing more than to be distracted by Sal's sharp wit and endless industry stories.

"*I'm* having dinner with some friends," he says, with a casual wave of his hand.

I only have time to realize that he planned this so I'd have a free night here and to get out the words "You jackass! *Did you talk to my dad*?" before Sal grins and the elevator doors slide closed.

"I'm not going to see Finn!" I yell at the sealed doors anyway, just as an older gentleman steps forward and presses the down call button. "I'm *not*," I tell the stranger before glancing at my room key and stomping down the hall.

I PUT MY bag down and after a quick search on my phone leave almost immediately to find him.

The sun setting over the water is nearly too beautiful to describe, and I wish someone was here with me to agree that it's unreal. The sky is fire orange at the horizon, fading to a deep blue-lavender with dappled clouds. The taxi drives me up along the coast from Victoria, past Port Renfrew toward Finn's house in Bamfield, situated right on Barkley Sound.

My head is still spinning and I want to see him more than I want anything else at this moment. I ask the driver to leave me at the dock, knowing if there's any light left that Finn is likely to be on his boat. But when I look out at the scores of boats tied to their slips, I realize finding him will be like looking for a needle in a haystack.

I wander along the slips, looking for the *Linda,* looking for someone who looks like they might know where to find Finn Roberts, Adventure Channel star-to-be. But the pier is quiet, and only the creaking of ropes against their ties and the water lapping at the hulls of hundreds of boats surrounds me. The thought that some of these boats are sitting here because their owners can't afford to take them out is sobering.

"You need some help?"

I turn, looking up into the sun-kissed face of Finn twenty years from now. I know his dad from the picture, but also because Finn looks exactly like his father: looming, broad-shouldered, hazel eyes steady and unblinking.

"You must be Mr. Roberts."

He shakes my hand, brows drawn in curiosity. "I am. And you are?"

"I'm Harlow Vega."

Stephen Roberts's face freezes, eyes going wide before he breaks into an elated smile. "Well, look at you." And he does. He takes my hands, holds my arms to the side, and looks me up and down. "You sure are somethin'. He know you're here?"

Shaking my head, I say, "He has no idea."

"Oh, you bet I'm going to enjoy this one."

Whether anyone else will enjoy this reunion? Remains to be seen.

He takes my arm and leads me down the dock, turning left to head down a long rickety pier. We reach the end, and stop in front of a boat with *Linda* painted across the stern.

"Hey, Finn," his dad calls out. "Got somethin' to show ya."

A blond head appears around a corner and I immediately recognize Finn's youngest brother, Levi. He's as tall as Finn, but not nearly as broad, and has messy blond hair and a baby face that I'm sure the television producers will lose their mind over.

Levi stares at me for a beat before busting out laughing. "Oh, shit. Finn! Come down."

Footsteps clomp on the stairs leading down from the top

house and I see his tall rubber boots over waders, and then his torso covered only by a soaking wet white T-shirt that is marked with grease stains. He's holding some type of gear in a greasy rag and his shirt is so wet I can see every single line of his chest. I can see his *nipples*. I can see the trail of hair that leads from his belly button down to his . . . good Lord.

Universe, you've got to be kidding me.

His face appears then, and my chest seems to cave in on itself. He has a grease smear across his chin, too, and his tanned face glistens with sweat. He sees me immediately, his face transitioning in a millisecond from relaxed curiosity to tight confusion. "Harlow?"

"Hey."

He glances at his dad and then over at Levi before looking back at me. I swear when our eyes meet my heart is pounding so hard I'm tempted to look down and check to see whether it's actually moving my shirt. He looks like he's in pain, and I want to know: *Is it me? Or did you actually hurt yourself fixing the boat?*

"What are you doing here?" he asks, carefully putting the gear down on a broad railing. He uses the dirty rag to futilely wipe his hands clean.

"I'm working with Sal. I had a free night, and since you left without saying goodbye to me, I figured I would come do it for you."

He closes his eyes, rubbing his forearm across his face as his dad lets out a low whistle, saying, "Didn't tell me *that* bit, Finn."

Finn's eyes snap to his father. "Dad, come on."

The eldest Mr. Roberts leans over, kisses my temple, and murmurs, "Keep at him, sweetheart."

My hands are shaking, my pulse racing, and Finn walks along the deck to the narrow ladder leading to the dock. Turning, he climbs down and slowly approaches me as if I'm either going to vanish or punch him.

He seems even more massive in his heavy waders, his muscles bunched from hours of exertion. "I didn't expect to see you here."

"I can imagine," I say. "I didn't expect you to leave so unexpectedly."

"It wasn't that unexpected, was it? You knew I was heading up soon."

I wince, looking away, and he takes a step closer to me before stopping.

I want so much to reach forward and put my hands on his face and kiss him. I miss him, and despite how angry I am that he left the way he did, I *love* him. I feel awful for betraying him and talking to Salvatore alone.

"I heard about the show."

He nods, pulling his cap off his head and scratching his scalp. "Yep."

"You okay about it?" I ask. Because yeah, I'm still angry, and yeah, I still want to hit him with something that will leave his voice about two octaves higher but, fuck, I love him and I *want* him to be okay.

Shrugging, he murmurs, "I suppose. Everyone else felt

pretty strongly in favor. Made the most sense." He looks up at the boat and then back to me. "Had some news people out here earlier today."

"That must have been wild."

He lets a smile flicker across his lips. "Yeah."

Seagulls call in the distance and the moment feels so eerily familiar though I know it's never happened. I just feel calm here with him. I like seeing him like this: near his boat, filthy, probably hungry. I ache with how much I want to take care of him.

"Finn?" I start, and he looks up from where he's wiping a spot off the back of his hand to meet my eyes.

"Hm?"

"I came here because the way you left town was really hard on me. I think I needed to tell you that." Swallowing, I say, "But the main thing I had wanted to tell you is that I feel really horrible for what I did."

His eyebrows slowly inch up but he doesn't say anything.

"I should never have gone to Sal without talking to you first. I should never have offered your boat up to *anyone*. It was wrong, and I'm sorry."

Nodding slowly, he says, "Okay, then."

I close my eyes, wincing at the sharp pain in my chest. He's so closed off. He's so *finished* with me.

"I just want you to know that I didn't do that because I thought you needed my help. I did it because that's what we do in my family when we love someone. It wasn't about trying to save you, it was about trying to find a way to save *us*."

He swallows thickly, his eyes dipping to my lips for a beat. "Yeah?"

I nod. "Yeah."

I was hoping there would be more said. I was hoping he would give me more than this, more than a handful of words that leave me nowhere to go. He's standing like a brick wall at a dead end, his posture telling me there's no emotion to be found here.

As we stand in silence, he looks me over, from head to toe, and under his inspection I realize how my outfit must look to him: cream jeans, navy sweater, red scarf. I must look like a WASP portrait of *Out for a Day on the Boat*. And I know I'm right when his lips curl into a sharp smirk and he says, "You look so out of place here, Snap."

Fire ignites in my belly and I suck in a breath, so wounded by his tone and his complete one-eighty and his ability to shut off his feelings like a switch. My problem? He was capital-I *It* for me. I don't know where to go from here.

"I might have thought the same thing once about you, in my town," I tell him, "but I never would have said it. I liked seeing you there too much. I liked the way you stood out."

"Harlow—"

I wrap my arms around my middle, turning to leave. But then I stop, and look back at him. "Before I forget," I say, "I'm not pregnant. Thanks for checking in."

Chapter SIXTEEN

Finn

"SHE DIDN'T EXACTLY look happy when she left," Levi notes, leaning back against the wall of the wheelhouse and studying me as I climb up the ladder.

I let out a little noncommittal grunt and hop over the railing. My stomach feels like it's been pumped full of battery acid. What the fuck just happened back there? Did I really let Harlow walk away?

Did I really forget she could have been *pregnant*? Even at the time it didn't seem like a *real* possibility, maybe because that fear was quickly overshadowed by our declarations, the party, and then the fights that followed.

I am the biggest, most self-absorbed asshole of all time. And just the memory of that night, of her climbing over me, my hands pushing aside her tiny scrap of lace and how easily I slid into her, how quickly we both unraveled . . . it rocks me. We hadn't been just fucking in the car. Already I loved that girl so much it made me reckless.

My little brother grabs his sweatshirt and keys from the deck. "You got everything you need done?"

I nearly laugh. Every day feels like it just creates more

things on my list of worries. I'm still reeling from Harlow's appearance at my boat and now she's gone. The boat's getting fixed, Levi, Colton, and Dad are all thrilled with our plan, but do they have any idea how our lives are going to look in four months when the film crew descends and starts taking stock footage of the area, of us? When they start following us into our favorite haunts? What happens when they set me up on dates with women and the only woman I want has just disappeared down the dock?

I'm the only one who hasn't signed every page of the contract. I've agreed to the show, sure. I signed my name on every page but one: I didn't agree to the relationship clause. I owe Salvatore for that one, too. Apparently it wasn't enough to break the deal, because after talking with him the network was happy to send the press release to *Variety* without it.

Tomorrow, the repair crews begin their full-boat makeover. I could leave town, leave them to it, and take another mental breather, but I won't. I'll be here every day, backseat driving, driving the crew crazy. A lot of the guys they've hired are local guys, guys I would have called myself if I had the money to fix the boat.

"Finn?"

I look up at Levi as he reaches the ladder.

"Don't be a fucking idiot. That woman was the most beautiful thing I've ever seen, and she came here looking for *you*."

I scrub my face, waving him away with my other hand. She did look beautiful, but Harlow's beauty isn't the only thing that knocks me sideways. It's her ferocity, her emotional honesty, it's that she's ten years younger than I am— younger even than Levi—and although I always scoff at what she considers *life experience,* she's still better at fixing her shit than I am.

———————

I SIT DOWN on my bed, the water from the shower still dripping out of my hair and onto my comforter. It's nearly midnight, but I don't think I'll be able to calm down until I fix this. A phone rings somewhere in San Diego and after an eternity, Lorelei answers.

"This is a Canadian number," she says by way of greeting.

If she's cutting to the chase, then so am I. "Harlow's even more pissed at me now, isn't she?"

After a little pause, she says, "The short answer is yes."

Hope spreads thick and warm beneath my ribs. "What's the long answer?"

"The long answer? *Yes, she is.*"

Laughing dryly, I say, "Thanks, Lola. That's helpful."

"You want *me* to be helpful? It took a lot for her to come see you today. Harlow doesn't stick her neck out for people she doesn't love—some people think she's selfish, but it's the opposite of that. She'll go to the end of the earth for you if she loves you. I'm pretty sure she loves you, and from what she said, you spoke about five words to her."

"That's pretty accurate."

Letting out a little huff, she growls, "You're a prick."

I laugh again, moving my phone to my other ear to drag my towel down my chest. "Yeah, that's probably accurate, too. It's a bad habit."

"I think she enjoys it, usually. But not when she's putting herself out there. I've literally never seen Harlow spend more than five minutes thinking about a guy. And I also don't think I've ever seen her so sad."

My stomach clenches and I feel nauseous. "Where's she staying?"

"No way. She's *sleeping.*"

"I'm not going tonight. I'm going tomorrow." Somehow, I don't expect our business lunch with Sal will be the time for Harlow and me to kiss and make up.

"If you go there, and make this worse, you know I will cut your balls off when you sleep."

"Lola."

Silence rings through the line for ten seconds. Twenty.

"Lola, I swear I'm not going to make this worse. I fucking *love* her."

"The Magnolia Hotel in Victoria. Room 408."

SALVATORE AND HARLOW have already been seated when the hostess leads me back to the table. I've never eaten at the Mark at the Hotel Grand Pacific, but I should have known it would look just like this: like something out of a glossy catalog for the beautiful tourist stops in Victoria.

I can immediately sense Harlow isn't going to look at me

much during lunch. When he sees me behind the hostess, Sal stands to greet me, and Harlow follows reluctantly. I shake his hand and we all sit. Apparently not even Sal expects Harlow and I to greet each other.

Her notepad is out and she's ready to play the role of the assistant. Maybe with anyone else she could fade into the background . . . though she's physically stunning and hard to ignore, so I doubt it. And with me, it would be impossible. She looks so unbelievably beautiful it constricts my throat, ropes something tightly in my chest. Her hair is down, she's wearing a sweater as green as an emerald, and tight black pants with these sexy little strappy heels. Jesus fuck, I want a picture of her in this outfit glued to my ceiling.

But I'm here for business and I really do want to be a consultant for the film. My noncompete clause with the Adventure Channel doesn't apply to film consulting, and I'm still so terrified of this unknown future that I'm grasping at any footing, any new contact. Besides, in our first conversation, Sal said he needed someone who could "talk fish from A to Z" and I don't know anyone better qualified to do that around here than me.

"How's the boat?" Sal says by way of official opener, and it actually makes me laugh. Seeing it myself once I was home . . . it was depressing.

"It's busted."

He laughs, this genuine, warm laugh I wasn't expecting. He looks slick but he speaks real, and I glance over at Harlow, seeing her in a new way. This guy is the real thing—a decent man in Hollywood—and he's plucked my girl up to be his right-hand man because he knows she's the real deal, too.

"Congratulations are in order," he says. "The show sounds great, Finn."

"We'll see," I hedge. "It'll be different, that's for sure."

For a beat, my eyes meet Harlow's and I wonder if she knows what I'm thinking, that I don't give a fuck about the relationship clause. I'm spoken for, whether the producers know it or not. But she blinks away, looking out the window, and I see her jaw flex. It's possible I fucked it up so much yesterday that even when I find her later, it won't matter.

I hope I'm wrong.

The waitress fills our water glasses, gives us time to look at the menu, and Sal and I chat casually about the area: the weather, the sports, why I follow the Mariners over the Blue Jays (they were my mother's favorite team), how often I make it down to Mariners games (as often as I can, which is hardly ever).

Harlow remains quiet—making note of useful information but otherwise aloof—and Sal doesn't push her to engage. I wonder how much he knows about what's happened between us. I want to catch her eye, tell her with my expression that we aren't finished here, that I have my shit together and my words have bubbled to the surface, but she hardly looks up.

The waitress returns to take our order and she's standing so close to me I feel her skirt brush against my arm. I slide over in my chair to give her more space, and Sal gestures to Harlow to begin.

"I'll order for the table, actually," she says and out of the corner of my eye I can see Sal look up in surprise and delight.

Pointing to him, Harlow says, "He'll start with a Caesar, have the chicken caprese for his main course, and iced tea, no sugar."

His eyes twinkle. "I was gonna get a steak, kid."

"Nope." She looks at him and winks. "Mila told me no red meat."

"Well, shit."

Pointing to me, she says, "He'll have the bisque to start—"

The fuck? She's not even going to ask me? "Actually—" I begin.

"The halibut for his main." She gives me a knowing look and my heart hurts remembering that perfect fucking day on the water with her. "And a glass of Chardonnay."

I blink. *Chardonnay?*

Beside her, Sal barks out a laugh.

Harlow hands her menu to the waitress, saying, "I'll have the filet, bloody, and a huge plate of fries." Glancing at me, she says, "Also a Stone IPA to wash it all down."

The waitress smiles, her eyes sliding over to me again as she collects the menu and leaves.

Harlow glances up, her lips twitching at my expression.

"Chardonnay?" I ask.

She licks her lips, giving me a sweet, wet smile. "You look a little parched."

"I was going to order the steak, too," I tell her, fighting a grin.

"Well, you can covet mine while enjoying your freshly caught halibut."

Sal is watching us with open amusement, his chin perched on his fist. "The audience is going to love watching you two."

"Not happening, Salvatore," Harlow says, still staring right at me.

"It *might* happen," I say back, unable to fight my smile anymore. "Seeing as how there was one particular page in that contract I didn't sign."

Her face registers surprise but she quickly hides it. So okay, I guess Salvatore left out a few details of our conversation, like where I made a fool of myself and told him I couldn't imagine being with anyone else. Ever. Harlow is it for me; I'll shout it from the top of Mount Fairweather if I have to.

"Well, relationship clause or not, we won't be interacting much in *any* form until you admit you were a complete dick yesterday."

Sal chuckles, and lifts his water to take a sip. If Harlow is comfortable doing this here, well, fuck it.

I lean my elbows on the table, saying, "I was a complete dick yesterday."

Harlow studies my face for a long moment, looking at my mouth, my forehead, my eyes. She blinks down to the table, drawing her finger around the rim of her water glass as she thinks. And then, lifting one shoulder in a little shrug, she ends this perfect moment: "I think you and Sal should probably get started."

CAREER-WISE, LUNCH IS a huge success. Sal has a million questions and I'm able to answer them all and give him some information it's clear he didn't even think to ask for. I signed an official consultant agreement—paying me a hefty five-figure consulting fee—so I can help immediately with set design and certain aspects of the film. I'm a little stunned over the complete one-eighty my life has done in the past three weeks.

Harlow-wise, the lunch was a bust. She took pages of notes, seemed to keep up with everything I said, and even asked a few good questions of her own, but after our brief back-and-forth toward the beginning of the meeting, she didn't really look at me again.

But it was more than I expected. To be honest, I expected her to ignore me entirely or at the very least for the conversation to never veer into personal territory in front of Sal. The fact that she couldn't help flirting with me gives me the confidence I need to drive to her hotel after dinner.

When the door to her room swings open, I think I've knocked on the wrong door and Lola was totally messing with me. But then I realize the mystery woman who has answered *is* Harlow in a huge bulky robe, a towel on her head and with her face covered in some white, cracking . . .

"Is that the kind of masque that ends in a *q-u-e*?" I ask.

She tilts her head, eyes narrowing. It causes the entire facial concoction to crack.

"What do you want, Finn?"

What do I *want*? I want her. I want her to open the door wider, let me in. I want to pull the tie open at her waist, pull off her robe, kiss her. I want to get back together and make it last longer than twelve hours.

But first . . . "I want you to wash the mask off so it doesn't look like your face is breaking."

With a sigh, she slams the door in my face.

The hall extends down for what feels like a mile and I wonder how many men have had doors slammed in their faces here. It's a pretty fancy fucking hotel. I'm going to guess a lot.

I lift my fist, knocking again.

It takes a long time for her to answer, as if she's walked away, and is considering leaving the door closed.

But then it swings open, and Harlow is immediately walking away toward the bathroom.

"Come in. Sit anywhere but on the bed. Don't look cute, don't get undressed, and don't touch my underwear."

I move to the chair in the corner, biting back a laugh.

"I'm rinsing it off because it's time, not because you told me to. If it didn't feel like it was breaking my face I would leave it on for the extent of your short visit just to piss you off, you enormous fuckwit." She walks into the bathroom, closes the door, and I hear the sound of running water as she starts the shower.

Holy shit.

I think she's going to forgive me.

Harlow emerges about ten minutes later, again wrapped in the robe but her hair is wet and loose and her face is scrubbed clean of the mask. I feel like I can't properly inhale, like the sight of her has short-circuited my most basic instincts: breathing, blinking, swallowing. She looks unbelievable.

"Did you touch my underwear?" she asks, walking to her suitcase.

With effort, I close my mouth, inhale, and swallow so I can speak. "Yeah. Rubbed it all over my sweaty chest."

She snorts and throws me a dirty look. "Don't flirt. I'm mad at you."

My smile vanishes without effort. "I know."

Reaching for a brush in her bag, she pulls it through her hair, watching me. "It's hard to stay mad at you when you come in here looking like that, though."

"That's . . . good, right?" I look down at my faded UW T-shirt, my old 501s, my favorite old red Chucks. I don't see anything special, but the way she's looking at me makes me feel like I'm wearing a tux. The knot in my chest loosens.

"Is this easier?" she asks quietly, adding, "Seeing me here in a fancy restaurant, or fancy hotel wearing a masque with a *q-u-e,* rather than trying to fit in down by your boat?"

The knot tightens again. "I was mad, Harlow. It made me act like a dick."

"I know. I'm just an insta-forgiver. If someone I care about says they're sorry, it's done."

"I'm not like that," I admit. "You'd already left by the time I decided you were forgiven."

She pulls her bottom lip into her mouth and sucks it, eyes wide and vulnerable. I know she has no idea she's looking at me this way, and it makes me want to open up my chest, let her see how fast my heart is beating.

I lean forward, looking around the room. "You know I've never stayed overnight in a hotel except for that Vegas trip?"

She stills, breath catching. "Not even for Bike and Build?"

"No. Some people did, but we stayed with host families or camped."

"Wow . . . that's . . ."

"That's been my *life*. Aside from the two years I spent in college, I was always here. I sounded like a dick when I said you looked out of place, but I didn't mean to imply that I don't *like* seeing you there. I just meant my world doesn't look like this. Doesn't look like *you*."

She puts the brush down and turns to rest back against the desk.

"I don't go out drinking every Thursday night and buy Starbucks every morning," I tell her. "I don't go on vacations and I couldn't call up a producer friend to come drop a ton of money on fixing my boat."

"You could now, probably," she says. "Your life is going to change completely."

"I know," I say, bending to rest my elbows on my knees. "I guess that's what I'm saying."

"That you're scared?"

I laugh, turning my attention down to the carpet. "Maybe not scared, really, just stepping into an unknown. It takes trust."

"You don't have to navigate this all on your own. I know I screwed up with you and Sal, but do you trust *me*?"

I look up at her and nod. "I do." She watches me, eyes softening and I repeat, "I absolutely do."

"All right. Then I'm getting dressed and you're taking me to a lumberjack bar."

My heart stalls, and then revs back to life as I sit up straight. "Just like that we're done fixing this?"

She nods. "Just like that." Swallowing, she adds, "I love you. We don't need to rehash. I messed up, you messed up. I'm sure we'll mess up again, it will just look different next time."

She grabs jeans and a sweater, underwear, and a bra from her bag and turns as if she's going to leave to change in the bathroom. Before I know it, I'm on my feet and moving across the room.

"Don't get dressed."

Harlow stops, backing into the wall. I slow a little, taking the last few steps to her over the span of what feels like a million rapid-fire heartbeats. I can see her pulse in her throat.

"Finn." She leans her head back against the wall, looking up at me as I step so close I'm only a few inches away from her.

"You love me?" I reach forward, finger the tie at her waist.

"Yeah, you idiot." She licks her lips, and then bites the lower one because, *fuck*, she knows it makes me hard. "I told you that already. You think it goes away after a few days, like a temporary tattoo?"

Laughing, I bend, pushing the heavy terry cloth aside to kiss her collarbone. She smells like shampoo and the soft smell I couldn't forget in a million years: honeysuckle and warm stone, Harlow and *mine*.

I loosen the knot at her waist and pull her robe open, groaning at the sight of her bare skin, golden and smooth.

Her eyes close and she moans hoarsely when I run my palms from her hips to her breasts and back again, pulling her forward into me.

"I'm sorry," I say into the warm skin of her neck. "I'm glad we're not rehashing, but I want to say it anyway. I'm sorry I split town, I'm sorry I didn't talk to you yesterday. And I'm so fucking sorry I didn't call to find out if we were pregnant."

She pushes me away so that she can look up at my face. "*'We'?*"

"Fuck, Harlow, you didn't do it alone."

Laughing, she agrees with a nod. "I'm sorry, too."

"Baby, that was two weeks of fucking *miserable*."

She falls silent, pressing her face into my neck. After a few seconds, she hiccups and nods wordlessly and I realize . . . she's crying.

I pull back to look at her, cupping her face. "Hey . . . no, don't. I—"

"I thought it was done," she says. I wipe my thumbs over her cheeks. "At the boat? I thought you were done with me. I wasn't sure how I was going to get over you. I've never had to get over someone before."

"I wouldn't have let it be done."

"You left, though." She looks up at me and two more tears run down her cheeks. "You just left and then wouldn't talk to me and it was terrifying because with you I realized I'm that person who finds their guy and that's *it*."

My chest twists and I tug my shirt over my head in a rush before pulling her against me. I need her skin on mine, need to get my heart as close to hers as possible, and she shrugs out of her robe, pressing into my heat, her arms going around my neck.

The Harlow everyone sees is a force to be reckoned with. This vulnerable Harlow is rare. She's just told me she feels what I feel—this is *it*, I've found my girl and that's it—and I don't want to fuck it up with her.

"We talk about everything," she promises into my shoulder. "And you don't ever leave me like that again. Promise me."

"I promise." I pull back and kiss her, a glancing touch across her lips. I mean it to be small, a seal on a promise, but her mouth opens and the sound that escapes is a sob mixed with a moan and fuck me, it's the sexiest sound I've ever heard her make because it's so *raw*.

In an instant her tongue is sliding over my lips, my teeth, my tongue and her pleading little noises are filling my head. She slides her hands down my body and presses her palm to the front of my jeans and I was already quickly getting there but under her touch I harden, needing her so much it feels like a match has been lit beneath my skin.

She slips free the buttons and digs her hand in, under my boxers, and, with a tight gasp, curls her hand around my shaft. I need my fucking jeans down at my ankles and her legs up around my waist.

I need her skin and her sounds and the sharp burst of her breath on my neck. I need her taste on my tongue and—

"I'm on the pill now," she says between her wild, sucking kisses. "I started it the day I got my period."

"Jesus *fuck*," I groan. "There is no better combination of words in the history of time."

She laughs, shoving my jeans down, and I kick them off with my shoes, stumbling against her and pressing her into the wall.

"I'll be slow later," I tell her, reaching between her legs. My fingers slide across her clit, down into the unbelievable slickness. *Fuck me.* "Later, I'll take my time but I just—"

"Stop talking," she says on a tight exhale. "I *know*."

Lifting her, I pull her legs around my waist and she holds herself there, watching me reach between us, rub the head of my cock over her. Up and down, barely in—fuck, *fuck*—barely out again.

"Look at that."

She sucks in a tight breath. "I'm looking."

The slight give of her body as I ease just in and out is a torture of bliss. My arms are shaking with how much I want to pound into her but she mistakes restraint for strain: "I realize this hotel thing is a novelty, but this one does come with a bed."

Laughing, I walk the two steps over to it and lower her onto her back, following closely so I don't lose the feel of her for one single second.

Her legs come around my hips and she pulls me down and in, guiding me inside her so fucking slow and hot, I have to stop when my hips meet her thighs because honest to God I could come right this fucking second.

She's staring right at my face, straight into my eyes; our faces are close enough that we're sharing a breath, back and forth. I lift my chin just slightly and I'm kissing her, and it's too intense somehow but I can't look away. I've *never* felt this. I want to tell her that but it sounds clichéd and plain. This feeling is so much larger than some trite words like *never before* and *no one else.*

"You're it for me," I tell her.

"Yeah." She nods, her upper lip glistening in the warm room and maybe also under the strain of this shared tension, this need to move and dig deeper and *feel.* I'm just terrified if I pull back even once, I'm coming.

Harlow writhes beneath me, rubbing and fucking up into me and I'm holding still, trying to keep my shit together but it's a losing battle. It's not going to take long for either of us. I'm so hard I'm nearly busting in her. She's swollen, hot and so fucking wet and I can tell by the flush of her chest that she could get off in under a minute rubbing on me like this.

She plants her heels into the bed and arches as I slide my hands beneath her shoulders, digging my hands into her hair, pressing my face into the damp strands. And then, under me, covered by me and filled *full* of me, Harlow fucks me like nothing I've ever had in my life. With her nails digging into my ass to hold me still, she circles and rocks up and grips me so tight—her body sucking all around me so wet, so good, holy *fuck*—gasping into my neck as she moves and growls and rubs herself right where she needs it, squeezing and tugging my cock while she gets herself off on me. She's grinding, I'm shoved in deep, and her mouth is pressed right to my ear like she's pushing every word in there, giving them only to me.

"So good," she gasps. "God, it's so good."

I'm barely hanging on; just waiting to hear the sound of her quick breaths and hungry little gasps that will tell me she's coming. "Get there," I manage.

She hiccups, and moans, nails digging into my skin, and with a relieved exhale, she comes so hard she shakes in my arms, pulling me over the edge with her. I can't be still anymore. I pull back and stab back in, fucking her hard now in long, urgent strokes as I start to come and she cries out into my neck.

I don't want it to be over. I don't want to move off her but for as long as her legs are, she easily weighs eighty pounds less than I do and so I roll to the side, falling beside her on the mattress.

"You know how gross hotel comforters are, right?" she says, breathless.

I close my eyes, still feeling warm and liquid beneath my skin. *"What?"*

"People who have sex in hotels—"

I reach over; press my palm over her mouth. "Shh."

She giggles under my cupped hand and licks me and *fuck,* I'm over her again, tickling and pulling her arms over her head and sucking at her jaw and her neck and her breasts. The relief hits me in a burst, like the wind has knocked open the window and blown across the bed: I'm here with her. The business may not have been saved in the way I wanted, but we won't lose our boats. My life is moving forward and I have the love of my life naked beneath me and everything will be okay.

But then I halt my mental uncoiling, because there's one thing we haven't discussed at all. "How's your mom?"

She stills under me, giving me a look that tells me the best time to ask this was maybe not when I was nuzzling my face between her breasts.

"Sorry, I swear I wasn't thinking about your mom's chest. I was thinking about how relieved I am and how everything seems to be sorting out, and then I thought about what you're going through. We haven't talked about it yet."

Harlow pulls my face up to hers and kisses me so thoroughly I have to pull away to get some air. "Thanks for asking me that."

"Well?"

"Let's get dressed," she says. "We can talk about it over beers."

She stands, and I follow her into the bathroom, sitting on the lowered toilet seat and running my hands up her legs, resting my head on her navel while she rubs some lotion on her face, ties her hair up in a messy bun. Now she smells like she did before, but also like the clean smell of her sweat and sex.

"You're thinking about how much you love me right now, aren't you?" she asks.

"Yep." I run my palm over her hip and between her legs. She shivers when I slip my middle finger into her, stroking slowly. Kissing her stomach, I mumble, "*Fuck*. Fuck that's hot."

"What?"

I look up at her. "I can feel my come in you."

This makes her laugh. "You're a dirty, dirty man." But she doesn't step away. And she can't hide the way her chest flushes and nipples grow tight.

"I like it," I admit. *I want to see it.* I don't admit that yet, though I don't know why. Maybe because if I give voice to the thought, I know we'll never leave this room tonight.

Her hands slide into my hair. "I like it, too. I like a lot of things I didn't know before."

There's a moment where I wonder if she's talking about the sex, or the rope, or something else, something bigger. Stepping away, she reaches for a washcloth and holds it under the faucet. "But don't get any ideas. You're taking me out."

———————

IT'S A HALF-HOUR drive from her hotel to my neighborhood bar but the trip seems to fly by in only a matter of minutes. What Harlow is going through with her mother is nearly identical to what I went through twenty years ago. Except she has the emotional maturity to deal with it far better than I did, and treatment is better now. Mom was diagnosed when I was ten, and I was alternately terrified of losing my mother and irritated by the responsibility I was left with because of her illness: Levi was only four, and when Mom died two years later, I was left to run the household for the two years it took my father to get his words back, to stop burying himself in sixteen-hour shifts on the boats.

If I could go back and do it all over again, I would do exactly what Harlow does, and I can tell by the doubt in her voice—Is she going over there enough or too much? What will her mother need when this second round of chemo starts? How long can her dad be the sole caregiver before he burns out?—that she needs to hear me say it out loud.

"You're doing it just right, Snap. If I could do it all over, I'd want to handle it just like you."

Her head whips to me. "Really?" she whispers.

"Really."

"I'm scared it's going to get worse."

I pull into the small parking lot behind Dockside and shut off the engine. "It probably will for a while. But you don't have to navigate this all on your own," I say, repeating her words back to her. "I know I screwed up with you when I left town, but do you trust me?"

Harlow leans over and kisses me once, full on the mouth. "I do."

For a Tuesday night, the bar is pretty busy, and I know it's because the weather has been unbelievable. Nothing makes for a thirstier town than warm weather in October, no rain, and a day of big fish.

We enter Dockside to a burst of cheers and shouts, congratulating me on the show. Fuck, I really hadn't considered this. I'd been so wrapped up in Harlow, I'd forgotten for a second that no one here would ever look at me the same. Leading her to the bar, I pretend I don't see every fucking head turn as she walks by.

The questions everyone wants to ask come from the bartender, Nick, who graduated a year before me in high school, went to Harvard, and returned here because he couldn't find a more beautiful place in the world to live. "Finn, who's the guest?"

"I'm Harlow," she answers before I get the chance.

"You Finn's long-lost sister?" says Kenyon at the end of the bar. "Please say yes."

Harlow winces with a playful apology. "I'm the mail-order bride. He told me he has a castle. Does he have a castle?"

"Sorry, kid," Kenyon says, laughing. "Just a fancy television show and a lot of groupies."

"Groupies?" Harlow asks, looking at me.

I order two beers and a basket of peanuts. "Come on." I guide her to two empty seats at the quieter end of the bar.

She sits down and turns to face me. "You have groupies already?"

"Kenyon is a shit stirrer."

"Because there *were* groupies?"

Laughing, I tell her, "There were some girls down at the docks today when the announcement came out."

"You mean the girls who are over there playing darts and staring at you?" She lifts her chin and looks across the bar.

I tilt my beer to my lips, surreptitiously looking at where she's indicating. There are a half dozen college-aged girls staring directly at us. "Yeah. That's them."

"Pretty sure they read between the lines on that *Variety* article." She lifts her beer and drains half of it. "Bet this bar is about to get a lot more business. Bet every place in this *town* is about to get more business. And I bet those girls are *all* over Twitter talking about you being here."

I hadn't considered any of this, that by doing the show we might be helping more than just ourselves. But I can't really focus on any of that with the way she's looking at me. I take another sip of beer, studying her. "You jealous?"

She laughs. "Nope. You just blew your wad inside me in under two minutes, about an hour ago. I think I have you locked down pretty tight."

"Gross. I fucking love you."

Harlow leans on the bar, gazing up at me. "Let's go get matching tattoos."

"Yeah?"

"Yeah. Mermaids or skulls. Your choice."

"Mermaids?"

"Yeah," she says. "Think of all the great conversation starters about your huge trident."

I rub my jaw, staring at her perfect fucking lips. The only marks on her skin will be from me. "I don't think so."

"You could get a hook."

A laugh bursts from my throat. "I'm not getting a fucking *hook* tattoo."

She falls quiet with a little smile pulling her lips up into a kissable curve. I bend, kissing it.

"You make me happy," she says.

Fuck. This girl. "You make me happy, too."

She straightens, eyes narrowing. "There will literally not be one other girl kissing you on this show or otherwise. Dates? Okay. But they have to be hilariously miserable to make good television and then you sneak out and come see me and put bite marks all over my thighs."

I blink, nearly choking on a peanut.

"Harlow, I told you I didn't sign that clause. I'm not dating other women on the show." I kiss her again. I'm hungry for it now, for the silk of her thighs on my teeth, for the way my teeth marks would look on that soft, delicate skin. Pulling back, I blink away, down the bar to clear my head.

"Won't you have to?"

"I think they're happy to have us signed on. I don't think Matt or Giles is going to push for me to stay single, actually. I think they're focusing the business story on me, and the romance angle on Colt and Levi."

"Well, yeah, *look* at them."

I growl. *"Harlow."*

She smiles, licking her lips. "You mean we don't have to be sneaky?"

Shaking my head, I ask, "Am I crazy to do this? I'm going to be a D-list celebrity auditioning for *Survivor* when I'm forty."

"Oh, come on, that's next year. Isn't it a two-year contract?"

"Ha."

"At least you'll have a hot wife."

"Wife?" My heart takes off, too fast. She reads my deepest thoughts, the ones that want to be settled, spoken for, sharing a bed and a home and a life.

"Yeah."

"You've already been my wife, remember?" Despite everything that happened in Vegas, there's very little I take more seriously than family. I step off my bar stool and she pulls me between her bent legs. "So you're actually proposing this time?"

"Just predicting." She leans her chin on my chest to look up at me. "I want kids."

Kissing the tip of her nose, I tell her, "I'm okay with that. But not for a little while yet."

"Three," she says.

I shake my head. "Two."

"Then they have to be the best two possible, so we should practice."

"Nightly."

"And daily."

I nod. "Vegas again?"

She lifts my arm, checks my watch. "I don't have anywhere to be until tomorrow at ten."

"I don't even have to work tomorrow," I tell her.

Harlow slaps a twenty down on the bar. "Then shit, Sunshine, we'd better hit the road."

treated as any sort of cultural revelation. He just enjoyed watching me having the time of my life, and I, in turn, was grateful that he got to see me so happy writing stories that are meant to make readers smile and escape the daily stresses of life for a slip of time.

In 1992, shortly before I left for college, my dad wrote me a letter to where I was working at a camp in Yosemite. He said,

> *I enjoyed talking to you on the phone last night—I have really come to appreciate and enjoy these moments where I am aware that I have my own special relationship with you. You know me in ways that I'm not always very aware of myself. It's only in my relationship with you (or Erin, although of course it's different) that the particular person that is Lauren's dad comes out. Somehow, Lauren's dad doesn't get as much practice as Dr. Billings or Marcia's husband. In spite of that, it always thrills me when I realize that "Lauren's dad" is a real person that you know, can predict, and frequently love.*

"Frequently" is an understatement, for sure. So, thank you, Dad, for being so wonderful that I didn't have to dig at all into the depths of my imagination to write a father-daughter relationship for Alexander and Harlow Vega that was full of love and support and loyalty. You are missed.

—Lauren

Acknowledgments

*T*HANKS, AS EVER, to our wonderful agent, Holly Root, our editor, Adam Wilson (who still probably doesn't know what hit him), the tireless and inspiring team at Gallery Books, our forever-helpful prereaders, Erin and Tonya, our amazing readers, all of the bloggers who support and promote us, and our husbands and children for their continued enthusiasm and patience.

Just after we began writing this book, Lauren and Erin's father passed away after battling illness for over a decade. Because Christina and I are more than coauthors—we are best friends—the loss threw both of us into a bit of a tailspin, and we were unable to work much for a few weeks. I'm hijacking these acknowledgments to thank Christina for being so steadfast and present for me. You're more than I could have ever hoped for, and always amaze me with the generosity of your spirit.

The last time I saw my father, he told me he had never seen me so happy and was so proud of me for chasing down this dream of writing. This meant the world to me. My dad—a professor, a psychologist, an epidemiologist—didn't care that what we write isn't heady literature or meant to be